D0754363

Yaficse
M2122se
McKillip, Patricia A
The sorceress and the
cygnet /
FRSN   FEB   2005

SECONDARY

FRESNO COUNTY FREE LIBRARY

Branches throughout the County to Serve You
You may return Library Materials to any Branch Library

PLEASE NOTE DATE DUE

Overdue charges will be assessed, ask at your
branch library. LOST or DAMAGED library materials
must be paid for

DEMCO

THE SORCERESS AND THE CYGNET

Ace Books by Patricia A. McKillip

THE FORGOTTEN BEASTS OF ELD
THE SORCERESS AND THE CYGNET

THE SORCERESS AND THE CYGNET

PATRICIA A. McKILLIP

ACE BOOKS, NEW YORK

THE SORCERESS AND THE CYGNET

An Ace Book
Published by The Berkley Publishing Group
200 Madison Avenue, New York, New York 10016

Book design by Sheree Goodman

First Edition: May 1991

Library of Congress Cataloging-in-Publication Data
McKillip, Patricia A.
    The sorceress and the cygnet / Patricia A. McKillip.—1st ed.
        p.   cm.
    ISBN 0-441-77564-0
    I. Title.
PS3563.C38S67   1991
813'.54—dc20   90-44103

Printed in the United States of America

10 9 8 7 6 5 4 3 2 1

THE SORCERESS AND THE CYGNET

PART ONE

RIDER IN THE CORN

CHAPTER

1

He was a child of the horned moon. That much Corleu's great-gran told him after, pipe between her last few teeth, she washed the mud out of his old man's hair and stood him between her knees to dry it.

"You have your granda's hair," she said.

"Tell him take it back." A thin, wiry child, brown as dirt otherwise, he stood tensely, still trembling with the indignity of being crowned with mud, tied up with Venn's granny's holey stockings and left in the sun to dry.

"I can't. He's dead now. His hair sprouts into dandelion seed. Moon seed." She smelled of smoke like a wood fire, he thought, leaning into her, and lavender and something dank but not unpleasant, like a cow barn. She was talking again, telling story as she stroked his hair with the cloth. Her own hair, proper dark, not moon hair, had a few white seedlings here and there. There were seedlings above her upper lip, and a mole like a black moon, which fascinated him, so the story he had to take out and examine later—years later—to understand it fully.

"He rode between the rows of corn on his great dark horse,

and all I could think was: His hair is white like the corn silk in
my hand. I thought how it might feel, under my hand. Hot from
the hot sun, and damp from his sweat. I stood there in the corn,
thinking those things for the first time. Everything grew farther
away, closer he came. His eyes were green, he wore green. I
never saw green the same way, after. Everything was singing:
My mam, a row away, was singing 'the little dark house falling,
falling. . . .' ''

"I know that," Corleu said, finding a place in the story to
stand, a stone rising up in a river while the quick blurred water
spun past.

"Everyone knows. Dark house falls to everyone. But that
day it sounded like a love song. Even the corn was singing, under
hot sun, leaves quiet like they never learned how to whisper
secrets, but whirring and buzzing from their shadows like blood
flowed in them. I held the ripe corn heavy in my skirt, and the
one in my hand I pulled leaf and silk aside with my teeth and
bit into, sweet and hard and full of sun. . . . He rode up to me
and stopped."

She stopped, too, suddenly; Corleu gazed up at her, feeling
as if the river had stopped.

"Go on. Tell story."

"Nothing much more," she said. There was more: He saw
it in her eyes. "Only how all the corn leaves pushed together to
hide us, and made the sky turn green. . . . And then he rode away.
And I had your granda. With his hair." She pulled Corleu
straight, scrubbed at his hair with the cloth. "He could foresee
in a bucket of still water, your granda. He could see with his
feet, they said. He could find anything in woods, any herb,
mushroom, flower."

"Who was he?" Corleu asked. "Who was rider in the
corn?"

She made a sound in her nose, in the back of her throat,
like a laugh, but she wasn't smiling. "So many asked me that
so many times. But how was I to know? I never asked, he never
spoke. 'Corn,' I told your granda. 'Corn was your father and sun
your grandfather.' '' She smiled then, her lined face rippling like
pond water. She touched his chin. "And old horned moon his
grandmother, who turned to see him just as he opened his eyes
first time, to see her. So all her power spilled out of her horns
into his eyes. Likely you looked at her, too, with that hair. But

you haven't learned to look in other ways. My son was reading petals by your age. He could see the simple things: weather, birth. He learned to fight young, too, like you. No place for the white raven among the dark.'' She stroked his damp hair flat. "And all Wayfolk are dark-haired.''

"Why?''

"Because long ago we wandered down out of the stars, that's how restless the Wayfolk are. Looking for new ways and roads and paths. We still carry night in our hair.'' She lifted his face between her fingers. "And eyes. Even though you stared at moon, you're one of us, with night in your eyes. And that's why women always put a braid in their hair, so the night and Wayfolk past won't flow out of it at sunrise.''

"Tiel doesn't braid,'' he said, thinking of her dark, straight, glossy hair.

She chuckled, hauled to her feet, and said something else it would take years for him to understand. "She will, one day. She'll braid, like all of us. But whose name will she braid into her hair?''

For all those years to understanding, it seemed to him that all else he inherited from his granda—or great-gran, more likely—was a gift for getting into trouble. "Moonbrain,'' he heard endlessly. "Corleu fell off moon. Limehair. Catch a cuckoo in Corleu's hair.'' Fists would fly, a small brawl erupt among the colorful wagons, always with the lank, corn-silk hair at the center of it, until someone's mam waded in with soup ladle or a pan of dishwater. He could turn even a simple game hobble-nobble. It might begin peacefully enough: all the dark-eyed, bare-foot, raw-kneed smallfolk in a circle, holding hands and moving around the moonbrat, who held his hands over his eyes, in a game as old as memory.

"In a wooden ring," the circle chanted,
"Find a stone circle.
In the stone ring
Find a silver circle.
In the silver ring
Find a peacock's eye.
Lady come, lady come,
Find my eyes, find my eyes.
Circle, circle . . . Blind can see!"

The circle jostled to a sudden halt; the blind dropped his hands. In front of him: Jagger, a stocky child with coarse straight hair and an eye for trouble. By rule of the game, Corleu must do whatever Jagger ordered, to get himself out of the circle. They stared at one another, mute, challenging, while the other children whispered and grinned.

Jagger gave his command at last. He pointed a grubby finger toward Venn's parents' wagon and said, "Go stick your head in that bucket of milk. Milkhead."

When the older children finally peeled the pile apart, there Corleu was on the bottom, with his hair rubbed so full of dirt he looked almost one of them. His nose was running, his eye wild, his fists clenched; Sorrel, receiving him into the wagon, sighed worriedly, for her fey son hardly looked human.

She cleaned him up and sat him down at the tiny painted table. She emptied a basket of dried flowers in front of him: wild rose, lavender, verbena, dandelion, hawthorn. "Pick the stalks out," she instructed. "And the leaves. Only leave the petals." She was a tall woman, with lovely almond eyes and a soothing, husky voice. She wore bright ribbons braided in her long black hair; that and the songs she sang had entranced Corleu since he was old enough to uncross his eyes. They had also entranced Tul Ross, a stolid, hard-working man who had fallen in love with her as she sang in the fields. Unafraid of her peculiar father and her own odd gifts, he had married her and had only said resignedly, when the past echoed in her newborn's hair:

"That's out of the way. Likely you'll have the dark ones now."

But she never did. She watched her son sniffing and picking at the petals, so gently they barely stirred under his hands. As he had watched her do, he blew over them, winnowed them with his breath, so that colors formed patterns on the wood. He sat silently again.

"What do you see?" she asked at last, curiously. He looked up at her, his eyes huge, shadowed.

"Face."

"Whose face?"

"Table's."

"What?"

He showed her with his finger: two knotholes and a scowling crack. She shook her head, baffled, and gave him one of his granda's books to read, for he had an odd, useless gift for that.

As smallfolk became halflings, they ceased tormenting Corleu and began trailing after him, for he also had inherited his great-gran's tongue. He told them the tale of the Rider in the Corn many different ways, always feeling his way closer to the truth of it, until one day they all stumbled into understanding, and the tale took off in wild variations. The Rider was a lord from Withy Hold. The Rider was an evil mage from Berg Hold. The Rider was a cowherd on a borrowed horse. There never was a Rider, only his great-gran's fancy, and the warm, sweet, singing corn. One of Wayfolk boys had fathered the bastard and Corleu's great-gran had looked at a white goat under the full moon, that's why his hair. Since by then, great-gran was dead, they couldn't go to her for the true story. He told them other tales, collected from Granda's books, or from listening silently in the dark while the oldfolk talked around fires on mild winter days in the deserts of Hunter Hold, where they met with other Wayfolk companies for the season, or in the barns and stables and cider houses on the sweeping farms of Withy Hold. One summer, he learned to take more than tales from the cider house.

He lay with Jagger and Venn and a crock of cider on hay they had, piled one hot midsummer night when they were all pushing into adulthood several directions at once, and all of them in the dark. Early in the morning, tales took a turn from fathers, girls and ghosts, to the stars above them, thick as sheep in a shearing pen. Living between earth and sky, little escaped their notice underfoot or overhead. Corleu, who was racing Jagger for height, but was yet all scrawny wire and muscle, took a swallow, slapped a mosquito on his cheek, and said,

"There's Peacock."

It was hardest to see: a spray of glittering eyes clustered near the almost perfect Ring. Venn grunted.

"I see it." He grunted again. "I see two Rings."

Jagger burped. "Where's the Blind Lady?"

"There is no Blind Lady," Corleu said.

"Blind Lady wears the Ring of Time," Jagger argued. "She sees out of the Peacock's tail." Venn giggled, was ignored. "So where is she?"

"In stories. In the sky you only see her Ring."

"How come she's blind?" Venn asked. From farmhands, shepherds, they all knew bits and pieces of the silent shapes of fire and shadow that haunted the night. Corleu said dreamily, hugging the crock against his chest:

"The Cygnet tricked her. If she looks straight at you, you die, because the end of time is in her eyes. So the Cygnet, when they were all fighting, tricked her into looking at her reflection in the full moon. So she went blind. Now she sees out of the Peacock's eyes."

Venn juggled his arm. "You'll split your tongue with book lies. Pass crock."

"I'm not! It's not lies, it's stories."

"It's stories," Jagger said. His voice was deeper, his jaw was shadowed, he held a weight of authority. "Pass the crock over."

"Stars don't fight," Venn muttered.

"These did," Corleu said. A dog barked somewhere, catching wind of them, then subsided. He shifted on the hay, an intimation of dawn creeping over him: Tul's furious face; haying under a blazing sun with the headache oozing out of his pores. But for now, night seemed on the verge of forever. "They fought the Cygnet. The Gold King. The Dancer. The Warlock. The Lady."

"For what?"

"For Ro Holding."

"Who won?" Venn asked fuzzily. Jagger nudged him with a beefy elbow; cider splashed out of the crock onto Corleu.

"You mucker, watch my hair—"

Venn snickered. "Been watching it, it's still white as bird shit."

Jagger's arm weighed across Corleu's chest as he started to sit up. "Don't brawl in the hay," he warned. "Bad enough we're drinking in it. Get on with story, I want to hear. Venn, you say another word I'll take your teeth for my sling."

"It's the cider in my tongue," Venn said meekly.

"It's a talkative cider," Corleu said darkly.

"Go on. Who won the star fight?"

"The Cygnet of course, you loon, it's the Holding Sign of Ro Holding. The others are only Hold Signs."

"Gold King is," Jagger said after a moment, calculating. "Sign of Hunter Hold. But not the others. Not the Dancer or the Warlock or the Lady. Hold Signs are the Blood Fox and the Fire Bear—"

"And the Ring," Venn said, catching up. "The Ring of Withy Hold."

"It's the Lady's Ring," Corleu said.

"What of Blood Fox, then?"

"Cygnet broke the Warlock into pieces and trapped him in the Blood Star. His shadow fell to earth, into the Delta, into Blood Fox's shadow. That's why they say: Beware the Blood Fox with a human shadow."

They were silent a little; the thick, blazing stars had edged closer, it seemed, to listen to Corleu's tales. The Cygnet, its broad wings spanning the sky at an angle, gazed with a frosty eye over its realm. Winking, the Warlock shifted, stars limning his shadow, which, oddly enough, was both in the sky and in the Delta, attached to a Blood Fox's pads.

Jagger said, "Fire Bear."

"Fire Bear chased Cygnet all over the sky, roaring fire at it, protecting Dancer. But the Cygnet stayed just ahead, until Fire Bear held no more fire, only that one last red star in its belly. Cygnet trapped the Dancer in ice on the top of the world. Fire Bear guards her. But there's no more fire left in the Fire Bear to melt the ice. So the Dancer stays frozen."

Jagger yawned. "Pass crock. There's Gold King, still."

"You've got the crock under your arm, crockbrain."

"Get on with Gold King. Then we throw Venn in the sheep dip."

"Gold King is trapped." Corleu yawned, too, hugely, trying to suck stars into his breath and bones. "The Cygnet trapped the Gold King in the Dark House. There it is, above the farmhouse. The black house with the lintel of gold and roof of gold."

"Cygnet trapped them all," Venn said drowsily.

"All."

"They're angry up there, likely. Being trapped so long."

Hay rustled as Jagger rolled suddenly, peered over the stack. "They're not the only things angry," he muttered. "My granny sleeps like a stump, but your da had an eye to your empty bed, Venn, and so did Corleu's. Your mam's out there, too, Venn."

Venn groaned, trying to crawl deeper into the hay. Corleu took a final swallow, passed the crock to Jagger. "Summer," he said, meaning the still, green-soaked air, the vast, glowing sky, the tales and touches that seemed to tremble constantly on lip and fingertip. Jagger grunted and toasted the moon.

Withy Hold for sowing and harvest, Hunter Hold for winter, and back again . . . and again . . . and then one year the wind changed direction, or the stars shifted a hair's-breadth, or some such, for two things happened, only one of which Corleu's mother had foreseen. Venn's younger sister, Tiel, crossed the camp one day carrying a bucket of water from the stream, and Corleu, chopping wood, glanced up to find that in the interim between her going to the stream and returning, the world had transformed itself under his nose. The wooden ax handle was of a finer grain; the ground her bare feet touched had never been walked on before. Even the air was different: too shallow to breathe, so that she seemed to sparkle as she moved through the morning. She glanced up at his staring. For a moment their eyes clung. Then she looked down quickly, the water trembling in her bucket, and for the first time in his life, he cursed his great-gran and the rider in the corn, for no one, he felt, of such dark, sweet, mysterious Wayfolk beauty, could love a head of hair like his.

He had reached his full growth by then; with his father's shoulders and his startling corn-silk hair and something of the stranger in the slanted cast of his face, he drew attention. But, giving and taking pleasure now and then with young women from farms or other companies, he had thoughts only for Tiel. He watched her, and realized that all the young men in their company were falling all over each other watching her. Then someone spoke a word that, for a little, drove even the thought of Tiel into the back of his mind.

Delta.

No one ever remembered who first spoke the word—maybe it had travelled with them from Hunter Hold—but there was talk of going south to the warm, misty Delta for the season instead of to Hunter Hold. Tul snorted; Sorrel foresaw and was baffled by her seeing. "Something falls," she could only say, and, used to water, leaves, seeds, something always falling out of the sky, no one paid mind. Talk grew stronger through harvest, swept from morning fire to night fire, until autumn, when nights began to chill and old bones began to ache, and suddenly it was true, they were turning south for the winter, toward the country of the blood fox and the sea and the ancient house of the rulers of Ro Holding.

Corleu was as amazed as everyone when his parents decided to leave the company. He was still whittling away at Tul's arguments the evening before their paths forked between known and unknown.

"Withy Hold in spring, Hunter Hold in autumn and back again," Tul said, "that's what's done and what's to be done. I never liked change. Swamps and bog lilies, that's all you'll find down there. Beetles big as your hand. Damp air like steam from a kettle, smelling of rot. That's no place for us. We follow sun and stars. You should come with us, not chase after some butterfly future."

Corleu shook his head. "Past is here," he said. They sat in the wagon Tul had helped him build. The back was open to dark and fire and tender songs yearning under wanderers' fingers for times and places that never existed. On his tiny table, Sorrel had spread her petals; scents of lavender, white lilac, violet, wove into the smell of burning applewood. Corleu picked out a harebell leaf absently, twirled it between finger and thumb, his eyes, intent and implacable, on his father's face. "You can't leave past behind you like a holey boot. We're all family and ghosts of family. You'll be without shadow, in Hunter Hold."

"I'll be without son, is what," Tul retorted. "Your place is with us, to feed us and drive our wagon when we get feeble and toothless. You come with us."

"I'm going south."

"Your mother has only you. What will she do for the little folk if you marry elsewhere?"

Corleu snorted. "Likely I'll have to wait till I'm bald to marry. Who in any company would want to wake to this head of hair every morning? It's got questionable past in it."

"Your granda married," Sorrel reminded him. "And in this company."

"My gran was fey to begin with. I'm going south. I want to see Ro City."

"What for?" Tul asked in astonishment. "Walls, stones, straight lines, roofs—why city, of all?"

Corleu shifted slightly, his eyes falling away from his father. "It's old," he said to the harebell leaf. "It's got past running straight back to the beginning of Ro Holding. It casts a long shadow."

"You're Wayfolk. What has a city's past of any kind to do with you?"

"I don't know." He dropped the leaf, ran his hand through

his hair. "Stories, maybe. Old stories. Old words. Books, maybe, like Granda's."

"You have books here."

"I've read."

"Well, what more reading do you need? What more can books give you?"

"I don't know," he said again, hoving against the chair he straddled until it creaked. "It's a fair question," he admitted.

"There's no work we're used to, in cities."

"I know."

"Then what are you using your head for, besides to hang your ears on? You can't eat story, or wear it, or bed it. Best come with us."

"I'm going south."

"It's your hair," Tul said recklessly, but Corleu only nodded.

"Likely, for once. The rider in the corn gave me an unnatural taste for words. But you have them all twisted. It's not me leaving you, it's you leaving me, for something done and done until it's a wonder we don't meet ourselves coming back on the road to Hunter Hold. You might like change; you never tried it."

"I never needed it," Tul said. "None of you knows what lies south in the Delta, and here's even your mother seeing against it. Change is for weather and geese and worn-out trousers. You stay with us."

"I can't."

"Won't. Stubborn as an old root ball, you always were. Your place is with us, not by sea or swamp or whatever unfurrowed place this company muddles across. You come with us."

Corleu started to answer, then did not. His eyes were hidden; the lamplight overhead drew stray shadows beneath the bones of his face, giving it a smudge-eyed, secretive cast. Sorrel gave him an opaque glance. She sifted petals through her fingers; a pattern of colors formed on the wood. "It's you being stubborn," she said to Tul. "And blind as a harrow after a hare. He's in love."

Corleu stirred suddenly, as if he had left a splinter or two in the chair he straddled. He could feel Tul's stare like a flush of fire over his face; he refused to look up. Tul found his voice finally:

"What's that to do with the time of day or the price of a turnip? You've been in love before."

"No."

"The world is full of pretty faces."

"No."

"So you'll stay," Tul said a trifle sharply, "and go south with the geese, to mope after some girl who will show you the back of her head while she smiles at true Wayfolk—"

"I am true Wayfolk," Corleu snapped, goaded into staring back at Tul. "I walked Wayfolk paths my whole life."

"You're looking to cross thresholds in Ro City. Wayfolk shy at doorposts. My da had to drink his way through doors."

"I can't help it. It's not the doors or straight roads or high walls or lintels I want—it's the past that built the city."

"How do you expect any Wayfolk woman to understand that?"

His hands closed on the chair back. "I don't know," he said tightly, holding the chair as if Tul were about to toss it and him into deep water. "I just want. Both."

"You're besotted."

"Likely. Likely that's a word for it. Wayfolk word would be 'moonbrained.'"

Sorrel breathed softly across the petals; they drifted across the wood, changing pattern, colors hidden, colors revealed. She studied them a moment, brows pursed; then she gave notice to the tension in the air.

"Tul." Her deep voice, half imperious, half pleading, eased them both. "It's our last night."

Tul muttered softly, yielding; Corleu slumped against the chair back. Three haunting notes from a reed flute caught his ear; then he named the song and could let it go.

"My lady walks on the moon's road,
Shod, she is, in peacock feathers,
All eyes, she is, all eyes . . ."

"Besotted," he sighed. "If that's to have your head so full of one face you don't even remember whose feet you're walking on."

"Have you said so to her?" Sorrel asked practically.

"I'm biding my time."

"Till when?" Tul inquired. "Till her hair is the color of yours?"

Corleu glared at him, then dropped his face into the crook of his arm. "Till I can drag my voice back out of my boots when I try to talk to her."

"Ask now. Tonight. If she says no, you can come—"

"Tul," Sorrel murmured, and then to Corleu, "You've only spoken to her all her life." Both men looked at her in surprise. She patted Corleu's shoulder. "Nothing's secret around here. Except to your father."

"She's different now," Corleu said, gazing at the swirl of petals. "Like she went somewhere without us and came back. She makes me forget words." He cast a warning glance at Tul, waiting for abuse. But his father only blinked down at the petals as if he finally saw the pattern in them.

"I don't want you to leave us," he said gruffly. "That's the all and that's the end."

"Then come. Come with us."

"No. Not to Delta."

"Why? It's only a Hold, not another world. By the sound of you, we're travelling toward some place outside Ro Holding, not held by Lauro Ro, beyond even the Cygnet's eye."

"How can the Cygnet see anything under that bog mist?" Tul retorted. Corleu, wordless, met Sorrel's eyes and saw the end of their lives together. He stared wide-eyed at the table. She gave him no comfort; she had seen it coming since he was born.

"Well," she said softly, intent on the petals, her voice snagging here and there on a word. "You'll always know where we are. Withy Hold, Hunter Hold and back. When you need us." Then she was still, not even breathing, so still that both men drew toward her. Her hands went out, staying them, before they disturbed her pattern.

"Strange," she whispered. "Strange . . ."

Corleu studied the breath-blown petals. Troubled, he only saw in every delicate, circling path, an ending.

CHAPTER

2

So the Wayfolk came down from the heart of Ro Holding
to the Delta. Corleu, plodding through days, one eye to
the road past his mare's rump, the other to the strange,
dark, tangled horizon, never knew exactly when they left the
clear, endless blue of Withy Hold sky behind and passed into the
Delta mists. There the sun was invisible by day; at evening it
hovered, huge and blood-red, above silvery, delicate forests. The
rich, steamy, scented air clung to everything, even time, it
seemed, until it moved like the slow, indolent water moved, deep
and secret. The bog mists, the great red sun, the lovely green
drugged the eye. The final, glowing moments of sunsets, trees
like black fire against a backdrop of fire, burned into memory;
Withy Hold paled, ghostlike, into past.

Tul had guessed it: In the Delta, the Cygnet was invisible.
In the Delta were low, sultry skies, smells of mud, still water,
the sound of hidden water, the sound of a great river breaking
up into roads and trails and ruts of water, black pools and back-
washes, before it drained into Wolfe Sea. Huge, shy, graceful
birds—yellow, rose, teal—cried at night in throaty, urgent

voices. Flowers of burning colors floated on dark water, left their imprint on the eye like the sun. Like the old river road they followed, Wayfolk were drawn from wonder to wonder toward what lay beyond the mists. But the mists never parted and the road ran endlessly into them.

Corleu, driving at the end of the line, eating the dust Jagger's wagon kicked up, felt a thought move, slow and fishlike, in his swampy brain. A warm weight sat on his head, his eyelids; sat on his thoughts, too, like hot light on water. The thought surfaced finally, making him lift his head, blink. The scythe-like, silvery leaves danced above his head, not a touch of autumn on them. We have been travelling forever, he thought surprisedly. Then the drowsy, sweating, perfumed air filled his veins again. The slow wagon ahead of him, with Jagger's gran peering out the back, and the dogs trotting behind it, grew smaller and smaller. He drifted in and out of a dream of blue sky. "Limehead," he heard someone call in the dream. "Catch a cuckoo in Corleu's hair." A bird had spoken, or the river. "Moonbrain. Corleu fell off the moon." He was on the haystack again, with Jagger and Venn, pointing to the Blood Fox prowling, huge, silent, dangerous, along the horizon, dragging the star-limned shadow of the Warlock behind it. "Delta fought Cygnet under the Hold Sign of the Blood Fox . . . Milkhead. Stick your head in a bucket of milk."

He raised his head, groggy, astonished at what he was hearing. A great blood fox flowed silently out of the shadows across the road under his horse's nose. The horse reared, jolting Corleu awake; hooves pounded down on the blood fox's shadow. Corleu, staring at the shadow's human hands, nearly lost the reins when his horse bolted.

He pulled at them, shouting; horse and wagon careened across spongy, shifting ground toward a broad, lily-choked swamp. Water loomed closer; the wagon reeled, nearly throwing him; he wondered if he should jump. Then both he and the horse saw something at the water's edge. The mare veered sharply away from it. The wagon groaned on its axle; things tumbled and smacked the floor. He got the wagon turned, its back wheel laying track within an inch of water, and he harried the mare back across the trembling ground to the road. He set the brake and jumped down, shaking, his head jerking back at the swamp where he had had a confused image of the blood fox's shadow, standing upright, black as the inside of nowhere, juggling stars in its hands.

He saw no one, nothing but the lilies, little burning crowns of light on the dark water, all of them just opened that morning, it looked, or maybe the moment before he saw them. He heard a noise behind him and spun; it was Jagger, loping down road.

"Gran said you tried to drive on water," he said. He had grown into a burly young man, grim, lately, a dark, puzzling force in the world, pent-up like a beer crock and apt to blow for no reason.

"Blood fox came out of nowhere," Corleu said, and saw again its human shadow across the dust. "Ran under the mare's nose, scared her."

Jagger grunted. "Would scare me. I'll send Gran to ride with you. She pinches if you fall asleep."

"I wasn't asleep."

"She said you were drifting."

"Maybe." He shivered suddenly, breaking out of a dream. "Likely that's all it was."

"What was?"

"Just a daydream."

"What? Blood fox?"

Corleu looked at him, then away, picking through shadow at the swamp's edge. The perfect lilies teased him again, irritating, like the whine of an unseen insect. "No. Thought I saw something, is all. It scared me. Jagger, how long ago did we cross over from Withy Hold?"

Jagger shrugged. "Days. Week or two maybe."

"A month?"

"Maybe."

"Two?"

"Why?" There was sweat on Jagger's face, dust on his shoulders; he did not want to tally time. "Do you have urgent business in the city?"

"Look around you."

"What of it?" Jagger demanded, not moving.

"Just look! We left Withy Hold in autumn! Where's the dead leaves, the birds flying south overhead, the flowers withering away? Where's the season? Feels like we've travelled into winter, but nothing dies here. Nothing dies," he said again, with a curious prickling of fear, but Jagger only looked annoyed.

"Winter's gentler in the Delta," he said brusquely. Corleu snorted.

"So gentle here that death tiptoes past the flowers. And where," he added, "is everyone in this wonderland? Could harvest all year long, here, if you drain a field or two. Yet we meet no one."

"Too far from the city."

Corleu eyed him askew. "You don't find it peculiar?"

"You've never been to Delta before, why should you find it one way or another? It's Delta, nothing we're used to—"

"It's Ro Holding, not the backside of the world! Winter travels, just like Wayfolk. It should have caught up with us by now."

"Winter." Jagger squinted at him. "A week or two out of Withy Hold—"

"Or a month or two—"

"We've been slow in this heat!"

"It shouldn't be this hot!"

"You've never been here before."

"No one has!"

"There's old road under your feet—"

"Road to where? We've been nowhere but here, days, weeks—the same sky, same trees, same flowers that always look like they bloomed just a moment ago when your back was turned. Just exactly where are we, here?"

"Delta," Jagger exploded. "You cob-haired gawp, where do you think? We've found a road leads out of the world? Have you been sitting back here with your face in the cider?"

"Don't call me cob-haired." His fists were clenched; he heard himself, the edge in his voice, the idiotic words, in sudden wonder. He and Jagger hadn't brawled in years. But there was something between them, like air tense with storm, and Corleu couldn't put a name to it. He eased his hands open, said more calmly, "It feels strange here to me, is all. Something does."

Jagger kicked at a clump of grass, blinking. "My brain's melting in this heat," he muttered. He added with an effort at thinking, "I forget you can't see moon changes under this mist. Women must know, though, they keep track of days. Except my gran." A corner of his mouth went up. "She thinks we're still in Withy Hold." Then someone stepped between them and his face went dark again. Corleu breathed in the scent of hair rinsed with lavender water.

"Da sent me to ride with you."

Tiel's hair fell past her waist; behind its darkness, and her sun-polished skin, the pale swamp flowers grew, thickly clustered, carved of ivory, without a bruise of time on them. Corleu drew breath, feeling Jagger's eyes boring at him. Someone else pushed among them, clung to Tiel's skirt.

"And me," said Tiel's youngest sister, her face and hands grubby from the bread and honey she was eating. Tiel, her face suddenly averted, lifted her up. The stiff, bulky line of Jagger's shoulders eased; he grinned fleetingly.

"Shall I send my gran, too?"

"Why not." Corleu took the child from Tiel, swung her onto the wagon seat. "Send the dogs, too." He added abruptly, as Jagger turned, "It was you, then, calling me."

"What?"

"You calling me names before the horse bolted. To wake me."

"I wasn't calling you names," Jagger said. "You didn't give me time."

Corleu was struck mute for a time by the bone in Tiel's bare ankle, by the gentle, light bird-gestures of her brown hands. The child did most of the talking. Tiel stirred now and then; the threads of her skirt dragging over wood grain seemed loud as language. She said little. Corleu felt the brief, dark, wordless glances she gave him, but she never let him meet her eyes. He wished another language would startle out of him, in the shape of small birds or pearls, for his head was as vacant of words as the sky. It's my hair, he thought hopelessly, remembering his father's warning. No one could love a head of hair like this. We could talk, once. What happened?

That was north.

"Shadow fox, fox shadow," the child chanted, and Corleu tensed, his eyes flickering across the road. But it was only a rhyme for a hiding game. "Hide your fox, hide your shadow—"

"Hide your face, hide your shadow," Tiel corrected. Corleu glanced at her. She leaned toward the child; the long, dark, heavy line of her hair hid all but the brown curve of her cheek. "Go on. Red star, blood star . . ."

"Find your eyes and see."

Find your voice and talk, you gabblehead, Corleu thought. The tall, graceful trees, thick with vine and moss, cleared ahead, gave him a glimpse of the wagons strung along the overgrown track, meadow feverishly green with dank, dark water beyond it, more trees.

"It's so empty," he breathed. "We've seen no one since we left Withy Hold. Not a traveller, a trapper, a boat—you can't walk a mile in Withy Hold without running into a field wall or stepping in a cow pile. Something hinting at people."

Tiel turned her head, let him meet her eyes a moment then; the dark, flickering glance dragged the breath out of him. "Strange," she agreed, but nothing in her voice truly considered the word. She was content, her eyes seeking colors. Her hair rustled against her back as her head turned. "It's so beautiful, it is odd no one has stopped here, of those who like stopping in one spot."

Corleu, watching her speak, almost stopped the wagon, wanting to taste and swallow the words coming one by one out of her full mouth. A wheel bumped over a stone; the child, climbing into Tiel's lap, clutched at Corleu's wrist with sticky fingers, dragged him back to earth.

"Dancer danced to a dancer dancing,
"Dance! said the dancing dancer,
"Dance the dancer dancing—"

"No," Tiel said, laughing. "Dancing, the dancer danced—

"Dancing dancer danced—"

"Dancer danced—ah, my tongue's muddled. Dancing the dancer—You say, Corleu."

"Dancing, dancer danced the dance."

"And danced," they all chanted. "And danced. And danced."

"Tell story," the child demanded, and Corleu's tongue went on without them:

"She danced on a hill, she danced in a rill,
She danced on a moonbeam, danced in a dream,
Danced on a star, danced very far,
Danced in a bear's den, danced home again."

"What bear?" Tiel demanded, smiling, her eyes full on his face. They were the proper color for the sky, he thought, not blue, but deep, warm, shadowy brown, for day, for night. He shook his head, smiling back at her. "Fire Bear, likely. I only tell them, I don't make them." "Yes, you do. I've heard you make them, with Venn and Jagger." Her face flushed suddenly, was hidden behind her hair. But she finished, "When you would sit by the fire late, behind our wagon. You thought everyone was asleep. But I listened." He felt his own face warm. "They weren't meant for you. Only for our potato ears and sheep brains."

"I know," she said. Her face came out of her hair, composed again. "Goat brains, more like. Bat-wing ears. But I liked—I like how you say things. How you see. Even asleep, I'd hear your voice." She was gone again, bird-quick. He swallowed, a blink away from letting the reins slide out of his hands, touch a strand of her hair with his fingertips, shift it aside to find her.

He said unsteadily, for he had never put it to words before, "All stories seem old to me, even the ones born in my brain. Likely it's because words are so old. Story words, that is. They carry bits of older tales with them. Like Dancer. She could be you, dancing. Or she could be the star Dancer, who brings you dreams from both the fair side and the terrible side of morning." He paused. "It's what I think I want to do."

"What?"

"Go to Ro City and learn more words." His mouth crooked. "Sounds silly. More stories, maybe. Something."

"But what would you do with them?"

"I don't know." He flicked a fly off the mare's rump with a rein. "Keep saying and keep saying them until I get all the way back to the first thing they mean." He glanced at her, wondering if she wondered what murky waters lay between his ears. But she only asked thoughtfully:

"Can you do the things your granda could? Or your mother? Foresee in water, in petals?"

"Me? No. I only got his hair." He slid it back between his fingers, to cool his face. "My mother tried to teach me petals, but all I ever saw in them was color, never any—never—" He faltered, his mind filling with petals then: dried roses, verbena, lavender . . . the pattern they had made under his mother's breath, paths circling, circling. . . .

Something—an echo—made him realize she had spoken again. "What?" he asked, then knew he had made no sound. He had gone away again, to some place chill, lonely, terrifying. "What?" he said again, and came back to the pale, heavy misty sky, the long afternoon. He shivered suddenly in the heat. His eyes searched sky, trees, water, for some sign—any sign—of change: a hill, a different kind of tree, even a wild swan or a stork flying south for winter. "I think," he said tightly, "I know where we travelled to."

"Where?"

"Trouble."

But she did not seem to notice the word. The child sat drowsing in her arms; her eyes had strayed from Corleu to a long tumble of orange and yellow blossoms, all fully opened, he noticed, all perfect, not one too young or too old for the moment he saw them.

"My mother foresaw this," he breathed.

"What?"

"This place. Day after day circling under this grey sky, no true sky for stars to point the way, no moon, no sun . . ."

"Yes, there's sun. Look. It's about to set."

The evening fire was beginning, the slow kindling of the horizon into gold, then red, then deep, deep purple before the black, starless night poured over them again. Tiel's eyes filled with the sunset; her face held the smooth blankness of a dreamer. She had forgotten Corleu.

It's this place, he thought, terrified. This place.

They made a loose circle of the wagons in a meadow. Children of all ages broke out of the small colored rolling houses, flickered like night sprites in and out of the twilight. "Corleu," a boy called, and then a girl: "Corleu." In the dusk their faces blurred past him; their changing voices were unfamiliar. Surely there were not so many smallfolk in the company, he thought. There were too many voices, echoes of the past, as if they had carried even his own, Jagger's, Tiel's childhood ghosts down from the north. Then he saw Tiel, chasing after one of the smallfolk, laughing, her hair rising in a slow, dark wave, then settling as she ran. The world went simple again, everything in its place, no mysteries beyond the mystery of Tiel's hair, rising darkly and falling. Then a girl said, "Corleu" behind him and laughed. He turned quickly, for that voice, that laugh, was long past and far behind. Someone circled behind him silently; he felt a long skirt whirl and fall against him, a brush of long fine bones: hands, back, shoulders against his shoulders. He turned to face her, saw only Tiel, walking away from him as she carried the child across the camp.

He drew a deep breath, moving through the still, heavy dusk as if it were thick with ghosts. He took the ax from inside the wagon, walked down the stream to cut wood. The underbrush rustled, as if someone walked beside him. The slow water murmured his name. He felt the hair rise on the back of his neck. "Corleu," a girl whispered: the young, flaxen-haired lord's daughter who had stopped him in a field one day. He smelled again the crush they had made of grasses, of wildflowers, mingling with the scent of her body. A flower or a finger brushed his mouth. He turned, felt again the quick, light touches of someone's body, circling him as he turned. Skirt wrapped around his ankles, a hip touched his. He dropped the ax, reached out with both hands to catch the dancer. No one was there. Leaves rustled, farther down the stream.

He came back under full night. Around the camp fires, he saw faces that bewildered him with their sullenness. *Where did you go, Corleu?* eyes asked. *Who have you been with?* They gazed at him without smiling, without moving, their bodies shadowed, only their expressions molded in both dark and fire. *You,* their faces said, with envy, longing, mistrust. *You.*

He concentrated the next day, as intent on moving into one simple moment after the next as if he were piecing his way step by step across a bog. The reins in his hands. The string of wagons—blue, yellow, white, red—with drying clothes flapping and children's brown faces peering out the backs. A woman singing behind him. The song stirred his memories. The deadly, silver smiles of scythes among the ripe wheat, the dry *hwick* of their work. Women bent, bundling the wheat; he and Tiel, Jagger and Venn, and Lark, their hands almost too small, picking up the bundles, leaning them together in threes. He, then Tiel, then Jagger. When Tiel's hands slowed, brought her closer to Corleu, then Jagger's movements would slow, until she was centered between them, then closer to Jagger. All afternoon, sun soaking into them; the whirling glint of metal; a baby crying; the smells of wheat, earth, wild flowers; their joking; Sorrel ahead, singing as she bound up the stalks. Singing of . . . what?

A baby's rhyme, a nonsense tale about a little black hut with a gold roof and a lintel of gold that tumbled out of the sky, and how you must never pass beneath the lintel, for if you do, you will see it is not a hut at all, but—

Corleu!

His head jerked. The world built around him again: mist, pale green, and the feverish colors of the flowers. His throat swelled with a silent protest. He felt the sweat on his face. Luckily the horses were still plodding in line. He thought of calling Jagger, but what could he say? I was dreaming again. You gawp. He concentrated. The reins in his hands . . . The little hut with the gold roof, falling, falling out of the sky . . .

He was still concentrating at the end of the day, so hard he had all but forgotten how to speak. Stop wagon. Feed and water horse . . . The water in the skins was low, so he slung them over his shoulders, walked through the camp as through a company of shadows, ignoring all claims on his name. Find flowing water, kneel. Open skins . . . Then, at the bottom of the shallow stream, he saw jewels flash. He stared at them, and finally recognized what he had not seen since Withy Hold: stars, reflected in the water, so clearly he might have picked them out like pebbles. If he looked away from them, they would vanish, something warned. So he knelt on the bank without moving, gazing at the ring of stars the Blind Lady wore on her finger. The water darkened; the stars grew bright, luminous, fire-white. They held all time, those stars, and he watched, his lips parted, scarcely breathing, for it seemed that any moment the dark within the stars would open, show what lay beyond the endless night.

Something struck him so hard he sprawled with a grunt on the muddy bank. Someone straddled him, gripped his shirt at the throat. His head rattled a few times against the ground before his eyes adjusted to the milky light that the moon shed behind the mists. He cried sharply, astonished, "Jagger!"

The weight shifted off him. Jagger was breathing heavily, a dark, aggrieved presence in the dark.

"Do you know," he demanded, "how long you've sat there? Just sat, like a rabbit cross-eyed under the moon?"

"I just got here, you muckerhead! I just came for—"

"It's full night!"

Corleu's breath stopped. He sat up; his eyes went back to the water. But the stars were gone; they never could have been there. He made some sound Jagger took as argument.

"You go off," he continued doggedly, "you're gone hours, you come back looking like you've been some secret place, with your ax but no wood, or your skins—" He picked them out of the mud, flattened by Corleu's back. "Empty. I had to follow you, to see where you go when you go."

Corleu rolled to his feet wordlessly; Jagger caught his wrist, nearly sent him into the water. Down the bank a blood fox's eyes caught some stray swamp light, flared amber red at them.

"It's this place," Corleu said. He was breathing so shallowly he could hardly speak. "This place. It's bewitched. I tried to tell you—"

"Not this place, it's you!"

"No—"

"You look at us all like a stranger, like something is swallowing you from inside. You barely talk anymore, even to her; you don't see us, not even her—"

"Who?" He jerked at the suddenly painful hold. "Who?" he said through gritted teeth. Jagger hauled him closer.

"Who. You blind owl. We watch her, she watches you, and you walk past her like she's smoke. It's you her eyes follow. And you don't—you don't even—you sit here staring at water while Reed and Dawl and Steof and me, we have to fight to lie in her path for her to walk across while she watches you—they all do. Watch you. You with that hair the color of—"

Corleu wrenched free. "Bird-shit. Slug-slime. I've heard all the white words there are by now. I can't believe you're standing there throwing your tongue around the color of my hair while you're knee-deep in trouble and sinking fast. Can't you see it? We blundered onto a road to nowhere; we drove our wagons outside time into a haunted place. Things are strange here. Things are dangerous."

"Something is," Jagger said tightly. "And it's you in danger. You've got us all smoldering and you're too spellbound to see—"

"It's not me!"

"It's you wandered out of the world, not us. Someone twisted your path for you, and if you don't find who, you'll keep on reeling through your days, trapped inside your head. I'd say most likely Steof, his mother knows things."

"No." He gripped Jagger's shoulders. "It's none of us!

Jagger, I've seen Blood Fox with the human shadow here. I felt the Dancer dance circles around me. Tonight you stopped me falling headfirst into the Ring of Time at the bottom of the water. It's a dream world we wandered into, and it scares my blood thin. We think we're heading south through Delta, but we're only circling and circling, that's why we never meet anyone, and why we never reach the sea, because there is no sea, there is no south, no north, we've travelled outside Ro Holding and not even the Cygnet itself can see into this land.''

"You're babbling," Jagger breathed. "You're moonstruck.''

"But what moon?" Corleu shook him furiously, rocking him off balance half a step. "We left moon and stars in Withy Hold!''

"You don't even care.''

"Of course I care. Why do you think I'm shouting myself blind, you stump-headed—''

"You don't even ask what I'm talking about.''

"What?''

"You just ramble. You don't care who.''

Corleu was silent, baffled by the mist in Jagger's head. He closed his eyes wearily, looking for words, and saw Tiel behind them, her hair so straight and heavy that when she swung her head it fanned the air and fell strand by strand back into place. He swallowed. "That's why.'' He opened his eyes to Jagger's night-hollowed eyes. "That's why you're angry at me. Because I followed her here, instead of taking my moonhead to Hunter Hold, out of her sight. But can't you see for once it's not Tiel matters, what matters is this place we—''

The night exploded in his eyes; he found himself trying to finish with his face under water. I should have gone to Hunter Hold, he thought bleakly. He felt Jagger's hands hauling at him. He turned and kicked hard; there was a cry and a massive splash. He waded out, dripping and coughing, saw again the chilling, red-washed stare of blood-fox eyes.

He woke near dawn, and, still half-dreaming, had all the horses loose and wandering off into the trees. Then he walked aimlessly across slow branch water, through perfumed woods— in circles, he thought likely—but he kept moving, until heat and weariness wore him down. He rested under a cascade of lilies flowing down tree branches into a small, deep pool. He sat shredding the perfect flowers, listening to the furious, distant shouting. "Corleu!" they called; gathering up the horses, they would blunder across him eventually. "Corleu!" He picked another flower, tossed it into the pool. It floated, turning delicately on an invisible current.

"Corleu."

Tiel stood beside the tumble of lilies. He stared at her; she looked like something the morning had just fashioned out of shadow and light and the mysterious, silvery green leaves. "Corleu," she said again, softly, when he didn't speak. "They're all angry with you. Jagger says you've gone moon mad."

"There's no moon," he said. But there was, he realized; she had brought it with her: moon and stars, the memory of the green-scented summer nights.

"Everyone is looking for you. Jagger says you should go back to Withy Hold, the Delta mists are driving you loony."

He shook his head. "This road goes one way only, and where, none of us knows yet." He barely heard himself; he wanted only to sit and look at her, in the bewitched morning, while the world turned circles around them.

"Delta," she reminded him, but there was the shadow of a question in her voice.

"No."

She paused, perplexed. Their eyes held in the silence. She swallowed. "Corlcu," she said, and, surprised, he felt as if no one had ever spoken his true name before. "What—what's to be done, then? If this is not true Delta, then where do we find it?"

"I don't know. But I can't just go on blind; there must be something to point, someone to say why all this, why this place that never changes, why . . ." But under her gaze he was forgetting why he cared, why they should not circle forever in that changeless, sultry, scented air. Her body had pulled back from him a little, disturbed at his words. But her eyes clung. Within them he watched doors open, one after another, revealing things he had never seen in her before. Her voice sank, barely more than a whisper.

"Maybe if you—if you come back with me and try to explain—Maybe, Corleu, maybe if—" She faltered into silence. They stared at one another, lost, he felt, in a dream within a dream.

He wanted to put his cheek against her long eyelashes to feel them brush his skin. He wanted to gather all her long, heavy hair into his hands until they overflowed with darkness. He wanted to circle her bare ankles with his fingers, her bare neck with his hands. He wanted to fall into her eyes with all the opening chambers in them, and keep falling and keep falling. . . . He whispered, "Tiel." And then she fell toward him, seemingly from a long distance, and as she fell, he felt himself yearn toward her as if a wind had pushed him.

The block of night across the small pool finally caught his eye. It had been dragging at him for some time: a square of black between his hand and her breast, a flick of dark over her closed eyelids, hidden within the braid his busy fingers had unwoven. He raised his head, one of her bodice laces between his teeth, blinking at strands of her hair that clung to his eyelashes. There it was, fallen out of nowhere: the tiny house. Four black walls, the gold roof, the lintel of gold. Standing without sound or movement in a riffle of mist.

He was still, so still that Tiel, fingers tangled in his hair, finally opened her eyes. She turned her head. Her lips moved silently, as if they were remembering a song. Then she sat up in horror, tugging at her bodice as if the lintel were an eye. "What is it?" she breathed.

Four stars its walls, one star its roof, one star its lintel, and the blue star its latch, so he had heard the lord's daughter describe it, in formal language, as she lay beside him, her ringed hand pointing out stars in a warm night tumbling with wind. The Hold Sign of Hunter Hold: seven stars that trapped the golden warrior's face of the sun.

The little dark house that falls from the sky . . .

He shuddered, feeling the cold tighten his skin, the bone-bare chill of recognition.

"Corleu!"

He dropped his face, kissed her numbly. "My mother saw it. Something falling. And she saw our path in her petals circling, circling. . . ."

"But it wasn't here when we came!"

"It was always here. It's the dream we're in." Still holding her tightly, he eased to her side, his eyes intent on the house. He breathed, "And there's the door."

"What door?"

"The door out of the dream."

She stared at him. "How do you know? How can you say that's the way out, just looking at it?"

"It's a door. It's the only door we've come across anywhere for weeks. You come in a door, you go out."

"No." She pushed against him suddenly, her face in his neck, hands gripping his shirt. "No. Wayfolk don't cross under doorways."

"Listen to me."

"No! I'm not listening!"

He kissed her hair, her jaw, found her lips again. "Listen," he whispered, and she stopped him speaking, plundering his words until he fell back, inarticulate. A stone, intruding between soft ground and his head, made him remember how to talk. "Listen to me," he said, blinking, hoisting to his elbow. "Listen. We're all spellbound in this dream country. Nowhere is where we're going. There's a door out. It's here, to be opened now— now, or we may be left here on our own in a world where nothing lives as easily as in one where nothing dies."

"Find Venn's mam, she knows things—"

"No. What if it goes? What if it's our only way and it disappears? My da was right. Not even the Cygnet can see through this mist. The only one can see in it and around it and beyond it is trapped in that little ancient house...."

"What are you saying? Whose house is it? Who is trapped?"

"And he trapped us...."

"Who?"

He had made the first movements away from her without realizing it: pulling up, beginning to rise. She grasped at him in horror, and he felt the blood lurch out of his face, at where his next steps would take him.

"I'll be back," he said, pulling her to her feet as he rose.

"No! Corleu, no!"

"I will." He pulled her against him, hard, and even then he felt the cold slide shadowlike between them. "Wait for me."

"How can you leave me?" she cried, as he loosed her, and, stepping away, he felt his whole body pull toward her. He caught his breath, dazed, her face and the house and all the colors of that enchanted world blurring together in his eyes.

"I don't know, I don't know, I don't know, I love you, I love you."

"Corleu!"

"I'll bring you back the stars. . . ."

He was running, half-blind, along the edge of the pool, when he heard her scream at him again.

"Corleu! It's the house! It's the black house with the roof of gold that falls from the sky! Don't go into it! Don't! It's the house you'll never leave!"

He ran faster. In another country, he heard oars in an oarlock, water stroked and lifted, words. He left all his thoughts behind, ran under the gold lintel, into the dark.

He stood with his eyes shut, waiting.

There was a smell of fish cooking.

Startled, he opened his eyes. He was instantly sorry. Inside, the small house stretched endlessly; the dark around him shimmered with vague colors, forms that he almost recognized until he stared straight at them, and then they dissolved, washed away by some invisible, lightless tide. He made the mistake of looking down.

All the stars in the night sky hung beneath his feet, as if he had stepped through the Ring to stand outside of time. He closed his eyes again, felt his whole body cry out, though his voice was frozen and made no sound. He began to fall back into the black, shining waters of time. Stars flowed past him like the bubbles of his final breath.

He smelled grass. He opened his eyes, lifted his head groggily. Sunlight he had not seen in weeks struck his face. Through the misty gold he saw Tiel again. He stretched his hand to her, tears of relief filling his eyes that he had fallen through all the worlds there were to find himself with her again.

Darkness fell between them before he could touch her. The

filigreed dome of night rose over him, with its vast humans and prowling animals. The Dark House hung above the Cygnet's outstretched wing: the four stars marking its walls, one star its peaked roof, one star its lintel, the seventh the door latch that Corleu had opened. Within the dark house . . .

Within the dark house . . .

Within the dark house he opened his eyes and saw the shrunken, dusty floorboards. Beyond the door he had flung open, perfect lilies tumbled from the tree-bough, down toward the pool.

There was the smell of fish cooking.

Within the Dark House he opened his eyes and saw beyond the open door the black, black night and the huge, northernmost star of the Cygnet's outstretched wing.

Someone was singing. It was a smallfolk rhyme, about a dark house falling, falling out of the sky, and how you must never enter it, for having entered, you will never leave. . . . He lay listening, his skin prickling with horror, because the door was open, he could have touched the dusty sill with his hand, but he could not move; he had leaped beyond the world into a child's song, into the story behind the song.

There was the smell of fish cooking.

He opened his eyes. He no longer saw the black walls, but he knew the Dark House rose all around him, beyond the mists, its four walls the night, its shining lintel the star that was the world's lintel.

There was the smell of fish cooking.

He sat up so abruptly that stars flecked his vision; he blinked fire into shape, water, a face.

A shaggy-haired man cooked over a fire beside the pool; from his battered pan came the smell of fish. Corleu's eyes flickered across the pool. The lilies cascaded endlessly; the petals he had shredded still circled slowly in the water. He could not see Tiel. He turned quickly, looking for the house, in a desperate hope that he had only leaped into a dream and knocked his head against truth so hard he saw stars. . . . A tinker's wagon stood where the house had been. The black horse that drew it was stone-still in harness, not even blinking; its hooves and mane were shaggy as the tinker's hair. Corleu could not take his eyes off the wagon. It was a tiny, rolling house, shadow-dark, with a peaked yellow roof and a yellow lintel; black stairs ran up into the open door. Painted in weathered yellow on the door was an ancient Hold Sign: the Gold King, with his furious, sun-round face and fiery petals of hair, imprisoned by the seven stars that formed the Dark House.

Corleu dragged his eyes from it finally to the face beside the fire.

It was a lean, swarthy face, with astonishing eyes of such light hazel they looked yellow. They smiled a little at Corleu; for a moment the smile was unfathomable. Then, in a shift of light, it was simply friendly. The tinker stirred the fish in the pan, cocked a dark brow at Corleu.

"Fish?" He ticked his fork against the side of the pan as Corleu stared at him. "Have a bite. Fish improves the mind. They say."

"Fish." His voice barely sounded.

"They say. Though," he added, "those swamp fish are ghostly things. Sweet, mind you, but pallid, as if they've been down in that pool for several hundred years. They might do for the brain, but they do nothing to improve the eye."

Corleu said nothing. He felt as ancient and pallid as the fish in the pool, something washed out of time's backwaters, without much brain to speak of, for he had been caught, it seemed, on a tinker's hook. Or had he? He cast a glance at the tiny, wheeled house; the Gold King glared fiercely at him, dusty and peeling. He swallowed drily. The tinker was filling his patched plate. His clothes were patched as well, with motley at neck and knee and elbow. He wore gold in one ear; a thin gold chain around his neck disappeared into his shirt. Words tossed crazily in Corleu's head. Tinker or King? King or tinker? He said finally, since the tinker had handed him a fish to deal with:

"Mist might do that to them."

"Mist?"

"Make them pale. For lack of sun. There is no sun under these mists. Except that on your wagon."

The tinker's mouth went up a fraction. "Likely you've hit upon the problem."

"Could cut these mists with a knife."

"To be sure. But," he added, raising the knife he cooked and ate with, "knife is not what's needed here."

"No?"

"No. Besides, you haven't got one. I noticed, as you slept. Not a knife or horse nor pot to your name."

"Not here. Wherever here is."

"A damp, muggy, empty place it is. Pretty, though. Smells nice."

"It wasn't empty—" His hands had closed; he kept his voice calm with an effort. "It wasn't empty. It had all my Way-folk company in it."

"Ah. Wayfolk, are you? You wandered off the road a bit."

"Far off. So far off I don't know anymore where I am."

"You're between earth and sky like the rest of us, walking from morning until the fall of night like all folk." He worked a fishbone out of his mouth. "Going from here to there, in one door, out the other, one place to—"

"Door." His voice shook as it seized the word. "In one door. What other door?"

The tinker crooked a brow. "It's a saying. An expression, so to speak. Are you sure you won't have a—"

"No. In one door, out the other, you said. A way in, a way out. That's what you said."

The yellow eyes, catching light, seemed to smile again. "You're a quick one, taking words up as fast as they fall. But, glancing around, I don't much see there's an in or an out here, unless maybe to the world itself."

"There's one," Corleu said. He was as tense as if he were poised to run for his life: A flower hitting the pool in the silence that followed his words would have sprung him piecemeal all over the ground.

The tinker glanced at the door, surprised. "So there is. But that's only my wagon with the one door in and out."

"It's a door. It's here."

"You're welcome to it. I'll be here waiting," he added, as Corleu got to his feet, "when you come back out."

Corleu paused. The dark house stood, weathered and tantalizing, a dream within a dream. He had yet to enter it, he had already entered it. It rose all around him, invisibly. Beyond it, there was Tiel, inside . . . another dark house, with perhaps inside it another dark house. . . .

And another . . . He was shivering in the warm air, as if the icy stare of the Cygnet's eye had rimed his bones as he fell past. He slid his hands over his face, murmuring, uncertain that Tiel would be anywhere in any of those houses, no matter how many he entered. He dropped his hands. The door was still there, beyond the tinker, who was still picking at his fish. He walked toward it. The tinker smiled; creases ran down his brown, stubbled cheeks, imprisoning his smile.

"Where are you going, Master Corleu?"

He felt his heart pound at the sound of his name. He did not dare look back. "To undo what I just did."

"Ah. Doing and undoing." Something in the tinker's voice caught Corleu mid-step, as if he had reached out long, clever fingers and gripped him. "You can't do and undo through the same door." Corleu turned slowly, the cold sweat gathering at his hairline. "You know that. Under that hair."

Corleu was silent, staring at the tinker behind the flames, with the gold in his ear and the flecks of gold in his eyes. Smoke billowed at Corleu; he blinked away tears, trying to see clearly through the harsh mist. He felt words push out of him, the last thing he wanted to say, the only thing he had left to say.

"That house," he whispered.

"My wagon?"

"Your dark house with the yellow lintel and the yellow roof."

"It's my house."

"It's the house of the Gold King."

"It's my house."

His heart beat raggedly; the colors of leaf and lily were suddenly too vivid. "Then you are the Gold King."

The tinker's smile did not change. He spat out a fishbone and said, "The dark house is a child's song. One of those songs Wayfolk brats are endlessly singing. If I were King would I live in such a tiny, dark, windowless house?"

"Not if you could find a door out."

"The Gold King is a moldy old shepherd's tale, one of those silly stories that get passed around the world like air, only if they were dreams and smoke they wouldn't be keeping such as the Gold King alive, would they, listening to his spoken name? Yes or no, Master Corleu?"

"Yes." Sweat, mingling with tears from the smoke, ran down his face. "No."

"If I were the Gold King, if I just happened to be him, eating fish in your company, how would I free myself?" He chewed a bite, regarding Corleu, knife pointed at him to invite answer. "How would I, do you think?"

"I don't—I don't know—"

"Think."

He licked dry lips. "You would likely find a door."

"I have a door."

"Then you would—you would—" He closed his eyes, finished in the dark. "You would likely find a moonbrained fool muckerheaded enough to enter your house, and get him to do what you can't."

"Ah. A muckerheaded fool who thinks, is it? Good, Corleu. And think this over: What, likely, would I ask you to do?"

If he closed his eyes tightly enough, to shut out every splinter of light, he could see Tiel again, under a tumble of green leaves and lilies, her hair unbraided, her bodice loosened over her soft, nut-brown breasts. If he closed his eyes still tighter, he could see her eyes smiling, he could see his smiling reflection in her eyes. If he shut out all light, maybe he could slip through the dark, back into memory. There he could linger forever as he had been, in some distant, former life, too stupid to do. There in that private green memory, he could bury himself instead of asking the question that was forcing itself like breath out of his mouth.

He opened his eyes; they were burning; his throat burned. "I don't know. What would you ask me to do?"

The tinker, finished with his fish, gazed at his reflection in the round tin plate. "Most likely just a small thing. Very small. Maybe I would . . . Yes. Maybe I would ask you to find something for me."

"What thing?"

"A little thing." He tapped the knife against his teeth, musing to himself. "A very small thing . . ."

"Where?"

"That's just it." He raised his head to smile at Corleu. "It's possible, Corleu, that I don't know where this small thing is. I've mislaid it, lost track of it, it went its way through time without me. It's entirely likely that you'll have to find it for me, as a clever young man who found his way through my door could do."

"Where?" Corleu whispered.

"Back, ahead, before, behind. It may be hidden in a stone, a star, another child's song. I have a few friends who might have glimpsed it, might have heard, might know exactly where. For instance, you might ask the Blind Lady. You've seen her silver ring. If you had something in trade, something she might wish for, as I have wished for this thing . . . For instance, you might give her what's on the peacock's feather. That's all we're in the business of here, you understand, Corleu. Trade. A bit of labor for me, a return to you of what I'm keeping of yours. A little something for us all."

"What is it you want?"

The tin plate in the tinker's hands was beginning to glow; light reflecting off it turned his face gold. His eyes, contemplating Corleu, were gold as coins. For a long time he looked at Corleu without answering, only smiling his tight smile, while the light crept over fire, water, lilies, even the black horse, coloring them gold.

"A small thing, Corleu. Just a small thing."

"But what—" He had to struggle to find air. "Tell me what—"

The circle in the tinker's hands was acquiring a face. The tinker covered his face with it like a mask. The gold light spilled over his hair. The eyes in the circle opened, blazing gold, tempestuous. The hot light flared into Corleu's eyes. He flinched away from it, crying out, "I don't know what you want!"

"Find it. . . ."

The world flooded with light. He threw his arms over his eyes, feeling the sun drench him, close around him like the hot, heavy, clinging embrace of the summer days he remembered. A voice blasted at him like a roaring furnace. He dropped his arms, trembling, feeling oddly scorched.

He stood in a vast hall of pure gold, no other color; the light cast no shadows. Upon a gold dais sat a gold throne; upon the gold throne sat the Gold King. Lip, eyelash, fingernail, he could have been melted and stamped for coins. His face was a mingling of tinker's face and the sun-face in the Hold Sign of Hunter Hold: wide-boned, wide-eyed, crowned with wild locks of gold hair. He wore a massive sword and armor spiked with points of gold at neck and wrist, knee and elbow. He was chained by one ankle to his throne.

Corleu stared at him, stunned.

"Don't fret, Corleu. You'll find it." The tinker-king moved restively, testing his chain, pulling it after him as he paced. "A quick young man like you, who can see through dreams and shadow-lands. Who knows? If you find this for me, I might see my way to rewarding you with other things you might have seen and coveted, along your way.'' He held up a gold-armored hand as Corleu opened his mouth. ''Now, don't be hasty. I know all you want now is your love beside you, and an open road through the Delta to the sea. I'll give you that, don't fear. But, as you search for this, you may begin to think a little, about what else you might ask for. I can listen, I'm prepared to be accommodating.''

''Why?'' he asked, his voice raw with bitterness and terror for Tiel. ''Of every sheep-brained fool in Ro Holding, why did you pick my life to fall into?''

The tinker-king laughed, swinging his heavy chain with an effort. ''You were easiest to spot, with that hair. You were always saying our names, stargazing, never thinking who might be listening. Why did you go into my house? You knew what it was. Everything you ever heard about that dark house said: 'Do Not Enter.' And what do you do? You get a little weary of looking at mists, of not seeing the sun or the stars that turn time in their cogs, so you throw yourself headlong against the oldest warning of all. Look at you, standing here while your love wanders in an empty garden without you. Who else would have left her there at such a moment? Who else in Ro Holding would have been that moonbrained?'' A sound came out of Corleu, half sob, half wordless agreement. ''Ah, I told you, don't fret. I need you, so I took you.''

''If you—if you harm her, any of them—''

''You'll what? Stop the dark house from falling? Stop the sun from rising?'' He turned again, grimacing slightly as he dragged his chain. ''It's a simple business, Corleu. You'll see. If you give me what I want, I'll give you what you want. But you must never tell. Listen to me. Don't speak. You must never tell anyone what you are looking for. Because, then, even if you find it for me, you will never find, either awake or dreaming, anywhere in your life, this little misty, timeless garden you have abandoned.''

''I don't know what you want!''

The cry echoed off gold walls, splintered in corners where lines of gold melted to a single point. Corleu, his unanswered plea bouncing all around him, felt himself fall again, the endless falling within dreams. Eyes watched him: the Peacock's tail, the

Blood Fox's yellow star, the Fire Bear's ice-blue stare. He heard his younger voice, telling story. . . .

The tinker sat beside his fire, roasting something small on a twig. Overhead the mists were darkening; the curve of gold in the chain around the tinker's neck caught, from somewhere, a stray spark of light.

"Bite?" he asked genially. The small thing on the stick was charred. Corleu's throat knotted at the smell. He shook his head, his eyes gritty from the harsh smoke roiling up from the spattering flames. He had fallen on his knees, supplicant to a tinker-king, but he had torn his voice raw with his last cry. He could barely whisper, as the thing on the stick dripped into the fire and the heat and the smoke billowed over him.

"Just. Tell me. What you want."

The tinker lifted the twig from the fire, slid the small, bloody, burned thing off and bit into it.

"The heart of the Cygnet."

CHAPTER
4

Corleu opened his eyes.

His face was in a puddle, one foot was in a stream, and the water in both places was freezing—that much he realized before several hands heaved him up and tossed him like a hay bale into the bottom of a boat. His head cracked against an oar; the breath was knocked out of him. Stunned, he could not move. The boat rocked under him; a pair of boots settled next to his ear.

"That's it. That's the last of it." The boat wallowed away from the bank. Current caught it. The oarlocks rattled and creaked.

"Petrified blood-fox spoor, she said," a younger voice objected. "She wanted that, she said."

"She may want what she wants, but nothing petrifies here. Things molder or get eaten here." The boot near Corleu's ear lifted, tapped his cheek. "This one is fresh dead. His skin is still on his bones."

"He never came out of the bog," the second voice protested. "Bones buried in the bog, she said."

"Where'd he come from, then? Fallen out of the sky?"
"We could toss him over, let a bog-hole chew on him, then pull him out again. He'd be authentic then. A true bog man."
Corleu caught his breath at the idea. There was a sudden silence; even the oarlocks were silent. "He's alive." A hand pulled his hair, tugged his head up. "He's breathing. He's bleeding quick blood."
"Well, how were we to know? What was he doing lying alive in this sour mire?"
"Throw me rope. Quick!"
Corleu moved dizzily, futilely. His hands were caught, knotted behind his back. When he opened his mouth to protest, a cloth smelling of old fish was jammed between his teeth. He was rolled onto his back. He blinked the faces above him clear against the misty dawn.
"He's not a bog man," a heavy-set, one-eyed man pronounced finally. "Nor marsh bones. Nor even dead."
"Toss him down the next sinkhole," a skinny young man with a wispy beard suggested. "Then we'd have it: dead bones out of the marsh."
The one-eyed man considered Corleu dispassionately. He shifted a twig from one side of his teeth to the other. "She won't pay for murder. I'm not climbing those stairs for nothing."
"She'll never know!"
"She'll know. I gave her murdered bones once, and she said they did nothing in her fire but weep and complain at her until she stopped and buried them. None of my fault, they never complained to me, so how was I to know? But she knew. Things talk to her."
"Then what will we do with this one? Heave him back on shore?"
"He'll be annoyed by now, likely. I'm too old for dealing with him if we untie him, and you're too puny. If we leave him here tied in this wild, that will be murder. Turtles would eat him if blood fox didn't."
Corleu chewed ineffectually at the cloth in his mouth. A grey-brown world slid past him. Tall trees with pale trunks rose out of the water, their long scythe-like leaves long fallen; the boat tacked unhurriedly around them. Carpets of rotting lily pads sent a bitter smell along the breeze. The dawn world rustled and cried with hunger. A snake, draped in deep blue scallops along

a branch, straightened like a whip and dropped into the water, narrowly missing the boat. An oar slapped at it. Water flecked Corleu's face. A thought was reeling crazily into his head: that this was the true Delta, of snakes and slow cold murky water and trees that had not only left summer behind but autumn as well. The boat passed vines cascading down from a rotten bough into the water. They hung limply, leafless, shrivelled with cold. He had a sudden vision of Tiel sitting under them, growing pale, drawn with despair, fading away like a ghost in a fading dream world. He pulled at the rope, gave a muffled groan of such fear and frustration and bewilderment that the eyes above him became almost human.

"Should we let him talk? Ask him what left him here?"

"No," the one-eyed man said. "Let her ask. She might find a use."

The boat meandered endlessly under the colorless sky. Great white birds cried hoarsely overhead, their wings rattling like old bones as they flew. Now and then a blood fox barked in the distance. They were travelling south, Corleu saw, with an eye on the current. Deeper into the Delta. Shivering with cold, he dreamed the sun, a fuming, hot-eyed, petal-haired face busy eating day and stars, the world, time. It fixed its furious gaze on him, said his name: *Corleu.* He jerked himself awake, heard a bird cry mournfully: *Corleu.*

The trees thinned; water shunted into a slow side channel and from there bled into a wide lagoon. They passed a great, dark tangled cave of tree roots where a huge tortoise older than Ro Holding, it looked, slowly blinked at them as it turned itself into stone. Its neck protruded from a shell ruffled with white agate; its jaws could have enclosed Corleu's face. Its eyes, velvety with age, pondered him and narrowed into slits of night.

The boat slipped through lazy shallows, among a grove of statues: old, worn, silvery stumps still rooted in the water, that some passing artist had whittled into shapes. A huge, long-legged egret gazed upward, its beak open as if to nibble at the sun. A squat toad sat on the water, its rolled tongue about to snap and snag the boat. A child, pulling her skirt above her knees, waded through dead lily pads; a lily trailed from her long hair. A naked man with the bunched, bulky shoulders and pointed teeth of a blood fox smiled at Corleu. He started; human blood fox became

tree again, its shoulders molded of broken boughs, one eye a
dark stain of pitch.

"Blood fox," the young man said, and Corleu turned his
head. A huge one gazed at them from the shore; the young man
stared back at it, an odd mix of hate and wonder in his eyes.
"Big. Look at its eyes. Evil. Beware the blood fox casts a human
shadow."

"That's a worn old tale. Blood fox isn't evil."

"It kills. I saw it kill a hunter once."

"What was hunter hunting?"

"Blood fox."

"So, then. Bad luck to kill a blood fox."

"They're bad luck. Look at its eyes. Blood fire in them.
Look at it. How it's watching. How it's watching."

"Delta belongs to the blood fox," the one-eyed man said.
"It laid claim long before us. Long before any Ro held Ro
Holding."

"It hates us. We took the Delta from it. We kill it, with
long knives and nets for sport."

"It doesn't hate us, any more than the little-boned animals
it eats hate it. Things are killed. Things kill."

Corleu shifted, trying to make himself smaller against the
cold. Shadow darkened over his closed eyes. He smelled damp
earth, roots that snaked over the banks to slide deep into the
water, weaving, in their ancient courses, doors, windows, path-
ways for the small animals. He smelled water everywhere. He
opened his eyes. Moss hung like women's hair from the tree
boughs, the only color to be seen; the sky seemed very far away.
Something swam after the oars, grabbed one; there was a tussle
between rower and water before whatever it was sank away.

"One of hers?"

"No. Old stone-back tortoise."

"Did you see its eyes? Old as Ro Holding."

"Older."

Hours later, the boat eased toward a dock. For an eye-blink,
Corleu saw a luminous woman, all in weedy white lace, sitting
in the prow of a long, graceful boat; the woman she spoke to,
all in black, lifted a pale face toward the passing boat. Then the
bright ghost vanished. A lamp hung on a mooring stump spilled
light across the dark; moths as big as birds flickered around it.
The men made for the light. On the hillside above the water,

Corleu saw a house; one thick, smoky window burned red as a fox's eye. The men pulled him to his feet. He stumbled onto the dock and fell, half frozen and dizzy with hunger. They hauled him up again, pushed him toward the rickety wooden stairway that curved up to the house. Before they could begin the climb, the woman, still sitting shadowlike in the long boat, spoke.

"You're late," she said coldly. "You took all day."

They all started. The one-eyed man said breathlessly, "Thought you were the ghost herself—"

"We've been talking." She stepped forward into the moth-stippled light. Her face, it seemed to Corleu—spare, proud, un-tamed—might have been the face of the dark, secretive woodfox, perhaps, or the beautiful, imperious wild swan. Her eyes, so pale they seemed to hold no color, went to Corleu's face. "What's this?" she said sharply.

The one-eyed man sighed hopelessly and was silent. The young one said brashly, "Bones, ma'am."

"Bones."

"You said bones out of the swamp. We found them lying, so we took them."

She gave an exasperated hiss, like an old swamp tortoise that just missed its prey. "You bubble-fish, I told you bones!"

"Yes, ma'am. We—"

"He's not even dead! Or is it just my eyesight going, too? Is he a ghost over his bones?"

"No, ma'am. He—"

"Are you?" She reached out, pulled the cloth from Corleu's mouth. He took a deep breath that did not smell of fish. Her eyes caught at him again; he kept looking for color in them. "Are you dead?"

He shook his head, though not with absolute certainty. "I'm Wayfolk."

"With that hair?"

Then he knew he was among the living. "With this hair."

"What would Wayfolk be doing in the Delta swamp in midwinter? Catching butterflies?"

He was silent. Her strange eyes were pulling his thoughts off balance, and suddenly he realized why. "They're like the mist we travelled in," he breathed. "As if you looked in at us."

"What?"

"It was never winter there. I thought it should have come,

but it was always warm. It wasn't Delta, where I was."

"Well, then, where was it?"

"I don't know. I kept falling. Sky, maybe."

"You fell out of the sky."

"Swamp gas ate his brain," the young man suggested, grinning. The woman ignored him.

"And what," she asked softly, "were you doing in the sky?"

"Talking to the sun."

She pulled her eyes from him abruptly; he swayed as if the world had shifted. "Bring him. He is obviously a lunatic, a runaway, most likely. No one will miss him. I might as well keep him to clean my hearth. Did you get everything else? Blindfish? The roots of bog lilies? Canaries?"

"There was the blood-fox spoor," the one-eyed man said heavily, and she glared at him. "Petrified. Things don't linger here to petrify."

"Tortoises do," she snapped, and he sighed. "Get the spoor. And bones. Old bones. I need old eyes to see out of. Do you understand?"

His head ducked turtle-like into his thick neck. They followed the woman up steps that hung together on a promise. The porch slanted crazily over the water; the windows sagged in their frames, looking neither in nor out, curiously opaque. The men deposited Corleu and the squirming sacks at the open door, then retreated to the top of the stairs. The woman heaved the sacks over the threshold herself. She turned to the men, who were eyeing Corleu with a morbid, fascinated speculation.

"Go," she said sharply, and they did so, old rails groaning under their feet. She touched Corleu gently. "What's your name?"

"Corleu Ross."

"Corleu. Come in. You didn't fall out of the sky dressed for winter, did you? Did they give you anything to eat?"

"Only that fish-blown cloth." He felt an odd resistance at her threshold, shadows dragging at him like water, and he stopped, finding the same resistance in his thoughts. But she put her fingers lightly on his wrist, coaxing him forward. "Never mind them."

"I have trouble with houses, is all. What are they?"

"Just my doorkeepers. My house wards." Dragging sacks

behind her, she led him through a short hallway, into a dark room
that smelled, he thought, like cider gone bad. She snapped her
fingers. Fat candles in fantastic holders lit themselves. Chairs,
small tables, books, seemed to arrange themselves hastily, as if
in the dark they had been wandering around. Corleu stopped
again, not knowing if his head or the room were shifting. Walls
had been torn away to make one huge room of oddly vague
dimensions. In the middle of the room was a fire pit, open on
all sides, with an enormous chimney straddling it. Several large
tables stood around the fire pit, cluttered with stones, knives,
glass pipes, crystals, nuggets of silver and gold, books, feathers,
clothes, jewels cut and uncut, small bones, bottles full of tinted
liquids and salts, jars with things floating in them—shadowy,
withered and half-formed things that brought Corleu out of weariness and hunger and memory to stand prickling with horror,
wondering what trouble he had just carelessly walked into.

The woman watched him silently. She was younger than
Corleu had guessed, a scant handful of years older than he. Her
hair, bound hastily at her neck with a gold clip, was long and
fine and so dark it reminded him of another such night he had
buried his face in. He whirled, to escape into the Delta night
again. But instead of the hallway between workroom and porch,
he found only a musty room full of doves sleeping in the rafters.

He turned back, bewildered, beginning to panic. The young
woman gazed down at the sack by her feet, ignoring him. The
string untangled itself, fell to the floor. Corleu, his heart pounding
sluggishly, watched the sack crawl like something living. Birds
fluttered out of the opening: yellow canaries, and tiny, iridescent
hummingbirds beating eerie, frantic, silent circles around the
room. They made no noise.

"Their tongues are in here somewhere," the woman said.
"I also need their wings. You will see to that."

Corleu flung a side door open. The room beyond it had no
windows, no other doors; it held a small black boat with a broken
mast and the constellation forming another improbable house
painted on its bow.

He slammed the door again, leaned against it. His heart
seemed to be circling above him with the desperate birds. The
woman was watching him expressionlessly.

"You can't leave," she said. "This house has a hundred
doors into itself. If you do what I tell you, I'll feed you and give

you a bed. In the morning you can tell me what you were doing
in the sky talking to the sun. Or if you are simply demented. If
you don't do as I bid, you can starve. Suit yourself. They're only
birds.''

Corleu ran down the hallway again. A door rose before him;
he threw it open and ran on, one arm raised to ward off whatever
might come at him. He came to another door, opened it, ran
down a longer hallway. Another door rose before him; he passed
through it, found himself back in the workroom.

He sagged against a table, spilling things, sobbing for breath,
and found that all the birds had come to perch on his hair, his
shoulders. He shook them into the air.

"Tear them apart yourself," he said furiously. "I'll starve."

She rummaged in the sack. Somewhere in the shadows a
clock ticked. The small birds fluttered down to rest in his hair
again.

She did not feed him for two days; he did not speak to her
for three. By then she had her bones and spoor and had taken
the bird wings herself. Slumped on her floor, growing numb to
both hunger and horror, Corleu watched her build her spell step
by step. She made a fire of dogwood and willow and hard black
gallwood. Tiny gold suns snapped toward the ceiling, gold lintels,
a sun-king's golden face. . . . The fire turned strange colors and
shapes as it ate her gleanings from the swamp. The shadows in
the room were tinted blue and purple; curtains and paintings
shifted uneasily. When she had fed the fire the last bone from
the marsh, it turned grey-white and shaped a skull without eyes.
The skull said one word and collapsed. The woman left Corleu
lying in the haunted dark and went to bed.

The next evening, tired of walking around him, she relented
and fed him. She guided him out of the workroom, deeper into
the rambling house and gave him a bed. The next day, while she
sat reading beside a normal fire, Corleu searched the house for
the one door that would undo. Rooms opened into rooms in her
house, none holding anything predictable. In one, all the chairs
in the house had gathered except the one the woman was sitting
in. Another room, with white walls and white curtains, held
nothing but a stuffed white peacock. One room seemed blown
out of glass. Frozen flowers tumbled around Corleu as he stood
in it. Delicate green ivy grew up the walls, soft purple lilac hung
overhead. He could smell lilac. Wondering, he closed the door,

then opened it again. Old tapestries hung from the walls now; a glass vase the color of lilac held a faded branch of lilac. He walked on, down silent carpeted hallways, opened another door at random. This room, for some reason, was filled from top to bottom with goose feathers. He sneezed. Pinfeathers startled into the air, drifted down like snow. He found a staircase and mounted it. At the top of the stairs he found a door with a sign on it that said "Do Not Enter."

He opened a door into memory. The tinker sat in the waning light, cooking something small over his fire. . . . Falling, falling through endless stars, he came up against another door. But which was this? In? Or out? He touched it, hands flat against the wood, as if he could feel a secret, trembling heartbeat within it. He was shaking at what might be within: the gold, armored king pacing the length of his chain, the smell of fish cooking . . . worse than either, what he had to find. But there was no undoing without doing. His hand slid to the latch; he opened the door.

Inside, the woman sat in her chair, reading. Her feet were bare; she nibbled a strand of hair as she read. She looked at Corleu; her pale eyes were as expressionless as water.

He spoke to her, for the first time in three days. "What are you?"

She shrugged a little. "I have been called everything from sorceress to bog hag. I know a great many things but never enough. Never enough. I know the great swamp of night, and sometimes I do things for pay if it interests me."

"And if—and if they can't pay?"

Her eyes narrowed slightly. "Are you bargaining with me?"

He swallowed. "Sorry. It's Wayfolk habit."

"But for what? You loathe what I do. What could you want from me?"

"It's—you know things. You have so many books. You must know other than burning owl bones. My grandfather knew a little. Country magic. But all I know is stories, and all they've done is get me into trouble."

She studied him curiously, as if he were a rare kind of tree frog that maybe she could use in her fire. She had a fine lady's sunless skin and slender fingers, though hers had chipped nails and blisters from the fire. Swathed in some black shapeless dress, all her thoughts hidden away in her lovely, cold face, she gave him again an illusion of someone who prowled or flew by day, and only walked, wept, spoke, in the darkest hour of night. She said finally, "You fell out of the sky. You talked to the sun. You ran all the way out of the world, it sounds like."

"Yes." His hands clenched, opened again. "I went into the wrong door."

"In this house?"

"Likely here, too. But even before they found me in the swamp. It was another house that said 'Do Not Enter,' plain as if it had shouted at me."

"Do you always open doors that say that?"

"I'm getting in the habit of it. So I went in, and now I must find something."

"What? Where?"

"I don't know where. It could be anywhere. So if a door like this one bothers to talk at all, even to warn, that's a door I need to open, to see if what it warns of can help me at all. Even you."

Her brows went up. She said drily, "Even the likes of me."

"I didn't mean—" He held his breath a moment, under that colorless, speculative gaze. "I'm used to a harmless magic. You know some terrible things. But you do know, and I'm short of knowing anything besides my name. I'll sweep for you, I'll clean your hearth, I'll do anything but kill for you, except for what you need to live. I'll cut wood, I know herbs and flowers, I can even mend your stairs. If you'll only help me, even only tell me where to begin—"

She shook her head, her fine hair sliding laxly over one shoulder. "I like my stairs that way," she said shortly. "They discourage company. I don't understand you. Begin what?"

"To look for what I have to find."

"And what might that be?"

"It's—just a small thing." His hands had clenched again; his eyes flicked past her as if shadows of his memories moved on the wall behind her. "A small thing. He said to ask the Blind Lady."

"What blind lady?"

"The Blind Lady of Withy Hold. He said to give her a gift."

She shifted, impatient, bewildered. "What gift? What small thing? What 'he' said you must find it?"

"The sun."

She made an unladylike noise. "You," she said, "may be too demented to be useful."

"No—"

"Demented people talk to suns."

"And to old burned bones that answer back." His retort left her wordless; he pleaded quickly, "You brought me in here. Likely you thought you could stand a few lunatic ravings."

"Or likely not—"

"I have no place to go, no one else to ask. Please. If you could only listen. Only that. Please." Her face promised him no indulgence. But she didn't stop him. "We travelled south this year from Withy Hold, instead of going to Hunter Hold, like always. We were bound for Delta, but somewhere we took a wrong turn."

"We."

"My Wayfolk company. Except my true kin—they went on to Hunter Hold."

"Get on with it," she said with some asperity. "I don't want details about all your barefoot siblings."

"I—my parents went to Hunter Hold instead, because my mother saw something in her petals, something falling out of the sky, and all our paths twisting and turning and going no-where—"

"Like your tale," she muttered.

"It was a beautiful place we came to," he said, skipping over the endless roads. "Nothing like the true Delta. Nothing. It was like the days in spring when you find everything has flowered and nothing has begun to die, so it seems that's the way the world must go on: always just breaking into blossom, and the air full of soft, sweet smells, and colors to wring your heart, after all the white and grey of winter. That's what this place was. Day after day after day. Nothing ever died. But once we left Withy Hold, we never saw sky, nor star, nor sun . . . just those colorless mists." His face was blanched beneath its color; he was sweating lightly, as if the warm, sultry air clung to him again. "We kept driving, driving, never counting days, never seeing sunlight except when it turned red at sundown, and then one day I saw it—how we must have driven past autumn into the dead of winter, and still we never reached city or sea, and still nothing in that land died. . . . I tried to tell them, but they were content there, they saw no harm. . . . Then I found a way out and I took

it. Alone. They're still all there. I can free them, he said. If I
find the thing he wants."

"How did you escape?" she asked, groping for a thread in
the tangled skein. "The color of your hair?"

"Something like," he whispered, so deep in the memory
he scarcely saw her. "There's a song."

"I might have guessed."

"One of those you're born knowing, you never remember
learning. The little dark house that falls out of the sky."

She nodded, impatient again and mystified. "I know it."

"You must not enter it."

"It's the house you'll never leave."

"Everyone knows it. But no one pays mind to it. I never
did either, until it fell." Her fingernail, ticking at the chair arm,
missed a beat. "There was no other door I could see. No other
way out of the dream world. Only that black house, with the roof
of gold and the lintel of gold. So"—he drew breath raggedly—
"I went into it."

She was motionless, in a way he associated with animals
fading into their surroundings at a scent, at something barely
glimpsed. "You did." Her voice was devoid of expression. "And
what did you find, in that little dark house that falls from the
sky?"

"The Gold King."

He had closed his eyes at the memory. He could not hear
her breathing, and he wondered suddenly if, exasperated, she
had taken her book and walked through a wall. But she was still
there, gazing at him without blinking, spellbound, it seemed to
him, sculpted out of air and painted.

"The Gold King is a Hold Sign." She picked words carefully, as she might have picked a path across a marsh.

"Yes."

"The yellow star its lintel, the yellow star its roof, the four
stars of red and pale marking its walls, the blue star marking its
doorlatch . . . The Hold Sign of Hunter Hold."

"Yes."

"It is a banner, a constellation, an ancient war sign. A song.
How could you walk into it?"

"Who am I to know that?" he asked her. "The likes of
me? How did the Cygnet get into the sky? How did the Gold
King's house get into a song? Maybe it was us put them there.

Or maybe they're the ones whispered to us that they were there.
Or something was there, hiding behind Cygnet, behind sun's face.
Something dark and powerful and terrible, that we hung faces
on to make them less terrible. The house fell. I went into it. How
is what I could break my mind over till I die. What matters is
that, standing here in front of you, I'm still in that house. What
I need is how to get out of it.''

Her face was so pale it reminded him of the waxen dream-
lilies. Her eyes were wide on his face; he saw color in them
finally, the palest trace of lavender. "That house," she whispered. "Here. In the Delta."

"In a dream."

"Why you? Why would the Gold King fall out of the sky
into your life?"

He swallowed, his throat burning. "I asked him. He said
no one else in Ro Holding would have been muckerhead enough
to enter his house."

She drew breath, moving finally. Shadows moved and
melted on the walls around them; he wondered, eerily, if they
were her suddenly busy thoughts.

"The Gold King wants you to find something for him. In
return for your people. What? Some treasure?"

"A small thing, he said. Being trapped, he can't look for
it.''

"A small thing."

"Something only he still values, after all this time, he said."

"The Gold King did." She slammed her heavy book suddenly, so hard he started. She caught his eyes in her unsettling
way. "A small thing. Corleu Ross, you may be a muckerhead,
but what kind of idiot do you think I am? The Gold King would
not tumble out of the sky in his ancient house to send you on a
goose chase for some bauble of sentimental value. I would guess
that what he wants you to find is powerful enough to rattle Ro
Holding like a weathercock in a storm. Tell me what it is or I
will not help you."

"I cannot," he whispered. "I cannot. I will never see them
again, he said. Never in the true world."

"But you do know what it is."

"Yes. I know."

She held him still under her scrutiny, as if she were trying
to see the mystery inside his head. But not even she could do

that, or wanted to; the intensity of her gaze lessened; he could move again. She nibbled a thumbnail; shadows shifted like smoke behind her. "This thing," she said. "Would you want it for yourself if you could find a way to keep it?"

His face twisted, as if he smelled smoke again from the tinker's spattering fire. He shook his head.

"Then, if I take it from the Gold King after he frees your people, you wouldn't fight me for it? Think. You might change your mind once it's in your hand."

"No," he said, brusque with horror. "It's a terrible thing. Likely even you won't want it."

She smiled a little, thinly. "Likely I will, if it's anything of power. In return for you finding this thing for me, I will help you with all my power. Which," she added, "is considerable, and not confined to this moldering backwater. I have taken it from all over Ro Holding."

"Are you Wayfolk?" he asked bewilderedly, for lords' daughters seldom rambled the length and breadth of Ro Holding, or took to living like a cuckoo in an untidy, haunted nest in a swamp.

She shook her head absently, already conjecturing. Her answer took his breath away. "Of course not. I am Nyx Ro."

5

He could not stop staring at her. Even though the door had moved and there was a hallway where he remembered stairs, and all the portraits hanging along the mauve walls were upside down, his eyes kept returning to her face, for never in his life had he thought he might be close enough to touch one of the three daughters of the Holder of Ro Holding. She ignored his staring, as well as all the white, closed doors they passed, until she came to one that had, maybe, one more grain of dust on it than the others, or it cast a slanted shadow. She opened it and they stepped back into her workroom.

"You never get lost?" he asked.

"No."

"You made this house, then?"

She shook her head. "I found it." She went to the fire; its embers glowed like a multi-eyed beast in the shadows. "It's quite old and full of memories, dreams, thoughts, reflections of time. But it's addled with age. It can't remember what's real and what's memory, or where it puts things; that's why they constantly shift." She reached for wood, then changed her mind before she touched it. "Make up the fire, Corleu. Use pear and coralwood, that will clear the air."

He was getting used to the stenches that came out of her fires, but this last had been formidable. "It smells like the dead were dancing in here," he muttered, raking the embers. "Why do you live like this?"

"Like what?" She was at a worktable, sorting through a pile of books that smelled of smoke and leather and ancient ink, and that flickered sometimes in the candlelight like star-fire and jewelled salamander tongues.

"Like this," he said recklessly. "Barefoot in a rickety house, summoning hobgoblins out of your fire, when you could be—"

"Shod in velvet, wearing pearls in my hair in the Holder's house by the sea?" She lifted her eyes; again he saw the faint wash of color in them, and then her narrow-eyed, sardonic smile. "I came here to learn what the swamp had to teach me. To look out of the stone-tortoise's ancient eyes and see what it has seen."

"But why?" he asked, thinking of the tongueless, fluttering birds. "It's a twisted power you get out of all this slow, deep running water, all these bog pools layered with dead things."

"Power is power. It's neither good nor evil, it's simply there to be used, either way. It's like fire. If you feed it silver it will shine like a summer's day and speak to you as fairly, and if you feed it gallwood, it will turn black and stink like the dead, and prophesy sickness, storm, misfortune. All that matters is what you put into it."

He dropped pearwood onto the grate with a clatter. "Bird skulls," he said tersely. "The beating hearts of fish."

"There's power in the living and the dead. Power in the bird's eye and in the eyeless skull. Not all knowledge is clean, innocent. I came here to learn, I don't choose what to be taught. If there is knowledge to be taken from the heart of a fish, I take it."

"Is that all you know? This mean, bloody kind of power?"

She was silent, absorbed in her reading, he guessed; he wondered if she had heard his rough question. She answered it finally, her eyes on the pages of her book, as if she were reading a tale from it. "In Hunter Hold, I lived among the desert witches, who are dedicated to the Ring of Time. Their lives are exemplary. I slept on bare ground, I wove my own garments, I ate nothing that possessed an eye or a heart. I learned how time is layered like tree rings, and how, with dedication and proper stillness in mind and body, you can see beyond the ring you circle at the moment. In Berg Hold, I studied with the oldest mage in Ro Holding, the last descendant of Chrysom.''

"Who?'' He was kneeling with his hands full of wood, entranced by the double vision of her: half unscrupulous bog witch, half the Holder's daughter, with all the history of Ro Holding in her name.

Her eyes flickered at him; her expression gave him a glimpse into his ignorance. "Chrysom was the great mage in the court of Moro Ro, who was the first ruler of Ro Holding—''

"I know that.''

"I'm overwhelmed. Chrysom built the house on the Delta coast, during the Hold Wars, where the Holders have lived for a thousand years.''

"The house that flew.''

"The house that flew.''

"The air,'' he commented, "must have been thick with houses once.''

"Don't take all day with the fire. Can you read?''

"Yes. My granda got into the habit. It was a place to get away from being teased about being a moon-haired bastard. My mother kept his books.''

"So you got his hair. He had some power, you said?''

"I didn't get that.''

"How do you know?''

He glanced at her, surprised. "I'd know by now, likely. I can't foresee in small ways, in dreams or petals, like he could. He could float herbs on water and forecast from their shadows. My mother could do those things. I never could.''

"You brought the Gold King's attention to you somehow.''

"I kept using his name in stories,'' he sighed. "How was I to know he was listening?''

"What was he like?''

"A tinker,'' he said tersely. Since there was no help forthcoming from Nyx Ro, he lit the fire himself with one of the fat candles that never seemed to burn down. The flame danced along the coralwood, spicing the air with a resin that smelled of oranges. He gazed into it, seeing again the brilliant, bitter gold face.

"A tinker,'' she repeated curiously.

"And a king made of gold, chained to his own throne."
She glanced at him, startled, catching a glimpse of something, then losing it. "How strange," she breathed. She went back to her reading. He watched her, as he tended the fire. Books piled up around her, threatening to topple as she worried at them, pulling them from mid-pile, flipping pages, then heaving them shut with massive thuds that sent dust flying and books swaying. Her hairclip was sliding down her back; her full sleeves kept tangling in her fingers; she would push them impatiently up one arm or the other, where they would slowly creep back down. He wondered suddenly at the power trapped in her, behind her intent, dispassionate gaze. He straightened; as if he had disturbed some delicate tension in the air, a pile of books sagged precariously.

"What are you looking for?" he asked tentatively, and got the sharp edge of her tongue.

"What do you think I'm looking for? I'm trying to find a gift for the Blind Lady."

"Oh." He slid his hand through his hair, blinking, and found a blood-fox skull gazing back at him from a shelf. "The Gold King said a peacock feather."

Nyx Ro lifted her head, looked at him with as much expression as the skull behind her. She slammed her book, then glared at a pile threatening to topple. "Why didn't you tell me?"

"I didn't know what you were doing."

"Do I have to tell you everything?"

"It's easier," he said steadily, "if you do. That way you won't have to shout at me."

"I'm not used to explaining things. Nothing around here asks."

"Nothing around here has a tongue to." He added, at her silence, "Likely I won't either, much longer."

"Likely."

"There's a stuffed peacock around here somewhere, could get a feather from that."

She folded her arms, still frowning at him, but no longer in irritation. "A peacock feather. Are you sure he said that?"

"Yes."

"Think. Remember the words."

He did then. "I'm wrong. He said: 'Offer her what's on the peacock's feather.'"

"Ah," she said softly. "That's clear enough."

"Is it?"

"You tell me. What is on a peacock's feather that a Blind Lady might want?"

He stared at her, his eyes widening. He shifted closer to the fire, feeling the old house shunt a breath of winter up from the cellar. He said after a moment, "The dark house of Hunter Hold fell in the Delta. Will I find the Blind Lady here, too, or do I go back up to Withy Hold in midwinter?"

She was still searching among her books, slowly now, absently, as if she knew what she looked for but had misplaced it and memory might find it before her hands did. She paused, favored him with a long, dispassionate gaze. "That's a good question," she said. "What do Wayfolk say about the Blind Lady?"

"What all folk say, likely. She wears the Ring of Time. She dealt death with her eyes until the Cygnet tricked her into gazing at her reflection in the full moon and she blinded herself. The Peacock guides her across the night sky with all its eyes. In Withy Hold, they say she weaves the threads of lives, meetings, partings, marriages, births, such. She weaves out of the dark and light of days."

"To the witches of Hunter Hold, she is only a tale. Time is not woven, they say, of threads that can be broken."

"In Withy Hold, they gave her gifts, long ago. To coax her into weaving fortune. One farm I worked had a giving place: a little ring of trees with a stone in it, where things were brought to her. The lord who owned the farm plowed around the trees, even though no one comes there now. He said it was a ring of time."

"You went into it," she said with sudden insight. He nodded.

"I wanted to stand inside time."

"What happened?"

"Nothing. What would? It was only story."

She bent over her books, found what she wanted at last, it seemed, for she read silently a long time, while Corleu kept the fire going and watched for a shift of light beyond the windows. But whether it was night or day, he could not tell, for all any of them gave was a reflection of the room. Nyx Ro closed her book finally. She stood silently, her arms folded, musing on something in the dusky shadows that hid the room's true dimensions. She said abruptly:

"Where did your grandfather get his hair?"

Surprised, he told her the tale of the Rider in the Corn, as he had remembered his great-gran telling.

"She died," he said, "before I was old enough to understand it, or ask her more. Something must have caught her eye about him besides his hair. But she was old, and years might have changed him from stableboy on a nag to a corn-lord on a stallion."

"Perhaps." She was still eyeing him, in a meditative measuring way that made him uneasy. "For someone who just came face to face with a story, you're far too ready to dismiss them. The Gold King's eye fell on you because you were looking at him, apparently, and what made you bring him to life is a mystery that may well have begun among the corn. Maybe you have some gifts, maybe not, but the Gold King summoned one of Wayfolk to find this treasure for him, not a powerful sorceress who might take too much interest in it. So. My hand must be on none of the work that may need doing for this. Everything must be done by you. Your hand on the wood the fire burns, your hand on the making and unmaking. Will you try?"

He shrugged. "I'll try anything. But you must keep in mind I'm still an ignorant gawp under this hair, and not even you with all your power can make a fish gallop."

"Don't be too sure," she murmured. She left her book lying open, came to the fire. "Find some warmer clothes around this house. You're going to Withy Hold tomorrow."   .

He nodded, not pleased but unsurprised. "I'll need a horse," he said. "Will there be one roaming somewhere in the house?"

"You won't need a horse," she said. "You'll bring Withy Hold to the Delta."

He stared at her. "How?" His voice had lost all sound.

"You will make a Ring of Time."

He wandered in and out of rooms the next morning, found clothes finally, in a trunk sitting strapped and ready for a journey in an empty room. He pulled out wool and leather and linen, hardly seeing what he put on, feeling, even after he had dressed, that there was something he had forgotten. But there were good boots on his feet and a heavy cloak over one arm, and a list in his head of all he would need for a long, hard journey north into winter. It would take more than the color of his hair to shorten the road to Withy Hold, and he expected to be hunting up a horse somewhere along the river by evening. The faint, melancholy sound of a reed pipe accompanied him as he left the room. He found Nyx Ro brooding over a book beside her fire. He stood watching her pale, still, secret face; the way her long, unruly hair slid over her shoulder; the way she picked at things with her fine, callused fingers—a bead, a button, a loose stitch—as she read. Her coloring reminded him of Tiel, yet she was unlike in every way: She was lonely, fearless, wild and powerful, and her knowledge was a vast country he scarcely knew existed.

She lifted her eyes, caught him watching. She said only, rising, "I thought you were a ghost, in those clothes." She went to one of her tables, cleared of all but a round bubble of a bottle and an odd assortment of things around it. "Come here, Corleu. This is where you will make your ring." He joined her silently. All the oddments around the jar were labelled in some painstaking, flowery, antique script. He read a label.

"Is that real?"

"Of course."

He stared at her. "Is this going to work?"

"Even," she said, "for the likes of you." She shifted, watched him from the far side of the table. He drew breath, feeling a wintry chill in his bones, as if by accident, moon-blinded eyes had met his eyes. "All you must do now is lay a fire within the jar from the things as I have placed them. Begin at the top of the circle, with the flaked moonstone, and go to the left from there."

He reached for it; as though it lay within a charmed circle, it seemed too far to touch. His hand fell, empty, on the wood. "I'm afraid," he said, not looking at her. "Of this, of the Blind Lady, of being in this house, of leaving this house. I'd go through this ring and run and keep running, likely, leave them all there in that summer place, if not for leaving Tiel there, too—"

"Tiel."

He looked at her then, wanting to swallow the name, put it back into his heart where it was hidden even from Nyx's strange, clear eyes. But her eyes asked, relentlessly.

"I left her," he said softly. "Tiel."

"Ah."

"For that house."

"I see." She seemed to: as if the green, peaceful private world had formed in the air between them. "Tiel," she said again, musing, curious; and at the reminder, or the rare gentleness in her voice, his hands eased open. He reached for the moonstone.

"The Ring of Time is a circle of stars, a silver ring on the Blind Lady's finger," she said as he worked. "The Ring has no beginning, no ending. Meddling with time, past and future, is a sorcery I have little skill in. But this Ring you are making is very simple; your hands do the work, not your mind. It opens only to the present, in another place. There are more complex rings, that open to remembered past. Two or three mages even wrote of Rings into the future. But they left no spell for that; if they returned at all to write about the future, they did not recommend it. They say little about their journeys, they seem to have lived brief lives afterwards . . . or perhaps they made the Ring a final time and stepped through it forever.

"For you, it will simply be a door opening there, and then back here."

Corleu, listening, was laying the strangest fire he had ever made in his life: a tiny thing inside a squat glass bottle that was so round he thought his breath might unbalance it. Into its narrow mouth he dropped filings of gold, of black dragon's bone, purple-green scales from the wings of a flying lizard, half a silver ring, a crushed pearl, twists of paper that held the dried tears of a weeper-owl, a single eye from the tail feather of a peacock, a long, silver hair.

"Do I drop myself in there last?" he murmured. "Or does time come out of the bottle?"

He added a bone button and a bit of amber enclosing a drop of wizard's blood that was the color of tarnished silver. He paused then, gazing at the fragment of amber, and wondering at the slow seep of time out of the tree that had enclosed and frozen a pearl of wizard's blood . . . and how time, too, had slowed within that magic drop of blood so that it had waited for the tear of amber to slowly weep around it.

"Time passes," Nyx Ro said, "in as many overlapping lengths as notes in a song."

He thought of Tiel then, caught in such a motionless pool of time. Dried, crumbled lily petals fluttered from his fingers down into the jar; he almost saw her there, a tiny young woman

with petals in her hair and a lizard's scale beside her for a pool.
But it was only an odd reflection in the glass.

"Could I walk through this Ring to Tiel?"

"She doesn't exist in any time you or I know. She is like
a thought in the mind of the Gold King. You would never reach
her through this Ring. You might see her reflected off a moment
of time, like an image in a mirror, but only that."

He shook pale fragrant powder of the hoof of the extinct
blue horse into the jar, and, finally, black dust from the obsidian
deserts in the barren southern regions of Hunter Hold, which had
been formed out of layer upon layer of volcanic fires.

"Breathe into it," Nyx said. Corleu leaned over the jar;
gold, obsidian, petals, swirled in his breath; the round glass
misted. "Now pick up the fire."

He reached for the fingernail of frozen silver fire that lay
like a dead leaf on a silver plate. Quiescent as it was, it burned
his fingers slightly, though with heat or cold he wasn't sure.

"The only thing complex about building this Ring is gathering the materials for it. That alone could take a lifetime. Sorcerers have died squabbling over a drop of spell-steeped blood
in amber. I was fortunate: I took mine from Chrysom's tower,
though it took me years to recognize it for what it was. Put the
jar there on the floor, in that silver circle. When you drop the
flame into it, step back quickly, or you will become part of
the Ring. Which may be an interesting fate itself, but you probably would not appreciate it."

The fire that kindled and exploded out of the bottle licked
the rafters: a flowing, changing loop of pure silver. It gave little
more warmth than something held for a long time in a closed
hand. Corleu could have stepped through it easily, though at this
point, he would only have travelled as far as Nyx's untidy table.

As he watched, mute with wonder, night dropped like a
filmy eyelid down over the center of the circle. He could no
longer see Nyx; she stood somewhere on the other side of darkness.

"It is complete."

He drew breath, watching silver fall like water through the
air, cast its glow on stone and wood and the threadbare velvet
on a chair. Nyx stepped from behind it; for a moment her eyes
were the same color as the falling silver.

"Good," she said, with as much expression, Corleu

thought, as if he had just made a broom handle. "Now, Corleu, you must envision where you are going, on the other side of this door. Think of the place in the field you stood in, long ago, where people left weavings, or fine thread for the Blind Lady to weave into their good fortune. It will be a silent place, bare now, stripped by winter, an odd lonely place where no one ever comes except those of us who felt her presence once. To others it's only a little ring of trees, and an old stone, once flat, but hollowed slowly through centuries by the weight of those gifts, by the touch of hands. You may have to move the wild grasses to see the stone. When you see it you will know. And in that place you will summon the Blind Lady. You will summon. You will summon . . . Go now. . . ."

He stepped forward into the Ring, and remembered, too late, what he had forgotten. "I have no gift!" he cried. Nyx Ro's words followed him through time.

"Offer her your eyes."

He stepped onto a field he had harvested.

The clouds hung heavy over it; he smelled snow in the air. The trees lining the edge of the field seemed to lift the cloud away from the earth with their bare branches. A crow, picking among the ice-rimed furrows, eyed him and startled away. In the distance, between gentle slopes of field, he saw the prosperous stone farmhouse, chimneys smoking, animals secured, gates shut. In late summer, the Wayfolk camped under the grove of trees behind the house. He could have walked there, found their wagon ruts, traces of their nightly fires. Then memory pulled his eyes to the crest of a hill a couple of fields away. The hill was plowed but for a small tangle of trees, brambles, underbrush on the top. The snowy furrows circled away from the little wood, ring after ring spiralling down from the top of the hill until it sloped away into other fields. Corleu began walking toward it.

In his memory the place was green, sun-soaked, still as a stone with heavy, late summer heat. He had gone in there years ago, looking for something. Someone? Tiel, maybe, though that long ago it would never have been her, luring him in there. Perhaps it had only been the thought of a few moments in the shade that took him away from his work, to fight through berry brambles and wild roses, long grasses, vines hanging from the trees in walls of leaves, encircling the place. The trees, he noticed then, grew in a circle.

He had been surprised at the silence, he remembered. He had stood there a long time without realizing time was passing, for it seemed that in the next moment whoever or whatever he had sought, or had summoned him, seemed about to move, to speak. But always in the next moment, never now . . . He heard his name shouted, in a world so far away the voice was like an insect's. And then he realized there were no insects in that hot, sweet-smelling place; there were no birds. Nothing rustled, nothing made a sound. . . .

Turning in sudden panic, he had tripped over something half buried in the grass.

Now, the vines and brambles were a brown weave that hid nothing. They did not give way easily, even then; he had to fight his way among them, old as they were, and so closely knit that rose twined with berry or grape indiscriminately. Emerging finally into the ring, he was battle-scarred, almost warm. A light, icy snow began to fall, whispering softly against the branches, the first noise he had ever heard in that place.

He went to the center of the circle. He found what he had tripped over so long ago, and he knelt down to uncover it, pulling the frozen weeds and grasses from it until he could see it: a dark round stone, slightly hollowed in the center, where over the centuries, gifts laid there had gradually worn away the stone.

You will summon, Nyx had said. *You will summon. . . .*

"But how?" he whispered. "I have no gift."

Offer her your eyes. . . .

Then he remembered, from so many past years that it seemed another life: a dozen grubby children clinging to one another, hand to hand in a circle spinning faster and faster around someone—Tiel?—who had covered her eyes with her hands, and was herself spinning dizzily as they chanted at the tops of their voices:

Lady come, lady come,
Find my eyes, find my eyes,
Circle, circle . . . the blind can see!

Breathless, still kneeling among the weeds, he put his hand on the stone. He heard the rhyme he spoke as if the grass had spoken it, or the snow, or the distant voices of children:

In a wooden ring
Find a stone circle . . .

Stone, trees, fields vanished in a fiery blaze of summer night. He saw her: the Blind Lady, who wore the Ring of Time and saw out of the eyes on the Peacock's tail. The Peacock's tail was a spray of white fire against the dark; its head was turned toward the Blind Lady, its visible eye was sapphire. The Lady herself had hair the color of the moon; strands of starlight wove from the Ring on her hand. She was beautiful and terrible, with her blind face and the constantly weaving strands of light between her fingers. Her head moving slightly from side to side, she seemed to search a darkness she could not see.

"Who summons me?"

The voice came from the stars, but the footsteps breaking the icy grass were behind Corleu. He turned on his knees, startled out of his vision, falling back against the stone. The face he saw struck him dumb.

It was an old woman's strong, fleshy, lumpy face. Her eyelids had sunk over her eyes; her face itself seemed to peer from side to side as if to smell Corleu or hear his breathing. She wore layers of old wool and linen—skirts and shifts and shirts, shawls and aprons of all colors, all faded, dirty. Frayed threads hung from every hem and sleeve, every seam, cuff and collar. She was big, shapeless, her hands gnarled and swollen with age. As she listened for answer, she gathered threads absently from a frayed vest, began to pull them, weave them. On one forefinger she wore a tarnished silver ring.

"Who summons?" she demanded again; her voice was deep, brusque. Her shoes, Corleu saw, were sewn of peacock feathers.

He found his voice finally. "I summoned you." He shifted hastily out of her way, when it seemed she would walk over him or through him. She kicked at the ground until she found the stone. She settled herself down on it with a sigh, and felt at her threads again.

"Corleu. Of the Wayfolk."

His heart hammered. He stared at the frail, colored threads between her twisting fingers; he wanted to touch her hands, beg her to be gentle.

"Well?" she said. "You summoned."

"I came—I—The Gold King sent me to you."

Her pale, shaggy brows lifted; her sunken eyelids twitched, trying to open. "He! Why?"

"I must find something for him, he said. He doesn't know where it is; he said you might. He said offer you what's on a peacock feather and you might help me."

She dropped her threads, groped toward him. "Let me feel you. For all I know of humans, you're all made of thread or light." Her hands roved over his hair, bumped against his cheekbone, his jaw. He felt the silver ring against his throat, cold or hot, like the silver fire he had dropped into the jar. "No, flesh and blood as ever. You came here once before, I remember."

"Yes."

"No one comes here. They used to, they brought me gifts to turn my weaving their way. Sometimes they moved me. They praised me, they called me beautiful." He felt her shake with silent laughter. "Was I or was I? I never knew. Why did you come here so long ago?"

"I don't know why. I thought the tree ring hid a secret. I wanted to know what. I was of that age, when everything seems to say something, even an old stone."

"And did it speak?"

"Nothing spoke. The silence spoke. I ran." The sleet had turned to snow, drifting down in another ageless silence. "I never forgot the sound of this place."

"It was me you heard, weaving."

"Likely."

"And you came back and brought me a gift. I can't see you, but that King had his eye on you. Well, where is it?"

"What?"

"My peacock feather."

He drew breath, his eyes flickering across the tangled ring around him. He caught one of her gnarled hands before it went back to its endless work. He held her fingers lightly against his eyes.

A quick wind shivered through the bare trees. "So . . . the King found a way to make you desperate, did he? Something you want badly enough to give me sight?"

"Yes," he said, and felt the snow slide like an icy sweat down his face.

"Tell me what the King seeks."

"What the Cygnet is hiding."

He heard her breath, a harsh, wordless sound. Her fingers twitched, as if to weave his eyelashes. "Yes . . . Oh, yes. He's been thinking, in that little black house of his. He's been thinking. . . . And he reached out and trapped you to do his bidding. You're trapped like him, like we all, or you'd be running like a hare by now back into the daylight."

"Do you know where?"

"No." He shifted, murmuring with despair, and her hand tightened across his eyes. "Hush, now, let me think. It wouldn't be lying around like a pebble, would it? Would it?"

"No."

"It's hidden too well even for my seeing eyes. But I hear thoughts and whispers along my threads now and then, from those who have guarded it through the centuries. Let me remember them. . . . There's a secret within a secret. . . . A web. There's a secret at the center of a web. Above that web the Cygnet flies night and day."

"A web—"

"That's as it comes to me, in broken words and memories. A web in darkness. It's not there, what you seek."

"Not—"

"No."

"Then what—"

"The secret of where to look is there."

"A web under the Cygnet," he repeated, bewildered, reaching toward her hand so he could see.

"Not yet, not yet, these are my eyes still."

"But you must tell more! I can't go looking at every spider web spun under the Cygnet's stars. You must know something more, something clear—"

"It's from my eyes that small thing is hidden. Not only from innocent Wayfolk eyes, but from such as fought the Cygnet. It's layered in secrets like an onion, not like a hazelnut you can crack with one blow. However"—she pulled his head back against her knee, her fingers weaving in his hair—"if you're this desperate, you may want to ask the Dancer. She sees into dreams, she may have seen more than I. Yes. Wake the Dancer at the top of the world. Offer fire to her Fire Bear and it will leave you alone.

She may know. It's all I can give now, but when you find what
the Gold King seeks, then none of us will refuse you. Whatever
your Wayfolk heart desires . . . or whatever heart you have by
then. Find my eyes, find my eyes. . . . The blind can see.''

CHAPTER

6

Screaming, he fell into a room full of mirrors.
Raising his head, gathering breath again with his throat raw from his last cry, he opened his eyes and saw, all around him, within mirrors ancient and ornate, framed plainly in wood or silver, oval, square, diamond, hexagonal, vast mirrors too heavy to lift propped against the wall with smaller mirrors strewn against them: crouching figures in torn silk and muddy leather lifting thorn-scarred faces, staring with black, empty eyes. For a moment he did not recognize himself.

The breath left him in a long, shaking sigh, with a sound to it like an unshaped word. He got to his feet; so did his reflections. He had an eerie feeling that even at his back his reflection was gazing at him. As he turned to look, all the images vanished.

He stood like a ghost in a room full of mirrors that took no notice of him.

"I'm dead," he said, startled. He heard Nyx Ro calling his name. Her voice sounded sharp, bewildered. He looked around for a door, saw only mirrors crowding the walls, a few hanging bannerlike from the ceiling, their faces blank as the Delta sky. He touched one; he could not even cast a shadow.

In sudden panic, he spoke Nyx Ro's name.

She appeared in one of the ornate mirrors. "I couldn't find you," she said tightly. "I heard you scream. I couldn't find you."

"I can't find a door." He turned again, searching, and caught his breath at the sight of Nyx multiplied, in threadbare blue velvet, her face waxen, a smudge of ash across one cheekbone. "I can't see myself at all. Only you."

"I can only see you," she said. Her arms were folded tightly; she was frowning, at once disturbed and curious. "I thought I knew every room in this house. Why didn't you come back through the Ring?"

"I did," he said tersely.

Her eyes widened. She said, "Corleu. Can you touch my hand?" She held it out to him; his fingers were stopped by cold glass.

"Am I some place out of time? Is that why I can't see myself? Should I break a mirror?"

"No," she said quickly. "Mirrors hold your image; they should be treated with care."

"These don't. They're all ignoring me. I saw myself in all of them, and then I vanished, as if an eye blinked somewhere, or they stopped thinking of me."

For a moment, even she stopped thinking of him. "How strange," she breathed. "How strange . . . A secret room within a house full of a thousand secrets. I wonder what it sees when no one is here?"

"If you wait long enough, no one will be here, and then you can find out, likely."

She held out her hand again. "I don't know why you're still standing there complaining. One of me is real. Find me."

He circled the room, touched her glassy hand in every glass. Finally, in a small mirror ringed in tarnished silver, he felt her hand close on his. He stepped forward. The mirror widened into a ring of motionless, icy fire. He stepped through it into her workroom.

The ring dwindled swiftly until there was nothing left of it but a tiny circle of silver that dropped back into the round glass jar. Nyx left it sitting within the circle painted on the floor. She looked for chairs; they had all gone elsewhere. Impatiently, she pulled a couple out of the floorboards, great, shapeless things smelling like mushrooms from the cellar. Corleu sat down gratefully; his eyes closed.

He was on his feet in an instant, pulling away from a glimpse of the Ring he had fallen into. Nyx watched him dispassionately. "Why did you scream? Did she try to harm you?"

"No." He wheeled at her abruptly. "You tricked me. I had nothing to give her but my eyes."

She shrugged. "It worked, didn't it? What did she give you in return?"

"Not much."

"Did you tell her what you were looking for? Did she recognize it? As something valuable? Something of power?"

"She recognized it, yes. A toad in a hole would recognize it."

"But she didn't—"

"No."

"Did she help at all? Was she angry with you? Did she not want you to find it?"

"Oh, she does want me to find it." He found a wall in front of him and paced back. "She does."

"Did she make any suggestions?" Nyx asked patiently.

"She said there is a web . . . a secret at the center of the web. The Cygnet flies over it day and night."

"And that's where it is?"

"No. That's where the secret of finding this thing is."

"A web . . ." She was silent a little, her brows puckered, a fingernail between her teeth. He looked at her in the candlelight, Lauro Ro's daughter, with her cold, curious eyes that, for all their look into power, had never glimpsed what there was to fear.

"It's not just story," he said harshly. Her eyes rose to his face.

"I guessed that much."

"If I give the Gold King what he wants, he won't just vanish back into words. Nor will she. Likely that's where the stories will end, because now they wear them like rags and tatters, but they'll grow too big, too powerful for us to keep them trapped in words."

She was gazing at him, motionless. "Are you warning me?"

"You don't know what it is I'm trying to find. I do."

"Well, Corleu, what use is there fretting until I do know? Are you going to stop looking for it? Leave your Tiel sitting there forever in a dream?" He was silent, trapped. "That's why I want this thing. I can use it against them, if need be. Was that all she said? A web?"

"She said to ask the Dancer."

She was still then, her eyes narrowed; he stood tense, waiting for her to catch a glimpse of what he sought. But she said only, "Sit down. Tell me a story, of Corleu and the Blind Lady. Maybe then you won't be afraid of the dark."

He sat. He dropped his face in his hands. "She was like . . . she was like this house. Old, rambling, crazed, untidy, like a beggar woman you might see at a crossroads, mumbling to herself, her fingers moving always, weaving, weaving . . . At the end, she made me look at her weaving. She threads even the stars into it. I saw the Ring of Time she makes, where all the threads there are flow together and you can't see one life, one star, from another, and outside that Ring there is nothing." He raised his head. "That's the Ring I fell through. I thought I would fall into that nothing."

She mused over that, twisting a pearl button. "Yet even she is trapped, Corleu. Even she. And what you saw is only another story, of the Weaver of Withy Hold. The Cygnet holds her powerless."

"And even that is only another story."

"Well, story or no, the thing you are looking for is real enough. Isn't it?"

"Likely," he said after a moment.

"So you move from tale to tale to get it." She studied the pearl, as if the light shifting across it wove a pattern. "A web . . . beneath the Cygnet flying day and night. Why does that tease my memories? Something I read when I was little, something I saw . . ."

"In your books, maybe."

"Then again, maybe I dreamed it." She drew herself up. "You'd do best to go ask the Dancer."

"I'd sooner find the web than wake the Dancer."

"Why?" she asked, surprised. "All the Dancer does is dream, beneath the ice."

"I'll have to carry fire to face the Fire Bear. And I'd sooner find the web than travel to the top of the world and wake someone who dreams sometimes like what appears in your fires.''

"You find the web, then," she said, turning. "Meanwhile, I'll find what fire you must take to the Fire Bear."

"I'm not going there."

"You'll go."

"I won't need to."

"You'll go," she said, and there was a flicker of something deep in her eyes, another glimpse into his seeking. "That's what they want."

Wordless, he watched her cross the room. She turned at the door. "There's food in the kitchen. I baked bread. Someone will come to the door tonight. My doorkeepers will give him what he has come for. If you stay in here, you may see one or two of them. Don't look directly at them; they take offense. Good night."

The kitchen, he had discovered, never moved. It could be found at the bottom of some stone steps, which sometimes moved, but never far from what they were attached to. Corleu carried books down with him, roamed through them for a web as he ate fresh bread and goat cheese and cold smoked river trout. The only web he found was cobweb. Wandering upstairs hours later for more books, he was startled by voices. Something vague and bulky in the shadows that looked like a misshapen hand or a forked root turned a pale eye at him and hissed. He stopped staring hastily, built up the fire and settled beside it with more books.

He woke in the morning, face-down in a book. Nyx was stirring the fire.

"You should never sleep between two spells," she commented.

He raised his head, blinked at the ancient writing in blue and gold and black inks. *Chrysom*, it said, at the bottom of each page, like a warning.

"I was looking for the web."

"You won't find it in there, that's spells only." She tossed fragrant wood on the fire and sat beside him on the floor, leafing through the pages of one of the books lying open. He watched her sleepily. She wore a long dress of stiff green cloth that rippled with light when she moved. Its top button was missing; he could see the ivory skin at the hollow of her throat, and the thumbnail of shadow below that. Her eyes were on him suddenly, chilly,

colorless, like a winter sky, like a slap of cold water.
  "Corleu. I know the fire you must bring to the Fire Bear,
but I haven't found yet where the Dancer sleeps."
  He sat up, groggy and stiff from the floorboards. "I'm not
waking the Dancer. She sleeps in ice beneath the Fire Bear."
  "Meaning what?"
  "She's under the constellation."
  "So is all of Berg Hold. And all of Ro Holding, nearly.
Where will you step to, if you go through that ring to Berg Hold?
What do Wayfolk say of the Dancer?"
  "If you think of her at the fair side of midnight, you'll have
good dreams; at the dark side, you'll have foul dreams. If a
woman's braid is undone during sleep, Dancer can draw memory
away. If you sleep with fresh lavender on your pillow for her,
she'll tell you who you will marry. If the lavender is withered,
she'll tell who will die. If she dances hooded in your dreams,
your life will change. If you see her face in your dreams, you
will die. The Cygnet trapped her in ice so she could not dance.
Freed, she never stops. Fire Bear would free her, but it has no
fire left in it, after pursuing the Cygnet. So it guards her."
  "But where?"
  "At the top of the world . . ." He paused, then shook his
head. "That's all I know. At the top of the world. You never
saw a likely place in your wanderings?"
  She mused, remembering. "In Berg Hold I visited the northern witches. I sat around their fires in the dead of winter in their
tiny dark huts smelling of tanned hides and smoke and bitter
herbs, and I learned how to foretell from the forked horns of
snow deer, and how to braid strips of leather into safe paths
through the snow, and how to understand the language of the
white crows, who gossip of bad weather, travellers, deer herds,
death. The witches made do with what they had against storm,
hunger, fever. They used to dance to invoke dreams of foreseeing.
To them, the Dancer came alive in those dreams; where she slept
in the ice was of no importance, that was only a tale. I also
studied with the mage Diu, who is the last living descendant of
Chrysom. He is very old; he went to Berg Hold to live in peace,
he said. But he taught me what I wanted to know, anyway, for
Chrysom's descendants have always spent time serving Ro Holding. He made nothing of the Dancer, for he slept little. He only
knew what Chrysom had written. The Dancer was a folk tale. A

constellation. Inconsequential.'' She turned a page, leaving Corleu to wonder at her down-turned, secret face.

"You were curious,'' he ventured. "That's why you went there. To Berg Hold, to live close to earth in the dead of winter. Just curious.''

She lifted her head, gave him for the first time a true smile. "Yes.''

"Were you always this way?''

Her eyes were clear again, expressionless, but not, he thought, offended. "I like to use my mind,'' she said.

"Does—does the Holder—'' The mist in her eyes seemed to chill into frost then, but he persisted. "Does she wonder—does she know—''

"Does she know that I'm in the Delta torturing small animals?''

"I wondered,'' he confessed, and she shrugged slightly.

"Oh, yes. She knows. After this, she may not want to see much of me again, but I think she will always know where I am.''

"How could she not want to see you?'' he protested. "You're her daughter.''

"She has Iris and Calyx. And she has Rush Yarr, who is not her son but might as well be. And she has Meguet. She can spare me.'' Her voice was dry, dispassionate. Corleu, feeling as if he had blundered into some complex, bewildering and totally unfamiliar country, said:

"You're like a story to us. The Holder of Ro Holding and her children: three daughters who wouldn't recognize their fathers from three fence posts, because that's the Holder's business and that's the way it is in your world. Once I saw a procession crossing Withy Hold when I was harvesting. We all stopped to watch it: long lines of riders in black, with other riders in fine, airy colors between them, and the Cygnet on a pennant as long as a furrow, flying like a black flame over them all. That's all I've seen of the Holder. Is she so cold or cruel or stupid that you ran away from her?''

The Holder's daughter shook her head, surprised. "My mother is none of those things. Maybe if she were, I could have lived in the same house with her.'' She added abruptly, frowning, when Corleu opened his mouth, "Enough. I don't like answering

to her, why should I want to answer to some Wayfolk man who
fell out of the sky?''

"Likely,'' he suggested, rising, "because of how I got
there.''

He wandered away to wash and change his clothes, torn by
the thorns and stained by the fields he had known in some distant,
lost life. When he returned, dressed in odd, rich, mismatched
clothes, combing his wet hair with his fingers, he found her in
the same place, beside her fire, so immersed in what she read
that she seemed only an illusion of herself.

But she raised her head after a moment. "I have work to
do this morning. You won't want to watch it. Take what books
you want with you. I'll find you when I'm done.''

Chilled, he took himself and an armload of books far enough
away, he thought, that not even the anguished bellow of a swamp
tortoise could reach him. In a small room containing an old velvet
couch, an empty chest, an empty picture frame and an empty
bird cage, he searched for a web until he fell asleep himself and
dreamed of Tiel within a fall of vines within the bird cage. He
woke and saw the sorceress's face above him.

He started, confusing himself, cages, small wingless birds.
Then he drew a breath, leaned back again. He lifted the book
that sprawled opened across his chest and said, "I found the
Dancer.''

"Where?''

" 'On the top of the world,' '' he read.
" 'On the top of the mountain,
*On the top of a cliff,
On the top of a stone,
Beneath the night,
Beneath the moon,
Beneath the snow,
Beneath the ice:
The Dancer sleeps.
In her breath,
The last breath of winter,
The breath of prophecy.' ''*

He closed the heavy book and sat up. "It's someone's—I
don't know—scraps of sayings, tales, bits of history, even rec-

ipes. Riddles. Accounts, where wild herbs were found. Such like that."

She took it from him. "Rydel. She was head gardener for Timor Ro. She knew some herb magic. Chrysom's grandson wrote of her. He thought highly of her. He wrote that she held secret powers of a kind not even Chrysom knew of, or would have understood. So I read whatever I could find that she wrote, or was written of her. But all her other writings are of herb lore, and no one else attributed such great mysterious powers to her. I have read these lines about the Dancer. I didn't remember them."

"Is there only one mountain in Berg Hold?"

"There is one peak much higher than the rest. There are many tales about what lies under its mists: ice spirits, the ghosts of travellers, the palace of the north wind, a real fire bear. I should have remembered that the Dancer and the Fire Bear are always together, even in tales. It's a grey barren peak in late summer, and by autumn you can no longer see it."

Corleu was silent, weighing the impulse to step out of the Delta onto the frozen peak of the world, to free the Dancer and ask her a question that might end his search, and then, with Tiel safe, to close his eyes and hope that the heart of the Cygnet and the heart of Ro Holding had no more to do with one another than a random pattern of stars had to do with a smallfolk rhyme. Impulse turned to desire; desire was nearly overwhelming. He said, his voice shaking, hearing the rustle of leaves in a place where there was no wind, "And if she doesn't know? You know where she will send me."

The green in his eyes resolved into the watery sheen of the sorceress's skirt, rustling as she shifted. She said only, "And if she knows?"

"And if she doesn't?" He closed his eyes, counted recklessly, deliberately. "Gold King, Silver Ring, Fire Bear—it's not only tales I'm stirring up. It's Hold Signs."

She was silent. He looked up; her eyes caught his, absolutely colorless. She made no movement, no sound. Suddenly terrified under that chill gaze, he thought she must have seen straight through his thoughts to the place where he had hidden his secret, and that, child born under the Cygnet's dark wing, she would kill him before he shook apart Ro Holding.

But she moved finally. Her fingers closed tightly on her

arms; her face, always pale, seemed ghostly in that pale room.
"How complex and fascinating," she breathed. "This is a power
like no other power I have ever encountered. If in the end I must
fight it, then I must understand it. And I can only do that if I see
it unmasked, open, not skulking behind poetry and folk myths.
If you don't finish this, the Gold King will find someone else
who will, someone who may not fall into my hands as tidily as
you did."

"You'd risk Ro Holding out of curiosity," he challenged
her, miserable and desperate. Her brows went up. Behind her,
in the frame that had been empty, he saw the night sky in miniature, the constellations of the Holds—the Gold King, the Silver
Ring, the Fire Bear, the Blood Fox—circling the Cygnet in its
flight. Circling among them were the lesser stars: the Peacock
leading the Blind Lady, the Mage shadowing the Blood Fox, the
Dark House, the Dancer guarded by the Fire Bear.

"Of course I'm curious," Nyx Ro said. "What else would
I be?"

"Likely if you're that powerful you don't have to be afraid."

"Not until you tell me what it is you want me to fear."

He looked away from her steady eyes, back to the night sky.
The frame was empty again. "If I knew exactly," he sighed, "I
could say. They're just tales, how could there be danger? Just
stars our eyes picked out and made into patterns so the night
would be less lonely with faces looking back at us. But because
of stars and smallfolk rhyme, I've lost everything I ever knew."

"It's only a step through time from here to there, from Delta
to Berg Hold, Corleu. From not knowing to knowing. And only
at the cost of fire. Will you wake the Dancer?"

Fire rippled inside the picture frame: a Fire Bear's soundless
roar, a tinker's fire. He saw the tinker's face in the fire, his yellow
eyes, his narrow, sidelong smile. He stared back at it, trapped
and shaken with sudden fury at his helplessness. He said abruptly,
"No."

"No? Corleu, it might take a lifetime to find the web, if
that's what you're thinking."

"What I'm thinking is that likely I'll have to give the tinker
what he asked for, but there's no reason to give him the world
and stars besides. I don't have to bring the Dancer to life for
him. All I must do is ask a question."

"So—"

"So." He met her cool, misty, slightly bemused eyes. "I'll wait for the last day of winter. She'll answer me truly and then she'll dream like always, and none of us will have to see her waking face."

Nyx was silent, studying him. Her head bent slightly; she turned, closed a couple of tomes and picked them up. She said only, "The work I do here might well drive you to Berg Hold long before the end of winter."

"I'll chance it." He heaved books into his arms. "If you'll let me stay."

"Only yesterday you would have given the world and stars to get out of here."

"That was yesterday." He waited for her to open the door, for she would find the workroom behind it, while he would find only another memory. "I can search for the web. If I find what that is, I won't need to ask the Dancer anything."

"You won't last here till winter's end," she predicted, and opened the door.

"I'll last," he said.

There was a woman leaning against a cauldron in the workroom.

Nyx stopped so abruptly in front of Corleu, he nearly dropped books on her; it was a moment before she spoke. The woman waited, her face composed. She wore black silk and leather; the Cygnet, limned and ringed in silver, flew in the hollow of her left shoulder. She was slender, broad-shouldered, tall enough to wear the long blade at her belt. Swans swirled up the metal sheath and over the hilt of the sword; one tried to soar out of the pommel. Her braided hair was pale ivory. Her face, broad-boned, sun-colored, reminded Corleu at first glance of the easily smiling daughters of the wealthy lords of Withy Hold. In the next moment she reminded him of no one he had ever met in his life, and he guessed where she must have come from.

"Meguet," Nyx breathed.

"The Holder sent me." She did not look at Corleu; her still, intent gaze was for Nyx. Nyx moved finally, to a table, and set her books down. She folded her arms. Corleu, following, saw her face as she turned. It looked bloodless in the candlelight; she was frowning deeply.

"Is the Holder well?"

"The Holder, both your sisters and Rush Yarr are all well."

The woman's voice, low and slightly husky, was quite calm under the stares of Nyx's assortment of skulls.

"I didn't ask about Rush Yarr."

"So you didn't." She detached herself from the cauldron with the grace of one intimately acquainted with movement. Her curious glance fell here, there; she picked up a bird skull, examined its clean, delicate lines, its empty eyes, as if searching for the magic in it. Nyx opened her mouth to protest, closed it again. Meguet put the skull down. "So you didn't," she said again. "I'll tell him that if you want. He'll ask."

"After all this time?" Nyx asked sharply. "Nine years?"

"He won't listen to reason." She touched a book or two, paced back to the cauldron, her movements light, quick, restive, like one troubled by walls, Corleu thought, or more likely only these, full of bones and smells. "He still loves you."

"What for?" Nyx said, astonished. The woman's eyes flickered at her; in the pallid light, Corleu caught a hint of their color.

"You must ask him to know. If it's important at all." She glanced into the cauldron. "You have a toad in your cauldron. A big, bloated moon of a toad."

"It's an albino," Nyx said crossly. "You've known Rush as long as I have. Tell him to stop. Tell him I said to."

"I will tell him. Does it jump?"

"It jumps out of everything but that."

"It looks too fat to jump."

"It jumps."

"Its eyes are sapphire. . . . He would have come with me, had he known."

"He should have come," Nyx said dourly. "This house would have opened his eyes."

"Perhaps. What do you do with an albino toad?"

"You feed it to an albino fire."

"Ah," the woman said softly. She reached into the cauldron with one hand, did something that made the toad give a deep, lazy grunt. "It speaks."

"As it will in the fire," Nyx said implacably. "If you are finished playing with my toad, perhaps you will tell me why my mother sent you."

"The Holder sent me to remind you that you will have been away from home for three years in spring."

"Three—" Looking surprised, she calculated, from dust

motes apparently. "Two years in the desert, last spring here . . . so it will be three years."

"In spring. The Holder asks that you remember your promise to return for the Holding Council."

Nyx was silent. She went to the fire, tossed a handful of wood chips from a bowl beside it onto the embers, and the harsh, charred smell in the air subsided. "Of course I'll come home," she said reluctantly. "I did promise. But I would think, under the circumstances, she would rather not see me in the company of all the Hold Councils."

"You think she should wait until you are doing something less disturbing and all the disgusting rumors of you have died down?"

Nyx met her level gaze. "You could put it like that."

"I just did. You're overlooking one thing. Your mother misses you."

Nyx's fingers found a strand of hair to worry. "I can't think why."

"She hoped you would come back with me."

"She must be getting tired of hearing comments about my life."

"That would be the only reason she wants to see you."

Nyx sighed. "If I go back now, we'll only quarrel."

"You've been here nearly a year. Is there that much to learn in this soggy backwater?"

"There are a few things left. Tell my mother I will come home in spring."

Meguet inclined her head without comment. Nyx studied her a moment, the look in her pale eyes unfathomable. She asked, "Is that the only reason you have come, Meguet? All this way through the swamp, up my rickety stairs? The Holder could have sent a message upriver; it would have reached me, my reputation what it is."

Meguet did not reply immediately; she seemed to hear a question beneath that question. "Your mother holds you in more regard than that. Even now. As for your stairs, I would think anyone as powerful as you could mend a stair."

"It discourages visitors."

"So it must. There are two morose trappers waiting for me in a boat at your dock, who almost refused to bring me here. They said you wouldn't want company."

"They were right."

Meguet's calm gaze did not falter. "Then I will leave you," she said softly. "It's getting dark and the trappers may not wait for me."

"How do you know it's getting dark?"

"What?"

"You can't see out of these windows."

"It was dusk when I came in," Meguet said surprisedly. She picked a heavy black cloak off a chair and swung it over her shoulders. The Cygnet, black and silver within a ring of silver, flew around her and settled at her back. She stepped into candlelight; the fire turned her pale hair silk, and Corleu shifted. A memory nagged him, a tale. Her face looked pale now; the things half-hidden in the shadows wore at her, or the odd sharpness in Nyx's questions. Nyx said more easily:

"I forget sometimes whether it's day or night when I work. Tell my mother I will see her in spring."

"I will."

"And tell the trappers to come back here in the morning; I will have work for them."

"I will tell them," Meguet said evenly. She held Nyx's eyes. "They say you are ensorcelled by this swamp. But, now and then, I think I actually see why you are here, why you burn albino toads. I may be wrong. I know so little of magic. But I do wonder, if any of us knew as much as you, where we would make the choice to stop learning."

A little color rose in Nyx's face. She did not answer, but words gathered in the air between them. Before she turned to go, Meguet looked at Corleu. He saw the color of her eyes. And then he saw the corn rows standing in the summer light, the cool, secret, shadowy world they hid between their leaves. He blinked, but he could not separate her from the tale: corn-silk hair and eyes as deeply green as his great-gran's green-drenched memory.

He swallowed drily, motionless under her gaze, not knowing how long they stood there silently, not knowing, from her expressionless face, what she thought. She turned suddenly, and almost dragged at him to take a step and follow her. Nyx stayed silent, listening to the fading footsteps on the porch. She looked as grim as Corleu had ever seen her. He asked tentatively,

"Who is she?"

"She is a far-flung cousin, Meguet Vervaine. She lost her

family early; my mother took her in, raised her with us. She has a penchant for weapons and for wandering. She goes where the Holder sends her, and she is the only person in all of Ro Holding permitted to enter armed into Ro House. She is a descendant of Astor Ro, Moro Ro's wife, who in a thousand years produced some varied and eccentric descendants.''

"Does she have power? Like yours?"

She gave him a brooding, searching look. "She has never shown signs of it. Why?"

"Just—how she looked at me, before she left. At me, into me, and out the nether side. As if—as if she might know me, but couldn't remember . . . Something like you're looking at me now, only it's not me troubles you, it's her.''

"She was in my house." Her fingers tightened on her arms; she stared at the dark empty hallway as if to see her cousin's shadow there. "My doorkeepers could keep even Chrysom out, and Meguet walked through them twice as if she did not even realize they exist.''

PART TWO

THE
GUARDIAN

1

Meguet Vervaine sat silently in the trappers' boat, to their three eyes wrapped in authority and glacially calm; in truth she was deeply troubled and sitting in a puddle. Expressions haunted her: Nyx's, seeing her; the face of the young man, whom she had never seen in her life, and yet who nagged at her, called her back the farther the river took her away. He was no one, she thought; Wayfolk, or part, with that odd hair; wanderer, who had found his way to Nyx's doorstep. Or, more likely, since Wayfolk were rare in the Delta, he had trailed Nyx across Ro Holding, promising this and that in exchange for . . . what? What could he have that she might want, enough to keep him with her? Mute, maybe; he had not spoken but with his eyes. If she kept him to bed, she would not have to listen to him in the morning. But he looked troubled, haggard, ensorcelled maybe, but by Nyx—who had run out of Chrysom's tower and out of Ro House and out of her own life in pursuit of freedom? It seemed unlikely she would extend her dark sorcery to humans just because for one year out of nine she had chosen to live in a swamp.

Meguet shifted; the trappers glanced uneasily at one another, unnerved by her as they were by the woman she had visited. The darkening water caught her eye; it went the wrong direction, she felt: away. The man's face had pulled at her, his dark eyes clinging to hers, stunned by something she could not see. She touched her pale hair, thinking of his hair. Wayfolk did not live within walls or in swamps, nor did they know those expressions, or have that hair. Nor had Wayfolk ever disturbed her before, hung in her thoughts clear and hard-lined as the moon over Wolfe Sea, tugged at her, like the moon tugged the sea, so strongly she said sharply:

"Stop."

The trappers eyed one another, wondering, obviously, how to stop the river. The one-eyed man asked gruffly, "Shall we turn to shore, Lady?"

"Turn back."

"Will cost," the younger man said timidly, and the older shoved at him.

"Will cost nothing," he said hastily, "to the Cygnet. But, Lady, how far back? Not to the house again?"

She nodded. "To the house."

The younger slumped over the oars. "It's not for the likes of you," he protested, "that witch's house. She's demented."

Meguet smiled thinly. "She is my cousin." They were silent then, rowing quickly, lest she reveal an arcane kindred power and find some unpleasant, peculiar use for parts of them.

They left her at the dock, gazing up at the opaque, dragonfly lights in the windows. What Nyx would say if she found Meguet spying on her was something Meguet chose not to contemplate. She heard a sigh behind her and turned, startled; the beautiful river-ghost in her water-stained tumble of lace sat in the prow of her boat and gazed mournfully mid-river. Meguet turned back and a blood fox's eyes flared in the mooring light on the bank. She grew still, not touching her sword, for the blood fox, like the swan, was of an ancient lineage, and had known the Delta before humans. To Delta folk of old family it was not so much bad luck as bad manners to harm their neighbor. When the red-washed eyes vanished, she went up the stairs.

She passed the odd shadows clinging batlike to the walls of the entryway; they were alive, she sensed, but did not consider her worth peeling themselves off the walls to challenge her. No one was in the workroom. She crossed it, under the empty stares of owl and goat and muskrat. She heard voices near, and froze. A few murmured words, silence. She heard no steps. They were together, Nyx and the stranger, nearby. She saw a door in the far wall and opened it a crack. The room beyond was empty. She slipped noiselessly into it. If Nyx found her, she could protest that she was only wandering through the house searching for her to talk further, to reason, to argue. It sounded innocent enough: They had been friends once. The walls of the room were blood red; a stuffed white owl watched her from its perch, looking alarmed, ready to ask its question. The room offered her eight closed doors to choose from. She opened one at random, bewildered, and felt, eerily, as she passed into a dense silence, that somehow she had gone too far: Nyx was not only in some other room, but in some other time. The room she entered was a twilight place, everything in it—candlesticks and chairs and heavy curtains—mauve; it offered her only one door. She pulled it open, expecting the owl room again, but found another room with a great canopied bed and one shoe set neatly next to it.

The door closed behind her; already, she guessed, the twilight room was changing. She stood blinking, bewildered, feeling more lost than she had ever been anywhere in the wilds of Ro Holding. The old house would ramble forever in its memories, like some fey old woman rummaging through her past. She would wander with it until she was forced to call Nyx's name for rescue. She closed her eyes, touched them with cold fingers, concentrated. After a moment, the Cygnet moved across her mind, the black swan flying against a circle of white. Instinct, and experience with that odd, secret habit, made her follow its direction. Eyes still closed she opened the door she had just come through and stepped into the room beyond.

Opening her eyes, she saw a hundred black swans flying around her. The vision lasted only a moment, and then the mirrors the swans had flown through were blank as sky. They changed again as she stood motionless, were suddenly busy with impressions. She saw herself in a small round mirror framed in silver, hung high on a wall. The big mirror beneath it reflected a room full of opened chests and wardrobes, rich clothes tumbling out of all of them. An ornate, square mirror propped against that revealed a room blown entirely, it seemed, out of glass. On every wall, in every corner, high and low, mirrors of every size framed the house's memories, some changing now and then, as if there were not enough mirrors, while at another moment it seemed that, as she stood there, mirrors were coming into existence around her, as if the house were baring its heart to one who could see.

Stunned, she could only stare, her eyes snagged by every peculiar revelation; not even growing up with Nyx's astonishing gifts inured her to this. She was able to move finally, a slight, unguarded sound coming out of her, when she saw Nyx herself, in an oval, wood-framed mirror on the floor. She knelt down in front of it. Nyx and the young man were in a kitchen; ovens and spits and blackened hearths lined the stone wall behind them. They sat at a vast wooden table surrounded by books, nuts, torn loaves of bread, smoked fish, apples, cheese, onions, pitchers of water and wine. Nyx, holding a half-eaten apple between her teeth, was flipping rapidly through a huge book. The young man was reading, his lips moving noiselessly, a frown, intent and anxious, between his brows. Wayfolk he certainly was, with his brown skin and black eyes; that he could read at all was curious. That he wanted to read buried deep in a maze of walls in the middle of the sunless Delta was astonishing. He was, Meguet decided, in dire need of a spell. Or someone he knew was. She leaned toward the mirror, studying him, feeling something cold, dispassionate, ruthless in the scrutiny.

The man lifted his head; for a moment he seemed to gaze back at Meguet, puzzled, uneasy, as if the mirror were water between them and he caught a strange shadow in its depths. Nyx removed the apple from her mouth and chewed a bite. "What is it?" she asked. "Did you find something?"

"Just a dead spider between pages." He rubbed absently at the pale stubble on his chin. Nyx still watched him, not, it seemed, with a lover's attention, but with a rather detached interest, as if he might, if coaxed right, predict, but then again he might not. "Nothing anywhere about a web. Not even in a rhyme for curing warts or jumping stooks."

"Jumping stooks?"

"In a wheat field. It's a smallfolk game."

"Oh."

He closed the books wearily, rubbed his eyes. "We'd get beaten for it when they caught us, but that was part of the game almost."

Nyx, uninterested in stooks, pushed her book aside, pulled another from the pile. "I thought you Wayfolk had a rhyme for everything."

"So did I." He poured water, drank it. There was dust all over his hands; Nyx had a streak on her face. They had, judging from the crumbs on the table, been at this mystery for some time. "It's a secret," the Wayfolk man suggested. "This web. So secret it's nowhere in these books. So it wouldn't likely be in a rhyme smallfolk gabble at each other."

"Nothing in this world is that secret."

The man's eyes flickered to her lowered head. He raised his hands to his face again, linking his fingers across his eyes. Meguet stopped breathing. She leaned forward, touched the cold face in the mirror, as if to draw his hands away, see what he was seeing.

Something is, she thought. *You know something that secret.*

His hands dropped. Nyx leaned back, contemplating him as Meguet was herself, so close to the mirror that her breath misted the cracked painted walls of the kitchen. Finally, Nyx spoke the young man's name.

"You can still change your mind, Corleu. You can wake the Dancer now, if you're fretting."

Meguet, repeating his name silently, felt something stir deep inside her, like the Dancer herself might have stirred, in her cocoon of ice, at the sound of her name.

"No." His hands closed; he said again, not looking up, "No."

"You're not fretting."

He raised his head at the bait; Meguet heard his breath. Then he came close to smiling, a taut smile that barely grew past his eyes. "No. I don't care anymore. The swamp is full of women trapped in mists, waiting for me. They can all wait till winter's end."

"Tell me," Nyx said curiously, "what she is like. Tiel."

He looked at her. "You wouldn't even see her face, likely, if you passed her," he said simply. "You'd see her dark skin and her dark hair and that would be all; your eye would say: She is Wayfolk. She—I could hardly see her face, when I—before I lost her. What it is like truly. She was like the world, like sky, like leaves, like night. Her face was my face. When that dark house fell and I ran into it, I never left her. I'm still there in that mist, like that ghost on the dock, like the Warlock's shadow in

the stars. I'm outside my heart, looking for the way back in."
He added bitterly, after a pause, "It was easy enough to leave.
I only had to go through a door."

Nyx was still, in a way that Meguet remembered: so still
the watery sheen on the fabric of her gown seemed painted; no
light trembled on the gold clip in her hair. Then her hand moved,
fell across the open pages, close to Corleu's hand. If she had
straightened a forefinger, she could have touched him.

"You had no choice."

"I should have stayed with her. I could have."

"Then there would have been no mist trapping your company, no falling house, no spellbound love, no timely meeting
with a bog witch—just a straight road through the Delta to the
sea, because if you were a man who could not recognize that
house, or had been warned by it, it would never have fallen into
your life. Though," she added, "that can't be a flea's worth of
comfort."

"Not even that," he sighed, and dragged at another book
on the heap.

Meguet watched, unblinking, scarcely breathing. It sounded
simple enough: the Wayfolk man in trouble, needing a spell; Nyx
helping precisely because it wasn't simple, and all her life Nyx
had loved nothing better than a challenge. That was all. Yet she
could not move; she held the mirror with both hands, her eyes
on the haunted Wayfolk face, learning every line and hollow of
it, for the words he spoke were illuminating, like lightning shed-
ding glimpses of a traveller's road, some dark, ancient landscape
within her mind.

The words almost came together, the landscape was almost
revealed.

The dark falling house . . .

The Dancer . . .

The Warlock . . .

The web . . .

For a moment, as she concentrated, every mirror in the room
showed her face: pale, intent, motionless, her green eyes narrowed, alert as a hunting animal after a scent. Then the road went
dark again, the words fell apart, meaningless. She dropped her
face against the mirror, wondering at herself, drawn upriver into
a room full of mirrors by a Wayfolk man with no power, just a

problem that, compared with Nyx's usual swamp sorcery, sounded remarkably innocent.

Yet she stayed, her eyes rarely moving from him, and bored herself into a stupor while they read. They spoke little more, finally closed their books with weary thuds, and Meguet slipped away, through the workroom before Nyx returned to it. She borrowed the ghost's boat and the dock lamp, and rowed herself downriver to the ramshackle inn where she had left her horse. The next morning, she sent the boat back upriver and rode out of the swamplands down to the sea.

She followed a narrow trail along the river, which widened and eventually became a road, a tavern at the point where it widened. Another half mile, and she caught a glimpse of Wolfe Sea, a line of deep grey running into the cloudy sky. The low swamp mists changed into a stormy winter sky over the city. The road beneath her crossed other roads now, fronted houses, buildings, boat docks. The river was growing broad, fanning out to mingle with the tides; sea birds and swamp birds wove overhead, with an eye to what the receding tide was leaving in the mud flats.

The road skirted wide around them; houses, shops, guild halls, warehouses, sprouted cheek by jowl, eye to eye across the road. The road itself was cobbled here, and in the late afternoon, crowded. Presently, the buildings yielded to a high stone wall that rambled along the road; ancient trees leaned over the wall, their bare boughs chattering together in the wind, like a private conversation between many very old friends. In the distance Meguet saw the sea again.

She heard it finally; the road wound around a curve in the wall and brought her to the gate of Ro House. It was late by then; the sea was very dark. A single red star broke through the clouds, hung low on the horizon: the Blood Star. The gate faced the sea; the waves turned sluggishly along the pale sand, broke with a frail, lacy line of silver that teased the eye and vanished. Beyond it, night fishers, their bows lamp-lit, flickered like fireflies on the vast restless dark.

The Cygnet flew diagonally across the gate, lit by torches on either side. Meguet rode up to it and dismounted. The Gatekeeper, who had seen her coming from his high perch on the wall, was already opening it.

"Lady Meguet," he greeted her, and swung the gate wide. "Welcome."

The house that the mage Chrysom had built on the curving shore of Wolfe Sea was a great, shining wheel of seven towers circling the high black tower above which the Cygnet flew on a pennant furling and unfurling, by day and night. The towers were built of granite and marble cut in Hunter Hold, of pale wood from the Delta and dark polished wood from Berg Hold and delicate glass blown in Withy Hold. A miniature city rambled around the tower walls, of stables, smithies, barns, kennels, hen coops, forges, tanneries, workshops, cottages with gardens in front of their doors. Some of the household and cottagers could trace their families back a thousand years to Moro Ro's time. Behind the towers the outer walls sprawled out of sight, for Chrysom had made room for fields, ponds, pastures, a small lake around which ancient oak mingled with the vast, dark firs he had taken as saplings from Berg Hold. Legend had it that he had built the house to move from Hold to Hold, eluding siege like a flea eludes a hound's tooth. At the end of the Hold Wars, the warlords had come to the Delta to pledge fealty to Moro Ro, in his house by the sea, and there it had stood since.

Meguet dismounted tiredly just inside the gate; the Gate-keeper held her horse while the stable girls ran across the yard. She lingered to talk to him. He was tall, muscular, with short, muddy sun-streaked hair, and eyes as silvery green as the scythe-shaped leaves on the swamp trees. He was a reticent man, with a clever, unerring eye, discreet despite the household gossip that found its way to him like water found holes in a sieve. He had opened the gate to Meguet for the ten years she had worn the Cygnet on Holder's business. Though he was swamp-born, as far as she knew, he always guessed where she had been when she returned.

"Has the house been quiet?" she asked him. A corner of his thin mouth slanted upward.

"In a manner of speaking." He wore the Cygnet at both wrists and over his heart, though on him they were apt to fly haphazardly, rucked up over his forearms, or half-hidden under a sheepskin vest. "I opened the gate a dozen times to the sons and daughters of the Delta lords. Most are still here."

"To see Rush?" Meguet guessed. "Or Calyx?"

"Both." He added, "And to see you."

She didn't ask who or why, having little interest in their neighbors. "Anyone else?" She liked to hear him talk. The rough, river-hatchling's voice ran just beneath ten years of household polish; it surfaced now and then, unexpectedly.

"Merchants," he said. "In and out again. A tinker, in but not out."

"A tinker?"

"He has kin, he said."

"Ah."

"The Holder sent word to the gate that she will see you whenever you arrive."

Meguet glanced at the third tower. Lights swarmed around it; the great hall looked aflame. "She'll be at supper." The Gatekeeper, eyeing something in her hair, seemed to weigh respect against inclination. He said:

"You had raw weather for a ride upriver."

Meguet looked at him. "I suppose you can tell from the mud on my stirrup which bog I stood in to mount."

"No." He reached out, picked a feather from her hair. "I've seen you wear mud from all over Ro Holding. But the small birds this color orange live only in one place."

Gazing at it, she thought of the small silent white birds caged in Nyx's workroom. She took it grimly, let it flutter free. He watched it fall.

"You saw the Lady Nyx," he commented. There was neither question nor curiosity in his voice, but she was irritated, at him for seeing a feather fall and thinking of Nyx, mostly at Nyx, for causing the tales that linked her to such small birds. She asked sharply,

"Is there anything else I've done that you need to tell me?"

He eyed her, his expression, in the torchlight, hard to read. "You sat for some time on the gutting board of a trapper's boat," he said. She stared back at him, impassive. Then she heard something beyond the tower-ring, across the back meadows and pastures: a weave of light and dark beating the air toward the small lake that lay hidden behind the thousand-year-old wood. She knew that sound, had heard that coming every year of her life.

"And you," she said, "forgot an entire company."

The spare, crooked smile flickering over his face again, into his eyes, made her smile. "Who?" he demanded. "Who entered or left missed my eye?"

"The wild swans of winter."

2

Meguet stood in the black tower, watching for swans. Her high chambers overlooked the tower ring, household grounds, sea and the city beyond. It was too dark to see anything; there was not a single star in the sky, not even a splash of moonlight on the lake to show her where it lay. But still she stood there, silent, tranquil, feeling them drop toward the water, a great gathering of black and white swans from the far north, who waited, it seemed, for the fiercest winds to ride across Ro Holding. She had never told anyone but the Gatekeeper that she could feel the swans come and go. In that house, with its long, powerful and eccentric history, it seemed an unimportant matter.

She turned away from the window. Her attendants moved quietly through the rooms, clearing away her supper, the bath water, gathering her muddy clothes. No one else lived in the tower; it was used once every three years for the Holding Council. It held Chrysom's haunted library, just above her, and beneath the tower, the maze where, legend said, his bones were buried. They were guarded, legend said also, by terrifying and awesome

beings, whom Meguet and Rush and Nyx had once wasted days
trying to find. Such tales clustered around the tower like the
thousand-year-old rose vines, making it the most peaceful place
in the house. The Holder and her children escaped to Chrysom's
library for quiet and conference; cottagers' children crept like
mice in and out of the exasperating and tantalizing maze. Other
than that, no one used it but Meguet and her hardheaded attendants, who feared neither ghosts nor the long spiral climb to the
top.

There was a tap at the door; word came that the Holder
would see Meguet in Chrysom's library. Meguet pulled on a long
black wool dress that hid the greater part of her oldest boots, and
set a braid, Wayfolk-style, to one side of her loose hair. Watching
her fingers move in the mirror, she thought of mirrors; Corleu's
face looked back at her, innocent and dangerous and bewilder-
ingly compelling.

She rose, went up the final spiral of stairs. There was wine
in Chrysom's library, and the makings of a fire and a view of
the night from every direction through the ring of glass windows
that circled the stones. The room still held obscure oddments of
Chrysom's sorcery; Nyx had taken some. It also held Rush Yarr,
who had built the fire and was standing at a window with a cup
in his hand, looking for stars apparently, but thrown back by the
utter dark onto his own reflection in the glass.

"Meguet," he said, recognizing her long, quick stride before he turned. He was a sinewy man with a lean, restless face.
He had hair the color of a blood-fox pelt and the blood fox's
amber eyes without the wash of red in them. His family, who
once fought Moro Ro under the sign of the Blood Fox, had
perished at sea in one of their own merchant ships. He had been
sent to Ro House at an early age, a year after Meguet had come.
There, he fell in love with the Holder's third daughter. The old
stones still echoed with their quarrels years before, for she had
not told him she was leaving, nor, returned for a visit, would
she permit him to travel with her. So, ghostlike, he haunted the
room where she had spent most of her time, waiting for her final
homecoming, trapped, Meguet thought, unable to love a woman
never there, unable to stop loving her.

He poured Meguet wine before asking the question she knew
was foremost in his mind.

"Did you find Nyx?"

"Of course I found Nyx," she answered. "The Holder told me to find her."

"Well?"

"Well what?"

"Well, is it true she is eating small animals alive and gossiping with the dead?"

"She was doing those very things when I walked into her house." Meguet sipped wine, and leaned her head back to look at Rush, who was pacing the length of the massive hearth. Ravens and gulls perched half out of the stone beneath the mantelpiece; the Cygnet, carved in black marble, flew above the fire. In that room, with its thousand-year-old collection of books and paraphernalia, Nyx had taken up residence as a child, reading constantly, spells seeping into her pale, luminous eyes, while Rush rifled through old jars and boxes, set minor fires and conjured up terrifying images in cloudy mirrors, which Nyx would summarily disperse. Meguet added with more sympathy, "She said she intends to come to the Holding Council."

"How kind of her."

"She's learning things, Rush."

"Learning what?" He was facing her suddenly, backed by fire and flying birds; something of Chrysom's had somehow gotten into his hand. "A mean, petty magic—pirates pay her to foresee storms, merchants pay her to foresee one another's misfortunes. She pays river-scum to bring her half-dead animals. She is Lauro Ro's daughter. Or at least she was. I don't know what she's making herself into now."

"A mage," Meguet said simply.

"I want to talk to her. Where is she?"

Meguet cradled her wine cup in both hands, contemplated the shiver of light across it. Something in her grew alert, as always when Rush was fretting over Nyx. She said calmly, "Nyx is in a house upriver. Any trapper could tell you where. If you really thought she would listen to you now, you would not be standing here talking to me. She is doing what she thinks she must."

"How can she think—"

"Be patient, Rush."

"She's in the Delta backwater, tearing the wings off birds and burning the bones of the dead." His hand clenched tightly around the thing he held. Meguet, very still, watched needles of firelight dart across it. "None of us knows her anymore. None of us. We saw her last nearly three years ago. For all of five days. And not for two years before that. She is tearing at the Holder's heart. And mine. And you say be patient."

Meguet closed her eyes briefly, against the headache that was threatening. "You could simply forget her," she suggested, not for the first time.

"She could be brought home."

"No."

"She belongs here. She could learn her sorcery here like she did when she was young."

"You weren't this bitter when she stayed for two years in Berg Hold. Or for a year in Withy Hold. Or in Hunter Hold among the witches."

"She was learning things of value then, not—"

"How do you know? How do you know what she was learning? Do you think knowledge always lies in safe, clean places where nothing or anyone is disturbed? That you can always learn by daylight and always sleep without dreams afterward?"

"How can you defend her?" It was as much plea as demand; he stood so tensely, waiting for answer, that he might have been something Chrysom carved on the hearth along with the crows. She picked her words with care; if he wanted a quarrel, she thought, he could go find Nyx.

"She has great power, I think, though it's hardly evident from what she does in the swamp. If she makes mistakes now, she may make great mistakes. But she—"

"Then she may harm herself, along with the swamp life. She should be brought home."

"Nonsense, Rush, you can't just walk into her house and—"

"Why not?" Rush demanded. "You did. So can I. So I will."

"No. You won't," she said flatly. "Because you know her too well. You know that she will only love you freely if you let her come back freely. That's why you are still here, shouting at me instead of her."

Rush was silent, his jaw clamped. He whirled abruptly, having no other argument but confusion, and flung the thing in his hand into the fire.

They both jumped, he in surprise at what he had done, and

Meguet because he had actually done it. She finished the movement on her feet. The fire made an odd, keening wail. She threw herself at Rush, who seemed too surprised to move, and knocked him away from the fire. Black smoke poured out of the hearth, obscuring the flames. Something snapped, and there was a stench that sent them both running to the windows.

They flung a few open before, weeping and choking, they headed up the stairs to the roof. The stones flashed green a moment; the smell followed them up, disgorged itself into the wind.

Meguet leaned on the parapet, wiping her streaming eyes. "I wish," she said tartly when she could speak again, "you would stop doing that."

"I'm sorry."

"One of these days you'll throw the wrong thing and blow Chrysom's tower back to the quarries in Hunter Hold."

"I'm sorry," he said again. He leaned against the stones beside her, dragging at the north wind. "It—it tears at me that you can see her, talk to her, and I can't."

She put her hand on his shoulder. "I know. But she barely even talked to me. I startled her, I think, coming out of this world into hers. . . . You'll see her in spring. It's not that long to winter's end. Perhaps by then she'll be out of the swamp, learning something less . . . dubious."

"Dubious." She felt him laugh noiselessly at the word. "There's nothing dubious about what she's doing. It's disgusting."

"Then how can you love her so? Can't you love someone else instead?"

"I've tried."

"And?"

"No one else in the world is a lank-haired, cold-eyed, sharp-tongued woman with enough sorcery in her to stand this house on its head."

"Is there anything at all you like about her?"

"No. Just the smallest finger in each hand, the color that comes into her eyes under a full moon, the way her mouth shapes certain words. My name, for instance. The way she laughs, which she did once, three years ago. A soft, summery chuckle like blackbirds among the rose trees. The way she wears the color green. The way she looks sometimes, like a wild thing listening for another wild thing. The way she reads, as if words are air to be breathed. The way she kissed me when we were barely more than children, out of curiosity, behind the closed doors of the hay barn on the warmest day of the year, and the way she looked at me afterwards, as startled as if she had just invented a world. The way the shadows of the doves flying up into the rafters crossed and recrossed her face . . ." His hand was between Meguet's shoulders by then, his fingers working at the knot from the day's riding. She tilted her head back, loosening muscles, and saw, beyond the curl of the great black pennant whipping above their heads, the full moon revealed with a swan flying across it. She caught her breath; in the next moment the swan had dipped down into darkness and the moon had disappeared.

"I suppose there is no hope for you, Rush Yarr."

"None." He paused, added with a shade of reproach in his voice, "I would have ridden with you to see Nyx, but you didn't tell me you were going."

"The Holder tells me when to come and go. She didn't mention you."

"Must you be so blindly obedient?"

"Always."

"Because she gave you a home?"

"Because I choose to."

"She gave me a home, too, and family. I am obedient and respectful, too, but rarely at the same time."

"You are of Delta blood. You have an archaic desire to rebel against the Holder."

"And you, descended from Astor Ro, desire to obey the Holder, speak meekly at all times with downcast eyes, and never look out of high windows."

"Astor Ro may have been afraid of anything not surrounded by high walls, but she fought at Moro Ro's side during the Hold Wars and she was not afraid to tell him when to change his underwear."

"How do you know that?"

"I read it in some old chronicle."

"You never read."

"I tried, when you and Nyx and Calyx all studied together. I never understood how you could. It made me feel strange."

He gazed at her curiously, his hand still. "How?"

"As if I had read everything before, and yet I never had. As if I remembered things I never knew . . ." She shivered suddenly and he dropped his hand. "Let's go back. The Holder is coming up. I want to see if there's a library left."

"What do you think that was?"

"What was?"

"What I threw?"

"I have no idea. Dead, it smelled like. A thousand years dead."

A silken green pall hung over the library. They opened more windows, let the north wind scour the air, blow the green shade out to sea. Rush, having enchanted away his anger, left Meguet alone to wait for the Holder.

She came finally, near midnight; Meguet heard her footsteps walk into a dream, and she half-woke, trying to rise at the same time. Lauro Ro's hand at her shoulder kept her still. The Holder crossed to the fire, and picked up a poker to stir the lagging flames. Of all her daughters, Nyx most resembled her, in her dark hair and her movements. The Holder's hair, wild, night-black, flecked with white, was coiled, braided, pinned into submission every morning; by midnight the Holder's impatient fingers had freed most of it. She was tall, big-boned, still slender; her eyes were dark as the Cygnet's wings and her voice could— and did once or twice—carry from the top of Chrysom's tower clear to the Gatekeeper in his turret beside the gate. She wore blue velvet that night, and rings on every finger, which sent jewelled lights spinning around the walls as she fanned the air under her nose with one hand. Rush Yarr considered her a throwback, in her darkness and strength and fearlessness, to Moro Ro himself.

"Has Rush been breaking things again?" she asked, opening a few more windows, and the damp sea winds danced into the room, waking Meguet further.

"He was upset about Nyx."

"He is always upset about Nyx. I am upset about Nyx." She gave the fire a final poke and turned, poured wine. "How is Nyx?" She handed Meguet a cup and sat down finally, near the hearth, with the poker and wood close at hand, for, like Nyx, she loved fires. "Will she come home?"

"She remembered her promise. She will come for the Council."

"But not before."

"No."

The Holder's mouth tightened. She pulled a pin of gold
and pearl out of her hair, shook the falling strand free. Her feet
worked out of her velvet slippers at the same time; she sat with
her unshod feet on the stones like a cottager while Meguet
stretched a worn boot to the fire and added, "I think she only
does these things to see that she is able to do them. That's what
matters to her. She's not destined for a life of petty witchery in
the swamps. But this may not be the only strange path she
takes."

"She's been away most of nine years," the Holder said
incredulously. "How much more of sorcery is there to learn?"

"I don't know."

"I wish I did know more." She brooded at the fire a moment,
her elbows on her knees. "Her father was ensorcelled," she
added, stunning Meguet, for the Holder never answered questions
about her daughters' fathers.

"A swan?" Meguet hazarded.

"No. A wolf in Hunter Hold. In the night hours when he
was human, he never spoke of any such knowledge. She didn't
get it from him. Or from me." She glanced at Meguet, reading
her mind. "I broke the spell over him. I don't know how. We
were both surprised." She smiled a little, remembering. Then
she looked at Meguet again, her eyes dark and fire, a long look
that took in more, sometimes, than Meguet knew about herself.
"But you have more to tell me."

Meguet, unsurprised, nodded. She took a sip of wine, held
the cup in her linked fingers. "There is someone with Nyx."

"Who?"

"A young man. I couldn't tell at first what he was; he was
dressed in rich, antique clothes. I learned later he is Wayfolk,
with strange pale hair and a dark, harrowed face."

"From watching Nyx work, probably. An apprentice?"

"Maybe."

"A lover?"

"I hope not."

"Why not?"

Meguet hesitated, received the Holder's full attention. "I
only looked at him once, and he never spoke. But something in
him drew me back into the house after dark. I could not ride

away and leave him there with Nyx, without knowing more. And yet there's nothing to know but that he's Wayfolk, with chaff from the fields of Withy Hold under his fingernails and a love named Tiel in his heart. On the surface.''

"On the surface," the Holder repeated. Her eyes were still now, expressionless, reminding Meguet of the ancient, equivocal night in a stone-tortoise's eye. "And under the surface? What exactly is my daughter living with?''

"I don't know. Neither does she. A Wayfolk man with a secret . . .''

"What secret?''

"I don't know.''

Memory, to her surprise, seemed as accessible as the memory of the house she had wandered in; small details became clear, including the landscape in her mind that the young man's piecemeal rambling had formed. She began with her unremarked entry into Nyx's house, and ended with Corleu taking the light out of the mirror, leaving Meguet in darkness in a room full of dark mirrors.

"I thought you might have sent me back anyway,'' she finished. "But even returning there, and listening to them, I have no idea what they're doing together.''

The Holder, still through the long tale, got to her feet in a whirl and prickle of lights. She poked at a log meditatively; Meguet could not see her face. The fire flared; she kept up a gentle but relentless nudging until sparks flew thick as stars up the chimney and Meguet cast a watchful eye at the ancient, mysterious, gleaming secrets along the mantel. Lauro Ro put the poker down abruptly, turned. The expression in her eyes startled Meguet; it was something like the impersonal, bone-searching gaze she had favored Corleu with.

"You followed the Cygnet into a room full of mirrors?''

Of all details her memory had woven together, it seemed least significant. "I didn't know which way to go,'' she explained, surprised. "It was like throwing grass into the air and following. I moved in the direction the Cygnet flew in my mind. That's all. It's nothing but a trick I play on myself. Sometimes when I'm lost impulse will find a path where reason can't.''

Lauro Ro sat down again. She pulled the last pins from her hair, tossed them into her lap. Her hair, tumbling forward, hid her face again. But her voice sounded more familiar. "They were searching those old books for a web?"

"So it seemed."

"Instead of waking the Dancer."

"It seemed."

"That's a constellation."

"His tale was full of stars."

"Is Nyx in danger?"

The question started Meguet. "From what? A Wayfolk man who grew up jumping stooks?"

"Then why did you go back?"

Meguet was silent, gazing back at the Holder. She pulled herself up restively. "I don't know," she said, scrutinizing memory to find the bone in Corleu's face, the fleeting expression that had turned her in her path. "Impulse."

"Grass in the wind."

"He disturbed me."

"Before he even opened his mouth?"

"Yes."

"So." The Holder watched her pace. "If the man himself is not the danger, who is the danger?"

Meguet halted mid-step, as if the shadow of a raven flying out of the stone had suddenly barred her way. She stared down at the shadow, whispered, "Is that what I saw? Why I went back?"

The Holder shifted; a sapphire light flashed. She raised her head; her eyes had changed: They grew wide, luminous, vulnerable, like the eyes of a deer catching sight of a hunter's arrow. She said nothing, left Meguet staring at her. Meguet took another step into the raven's shadow, and stopped again.

"Do you want me to go back there and talk to Nyx?"

"Was Nyx settled there for the winter? Or will she move again before spring?"

"She said she has work to busy her there until spring."

"I can imagine," the Holder said, darkly. "I could call her home, I suppose. She could glare at me and pick bats apart in the middle of the night." She stirred the fire with unnecessary force, scattering embers onto the floor. Meguet kicked them back in, leaning wearily against the stones. She felt bone-tired suddenly, ready to sleep where she stood, propped among the stone birds, beneath the Cygnet.

"How did the Wayfolk man get his hair?" she heard, a riddle in the dark, and realized that her eyes were closed. She said:

"Yes."

"What?"

She opened her eyes, saw her own hair milky in the firelight against her black gown. "There," she said, "is the question." She dragged her hand over her eyes, remembering. "I looked at him, he looked at me. He recognized me. That's what I saw in him. Why I turned back. We recognized each other."

"From where?" the Holder asked. "Have you met him before on your travels?"

"No. Never."

"Then how?"

"That," she said, "I will find out."

"Just be careful," the Holder said somberly.

"I am always. And he is only Wayfolk."

"He may be only Wayfolk, but he is with Nyx, and she is wandering in dangerous country. One of these days she may call up something she didn't expect. She may have already, by the sound of it. Take Rush with you. You should not go alone."

"I would rather take the Gatekeeper," she said, surprising both herself and the Holder. "Rush would only fight with Nyx."

The Holder looked at her silently, her expression unfathomable. "My Gatekeeper?"

"He knows the swamps." She kicked a cold ember back into the hearth. "There are fewer travellers in winter, for him to open the gate to."

"He will not leave the gate. They never do."

"If he will?"

The Holder was silent again, her eyes on the fire. "If he will go," she said slowly, "take him." She shivered suddenly, then gathered pins in her lap and stood. She put her hand on Meguet's shoulder, kissed her lightly. "Watch over my spellbound child. But be careful of her."

"I will."

Asleep finally, Meguet dreamed a moon, and a strange pattern of stars beyond her window, in a windy, blue-black sky. A ragged edge of black cloud detached itself from the wind and sank earthward. As it neared her window, the winds stilled. Moonlight drenched the sky. The casement opened: A wild black swan lighted on the ledge, drew in its wings. It filled her window, huge, mysterious, darker than the night behind it. It watched her. Dreaming or awake by then—she hardly knew—she watched it.

3

She was forced to wait before she went back upriver. Cold rain fell for days; the entire swamp, yellow-grey with mud, seemed to be sliding into the sea. She and Rush, both restive, took to the armory and threatened each other with antique weapons. Sons and daughters of the Delta lords, descendants of swamp dwellers and half-wild under their wealth and manners, joined them, looking for any sport in the drenched world. Meguet gave lessons to young men whose eyes constantly looked past her for a glimpse of Calyx, and then were suddenly on her, unbraiding her neat hair and studying her flowing, muscular movements. She treated them with a grave courtesy that was dampening, left them searching for Calyx, who was always elsewhere.

She forded the rivers and pools in the outer yard one day near dusk, when the hard edge of the rain had dulled. She surprised the Gatekeeper as she came up the steps along the wall to his turret. With thick sheepskin on the stone seats, a three-legged brazier between them, and their own voluminous, bulky cloaks, there was hardly room under the peaked stone roof for both. But he seemed pleased, if mystified, by her company.

"Lady Meguet," he said. "It was brave of you to cross the yard. Some of the cottagers were fishing in it earlier."

"I don't doubt." She held her hands to the brazier, looking curiously around at the scalloped edgings of marble on the open ledges, and along the roof. "This place was enormous, when I came last."

"Before my time, then. Or I would have remembered you coming."

She smiled. "It was another Gatekeeper, yes. An old man with white hair and black brows. I have forgotten his name. Or maybe I never knew he had one beyond 'Gatekeeper.'" She paused, saw the flicker of smile in his eyes, and surprised him. "Hew."

He blinked. "Yes. Most don't know that, beyond the cottages."

"I asked the Holder."

"Oh." He cleared his throat. "She remembered my name, did she? After ten years?"

"She must have considered it important."

"And you," he said mildly, "have found it suddenly important to know."

"I asked her," Meguet said, "ten years ago, the first time you opened the gate for me alone."

He was silent; she watched a wave, storm-ridden, stumble wildly against the sand and fall a long, long way before it stopped. He reached for a little ebony pipe on the seat beside him, and found a taper. He met her eyes. "What can I do for you, Lady Meguet?"

"The Holder said you may not do it."

"Ah." He carried flame to the pipe with the taper; light flooded his hands, the lower part of his face. She realized then that he had been young, too, when she asked the Holder his name: a boy, straight out of the backwater, catching crayfish one day and guarding the Holder's gate the next. "There is only one thing I would not do for you," he said simply, and she sighed.

"You won't leave the gate."

"I can't."

"But why? You leave it nights to sleep, don't you? Do you? You do sleep."

"Sometimes here, other times I have a small cottage . . . ."

He studied her, his brows crooked. "I can't," he said again. "But tell me what I can do."

"Tell me what binds you here," she demanded, frustrated. The rain pounded down again; he shifted the brazier from the open window, his eyes straying by habit to the massive closed gate. He puffed on his pipe a bit, then said apologetically at the smoke:

"It keeps me warm, and awake when I'm up late, waiting. . . . Nobody ever asked me that before. Not like that, anyway."

"Is it secret?"

"Even so, I'd tell you. Because you know what you're asking. The old man—the other Gatekeeper—came looking for me upriver. He had yellow eyes; with all that white hair he looked like an owl. I heard he was coming; word travelled faster than him, that some bird-haired old man wearing the Cygnet was stopping everyone, man and girl, and saying one thing to them. I was standing in my boat, hauling in a five-foot pike when he found me. He spoke. That's the last I saw of the pike."

"What did he say?"

"He said, 'I have left the gate.' I remember rowing downriver in such a panic I nearly wrecked myself among the ships coming into the harbor. That's the last I saw of swamp and the first I saw of the city and the Holder's house. I didn't stop moving until I had shut the open gate and climbed up here to watch." He smiled a little. "Later that evening the most beautiful woman in the world came up the steps and brought me supper. She asked my name and welcomed me into her house."

Meguet leaned back against the stones. "What a strange tale. So you were born Gatekeeper."

"Seems so. One day, I'll do the same, leave the gate wide and hobble around the Delta until someone drops crayfish net or butter churn or bill of lading and runs to close the gate."

"What happens if you leave?" she persisted. "For only a day or two. Three."

"Makes my heart pound, just the thought. But why? Why me, of all?" Then he answered himself. "The swamp." And then, "The Lady Nyx."

This time his guesswork did not annoy her. She sighed soundlessly, sliding her hood back, for the brazier had heated the old stones well. "Nyx," she said softly. He waited, pipe

going out between his fingers, his odd, slanted, swamp-green
eyes grave. "I think she may be in trouble. The Holder wants
me to go and talk to her, but not to go alone. I thought of you.
You know the swamp."
    "So do you."
    "You know the tales spread about her."
    "So does everyone."
    "But you would not spread others, if you saw her. You
would be discreet, you would not be afraid of the swamp, and—
I think—you would not be afraid of Nyx."
    "I've seen swamp magic." He relit his pipe, added, glancing
across the yard, "It's a bloody, ugly kind of thing, some. But I
can't believe you'd be in danger at all from Lady Nyx."
    "She has someone with her."
    He said, "Ah," softly. Then: "The Lord Rush Yarr knows
sorcery. He is not afraid of Lady Nyx."
    "I'm afraid of his sorcery. And his temper. Nyx would toss
us both out of her house and guard the door." His eyes were on
the yard again; she turned, saw some of their neighbors bundled
faceless, splashing through puddles toward the gate. "If you can't
come, I will ask him, though. He doesn't know enough to fear
the swamp; he won't be discreet with Nyx, but at least he cares
for her."
    "I'm sorry."
    "Do you miss the swamp?" she asked suddenly. "Your
freedom?"
    He smiled. "That's why I like to see you come and go.
Hear where you've been, travelling around Ro Holding like a
tinker." He flushed a little as she laughed. "Sorry. I had one on
my mind."
    "I never met a tinker who roamed as far as I do."
    "This one might. Hunter Hold Sign on the back door of his
house, and Withy Hold on the side. He could put Delta on the
other side while he's here."
    "It's easy enough to paint a sign."
    "Or tell stories to the gullible." He put his pipe down as
the riders neared. "At least he did tell them. Mended pots and
told tales, cottage imps in and out of his house. It caught their
eyes, his little, black, rolling house. It caught mine."
    "You said he had kin?" she said absently, pulling her hood
forward.

"No. He said."

"He didn't? He lied to get in the gate?"

"He claimed kin, I heard. But by the time he did his business and told his stories, kinship got confusing. Everyone knew he had kin, but no one claimed him. When they got that sorted out, he had disappeared."

"He left the house."

"No. I never opened the gate for him to leave. He's hidden somewhere. Not even the cottage brats can find him."

She waited for him to rise, followed him out into the rain-spangled torchlight. His story irritated her: too silly to heed, too disturbing to ignore. "A tinker," she repeated, "in hiding in Ro House. Tinkers don't do such things. They mend and move on. He must be somewhere among the cottages."

"You must be right." He stepped to the gate as the riders came up, bid them good night courteously, not missing a name or a half-hidden face. "He could put that dark house in the shadow of a wall, and you'd miss it." He swung the gate shut again, faced her, the rain sliding down his bare head, wet hair hugging the lean lines of his face. "Or I would."

She shivered suddenly, gathered her cloak close. "You wouldn't," she said. "You put him into my eye. Now I'll be looking for him. A little black house in the shadow of Ro House."

The heavy rain turned to snow the next day, to everyone's astonishment, for it rarely snowed along the coast. The Holder's children gathered one by one in Chrysom's tower to watch it fall. Even Iris, who thought Chrysom's library gloomy and sorcery incomprehensible, joined them and was entranced by the pale sky falling endlessly into Wolfe Sea. Meguet, staring out at the weather, was not entranced. Her eye fell on the Gatekeeper, in his turret across the empty yard. Even in that cold he kept watch.

She heard her name spoken; Rush was describing the sword-play lessons to Calyx.

"They are all in love with Meguet," he said, "at least while they are with her, and she scarcely sees them." He smiled as Meguet turned; he was slightly drunk. "Meguet loves no one."

"So do I," Calyx sighed. "They all have homes, don't they? Why can't they stay there?"

"Really, Calyx," Iris said. "You might like marriage." Iris, the oldest of the Holder's daughters, had deep chestnut hair

and violet eyes, and a head for the myriad small details that
fretted each Hold or kept them peaceful.

"I will never marry," Calyx said. "I am going to live in
this tower and write a history of Ro House." She sat leafing
through an ancient, cracked book, looking like a winter rose,
with her fine, silk-white hair, her skin flushed like dawn over
hoarfrost on the top of the world. She had eyes the blue-grey of
the northern sky, and bones so fine only the smallest of rings fit
her fingers. Though the Holder had never told her, it seemed
obvious where her father had come from. He was, Rush suggested, one of the ice-spirits of Berg Hold, who lured travellers
to their deaths with their stunning beauty. Calyx agreed that, if
nothing else, he had probably got the Hold right.

"You're already too much in this tower," Iris declared. "It
can't be healthy."

"Meguet lives here. So I will."

Iris eyed Meguet a moment, found answer to her own satisfaction. "Meguet is permitted to be eccentric by heritage."

"This entire family is eccentric," Calyx said, delving back
into her book. "We have no known fathers, Nyx is a sorceress,
Rush is hopelessly in love with a sorceress, and Meguet wanders
everywhere and lives among ghosts. Our mother never married.
I take after her."

"Our mother never sat in a tower to avoid suitors."

"They bore me. I would rather read history."

Rush slipped the book out of her hands. "What is this?"
he asked, leafing through it. "There seems to be a lot of vege-
tables in it."

"It's Rydel's book on the growing of herbs and roses. I
thought I would."

"Would what?"

"I found a tiny, overgrown walled garden behind the back
tower; Rydel wrote that Astor Ro had one that was latticed with
vines, so she did not have to see the sky. I think this was her
garden. Rydel planted roses there; perhaps some are still alive."

"After three hundred years?"

"The rose vines on this tower are a thousand years old."

"But Chrysom planted those. They must be magic."

"Why must they be?" Iris demanded. "I don't see why
everything in this tower must be somehow touched by Chrysom.
He's been dead for centuries."

"This entire tower is spellbound," Calyx said composedly. "That's why I like it. The roots of the rose vines are fed by Chrysom's bones, buried in the maze."

"Oh, really, Calyx," Iris said in disgust. Rush laughed; Meguet, glancing at him, realized how rarely he did that, these days.

She poured herself wine, sat where she could watch snow and fire at the same time. Rush paced a little, restlessly, behind her. His feet stopped finally; she felt his hands on her shoulders.

"You look beautiful in that green," he said. She dragged her thoughts back from the swamp, watched him thoughtfully as he moved to lounge on skins at her feet. He met her gaze. "Am I right," he asked, "that you love no one?"

She did not answer for a long time. "You," she said, "love everyone and no one. I love no one and everyone. Even you, Rush Yarr. As you sometimes love me. And sometimes Calyx. But always Nyx."

"So," he said, "you are not indifferent to the young blood foxes you teach."

She smiled. "Of course not."

"Don't you want to marry, leave Ro House for a home of your own?"

"No," she said. "Marry, perhaps. But leave this house? Never. It is my heritage, I think. So old, I am tangled in these old stones. I can't separate myself."

"One day you might," he said, his brows knit. "One day."

She shook her head. "I can't explain it," she said, indifferent to explanations. Calyx, listening, said gravely:

"Meguet is born to love a swan."

"What?" Rush said, turning. Meguet looked at her, startled. Calyx gathered strands of imagination, began weaving them.

"A swan. One of the wild swans that come down late from Berg Hold. A great black swan, who comes once every three years to the lake. Once every three years, in the hour just before midnight, he takes on human form, and one year—perhaps this year—Meguet will stray to the lake under moonlight and find him, in the thousand-year-old wood where the trees will shift and hide them from all view. The mage who ensorcelled him is dead, and no one in the world is powerful enough to free him. So he is in despair of ever regaining human form. Meguet, finding him, will be his only solace, his only happiness. But, unbe-

knownst to him, there is someone even now growing powerful
enough to free him, someone no farther from them than the
Delta swamp—''
   Iris, intrigued by the tale, interrupted harshly. ''Oh, Calyx,
she'd be more likely to burn his liver for him than turn him
human.''
   ''She would not!'' Calyx said indignantly. ''Iris, I can't
believe you believe every stupid drunken trapper's tale you hear
about Nyx.''
   ''They're true,'' Rush said shortly. ''Meguet knows. True,
Meguet?''
   Meguet sighed noiselessly, disinclined for a tempest. ''Nyx
would recognize an ensorcelled swan if she saw one.''
   ''Yes, but the question is: What will she do with it?''
   ''Stuff it and roast it for supper, I suppose.''
   ''Poor swan,'' Calyx said temperately, opening her book
again. ''An unhappy end to an unhappy tale.''
   ''Anyway, Nyx may be wicked, but she is not disgusting,''
Iris pronounced, contradicting herself, and Rush, as always, rose
to the bait. Meguet moved from between their argument, to sit
next to Calyx. Calyx knew odd things and Meguet had odd questions. Calyx smiled at her. The swan had met its destiny and she
was already back among the roses.
   ''You know that garden, Meguet. Don't you? Where the
tower rooms had no windows above the garden wall, so that she
would not have to look out.''
   ''Yes,'' Meguet said. ''I read about it once, and I searched
for it. I wanted to look at the world out of Astor Ro's eyes. She
fascinated me: such fear and such courage. I could read Rydel's
books; she talked so much about plants instead of history.''
   ''Which book was it?''
   ''I don't remember. Odd things, she wrote of, everything.
I think Nyx took it. She rambled about her gardens and Timor
Ro.''
   ''Timor Ro said she had mysterious powers.''
   ''Sorcery?''
   ''Something like, but even more powerful. Chrysom, Timor
Ro said, stood in her shadow.''
   Meguet raised a brow. ''All she ever did was garden.''
   ''Mysterious, secret powers, they were.''
   ''Calyx, you're inventing this.''

"I'm not. He said she used them only for Ro Holding."
"Did he say what powers?"
"No. He said such things were not to be known."
"He must have meant her peach brandy. Calyx . . . if some-
one spoke of waking the Dancer, what would that mean?"
"The Dancer trapped in ice by the Cygnet," Calyx said
promptly. "Guarded by the Fire Bear."
"In the sky?"
"On the top of the highest peak of Berg Hold."
"Berg Hold," Meguet repeated, oddly startled. There was
a place, not between lines of a tale, but in Ro Holding, that a
Wayfolk man might find if he persisted. "How would—how
would the Dancer be wakened?"
"Only the Fire Bear can free her, and it has no more of its
fire."
"Then how—"
"But, she may be wakened on the last day of winter."
"Why the last—"
"Then, if you bring her a question, she will wake just long
enough to answer or predict, without moving from the ice. Which
is safest for us all, since, freed, the Dancer dances chaos into
the world."
"Why chaos?"
"Because she is no longer trapped in dreams; she can turn
all our waking lives into dreams, and nightmares." She read a
page or two, while Meguet, frowning, imagined the Dancer danc-
ing free.
"Why the last day of winter?" she asked. Calyx pondered,
smoothing a single shining hair back into place.
"Perhaps," she suggested, "because the constellation of the
Dancer sinks out of sight during spring, leaving only the Fire
Bear visible, watching her over the edge of the world."
"How do you know these things?"
"I watch the stars," Calyx said simply. "Sometimes it
seems that all the constellations exist in a strange, ancient tale
that we only catch glimpses of, in our short lives, while they
move slowly as centuries through it."
"A piecemeal tale," Meguet murmured, and thought of
another piecemeal tale she had heard from within a mirror. "But
what, I wonder, is the tale?"
She and Rush went to the armory awhile, and then, sweating,

tired, still armed, they flung cloaks over their light shirts and went riding to cool themselves. The sky had emptied itself for a time of rain, snow, wind, and there was nothing left in the pale, silken clouds to fall. The air was still; only a thin, dark thread of crow flight seamed it now and then. They rode across field and meadow, an unbroken plane of white, passing birch a shade whiter than the snow. The thousand-year-old wood, a dark, glistening green powdered with snow, seemed the only color left in the world. They rode to the edge of it and paused, questioning one another silently. The tangled, massive, sweeping boughs had caught most of the snow before it touched ground. The snow itself had caught the frail winter light, leaving a dense, sweet-smelling shadowy world among the black trunks that rose toward a green-black mist higher than Chrysom's tower. It looked, Meguet thought, like a giant's garden.

She turned her horse into it; Rush followed.

"We just left the world behind," he said, glancing back: Towers, gardens, pasture, sky had all vanished.

"Speak quietly," Meguet warned him. "The trees are more restless in winter. Cold wakes them."

Rush stared at her. "It is true, then. I never believed it."

"That they shift?" She looked at him, amused. "Why would you believe everything else that Chrysom said, and not this?"

"I don't know. Moving trees? Maybe if they roamed under my window I would consider it."

"You'll consider it if they start," she said softly, and he eyed her again, askance.

"You've been caught in that?"

"Only twice."

"Twice!"

"Sh."

"What's it like?"

"It's like being lost in a forest the size of Berg Hold. . . . The trees shift, and all their memories move with them, century upon century of dreams, until you don't know anymore what's tree and what's only a dream of tree."

"It's only a small wood."

"I know. But Chrysom took them from the northern forests so long ago there must have been a sea of trees bigger than Wolfe Sea. It's that they remember, I think, and that's the memory you get lost in."

Rush shivered lightly. "Cold," he commented. He reached out to touch one swollen black trunk. Knots and boles like small animals ran up it, peered, frozen, at the riders. "Cold," he said again, as if he had felt the heart of the tree, and Meguet had a sudden image of tree roots, chilled in the unexpected weather, stirring just beneath the earth. She picked up her pace a little. The swan lake lay just on the other side of the wood. Like the trees, the swans were born to a land of fierce winter; the snow, it seemed, had followed them south.

"Rush," she said impulsively, keeping her voice low, and hoping he would, "I must ride back upriver as soon as the weather clears. To talk to Nyx. The Holder told me to take someone. Will you come?"

He was watching her as he listened, his face as cold and set as the wrinkled faces of the trees. "Why?"

"Why what?"

"Why do you need company? You never have in your life. Why, to see Nyx? What is she doing?"

She drew breath, her mouth tight. "Rush. Don't shout here."

"I'm not going to."

"You are. Just say yes or no. Shout among the swans."

"I'm not—"

"You are. Please. Say yes. Say no. Then don't say anything more."

"Why—" She stared him into silence, saw his eyes widen in comprehension. He unclamped his jaw, said, "Yes," and watched the trees in an uneasy fascination.

They were nearly through the wood, with a tree or two between them, when Rush vanished. He was there one moment, and then, obscured by two trees aligned by eyesight, if not by distance, he was simply gone. Meguet circled the trees several times, called him softly. He was nowhere, it seemed, or she was. She reined, feeling the blood run quick and cold through her. Trees filled her sight wherever she looked. She moved forward, she thought, toward the lake. Trees shifted in front of her, faded as she circled them, or did not when she rode up to them. She cursed softly, helplessly, feeling the chill damp air clinging to her. "Not now," she pleaded, numbly. "Not now." But trees and the dream of trees rose in her path, huge, tranquil, ancient and endless as the forests of a world a thousand years younger.

She called his name desperately, careless now of their peace, and heard a rustle like wind around her. She smelled wood smoke. She turned toward it with relief, without thinking. Trees opened in front of her to dense shadow. Within shadow was a denser shadow: a small black wagon like a house, its slanted roof painted yellow, Hold Signs on back and side. And in front of it, roasting a swamp lizard: a tinker.

He lifted his black shaggy head, smiled. Gold gleamed in his ear, around his neck, and, she imagined, from his eyes.

"You'll pardon me, Lady," he said. "I'm a solitary man. Crowds like that in the yard when I entered frighten me."

Meguet stared at him. There seemed a patch of sunlight beside his fire, or some odd reflection from the flames. "Why did you come into this house?" she asked, for he was no tinker, nothing she had ever encountered.

"To patch pots."

"We have no need of another tinker."

"You never know," the tinker said. He turned his spit thoughtfully. The lizard's eye, open and emerald green, regarded her.

"You must come with me," she said, dragging her eyes from the lizard. "In the name of Lauro Ro."

"Why?" the tinker asked, wide-eyed. "I have done nothing more than pass through her gate."

"She has a pot to patch."

"She has, in this great house, a tinker for every broken pot."

"She has not yet had you to mend a pot for her." The patch of sunlight appeared to be moving with the tinker. It was his shadow, she realized suddenly, a subversion of light that left her breathless. She kept her body very still, kept her face calm, though it felt cold and white as snow. "You must come with me. The trees are shifting, it is not safe here."

"You are armed," he said surprisedly, and the jewel in the pommel of the sword she wore winked as at a touch of light in that dark place.

"It is my right to bear arms in this house."

"Against a poor tinker?"

"You troubled the Gatekeeper, who has an eye for trouble. You are skulking like a thief in these woods without a broken pot in sight. Since you did not give your true name to the Gatekeeper, you must give it to the Holder, for you are in her house."

He did not answer her. His yellow-gold eyes seemed to reflect fire as he gazed at her. A corner of his mouth had crept upward in a smile. "And you?" he said finally, softly. "You looked straight at me, through those shifting trees; your eyes picked me out of the shadows. Who are you?"

"Meguet!" Rush called, from some place far away, within trees, behind trees, encircled by trees.

"Meguet," the tinker repeated thoughtfully. He turned the spit again; the lizard's eyes were faded now, filmy with smoke. "Meguet," he said again. "Pretty. But who? Who dwells behind your eyes?" He fingered the lizard, picked an eye out of its head, tossed it into the air. Falling, turning, turning in the air, it flashed now emerald, now coin-gold.

Sudden, dark, overwhelming anger drove Meguet forward, past revulsion and fear, to the fire and the charred, one-eyed lizard, and the tinker who dared his ugly sorcery within the Holder's house. She drew the sword at her side, thrust it down through the flames until the tip rested against the tinker's heart.

It was Moro Ro's great sword and it shook slightly in one hand, but the tinker seemed impressed. He looked up at her, still turning the lizard's eye between his fingers. "Meguet," he said curiously, his eyes full of yellow light, and suddenly her mind was full of light, as if the sun had struck her.

"Meguet!" Rush shouted behind her. The fire flared silver, swallowed the lizard, Moro's sword. Half-blind, she swung her horse, confused, trying to see Rush. She saw the tinker's wagon; its back door with the gold sun on it slammed shut. Then the air cracked oddly around her, as if a tree had snapped in two. The dark walls of the tinker's house crawled with flame.

She cried out. Rush tugged at her reins; she jerked free, turning back to stare at the tiny house, with its four black walls and its yellow roof and yellow lintel, until the silver flames engulfed it and Rush wrenched at her reins again.

"Meguet! The trees!"

They were rustling, sighing, drawing back from the fire. "Meguet," Rush pleaded. "He's burning in his house." He looked shaken, white; as usual, Meguet realized, his sorcery must have gone awry. The flames were dying already, without reaching toward the tree boughs; that much he had done right. She let him lead her finally. She glanced back one more time, incredulously, to seek a hint of what she had glimpsed in the fire-chewed bones of the wagon. The lizard in the fire moved its head to look at her. Both eyes were in its head and they were yellow-gold.

CHAPTER

4

"You burned a tinker in the thousand-year-old wood?" the Holder said incredulously. Half the household had stood in windows and doorways, on the parapet wall between the back towers, watching the silver smoke rising out of the trees. Household guard, riding out to investigate, had found Meguet and Rush emerging from the trees, grim, silent, exhausted from the twisting paths of the disturbed and dreaming trees. The Holder, the guard told them, would see them immediately.

"He was not a tinker," Meguet said abruptly, breaking a silence that had lasted from the wood to Chrysom's library, where the Holder and Calyx had been watching the oddly glittering smoke. "And he is not dead."

Rush stared at her. "He's dead. Whatever he is. I burned his house with him in it—"

"Why?" the Holder asked sharply. "What had he done? In Moro's name, why did you set fire to a tinker?"

He closed his eyes. "I did not intend to. I was trying to circle his house with fire. Not burn it down."

"Then why—"

"I missed."

"Oh, Rush," Calyx breathed, hands over her mouth. "You never could do that right."

"He's not dead," Meguet said wearily. She began to tremble suddenly; methodically, she tried to unbuckle the sword belt dragging at her side so she could sit. Her hands shook; the buckle would not loosen. Calyx's hands moved under hers, flicked it open; she sat down finally, the sword across her knees. The Holder touched a pin in her hair, frowning down at Meguet, then swung back at Rush.

"Why?"

"He was threatening Meguet."

"A tinker?"

"She had drawn her sword against him."

"So Meguet was threatening the tinker. And you set him on fire. I gather this was no ordinary tinker. Meguet, why did you take up arms against a tinker?"

"He isn't a tinker."

"Wasn't," Rush murmured.

"He isn't dead." She heard him gather breath; she leaned forward in the chair, gripping its arms, gazing at him. "The yellow star its lintel, the yellow star its roof, the four stars of red and pale marking its black walls, the blue star marking its door latch. That's the house you burned, Rush."

In the silence, the Holder pulled at a pearl hairpin. The pin came out; a strand fell. "That's a Hold Sign," she said harshly. "Meguet."

"Yes." She met the Holder's eyes. She was still trembling; the jewels in Moro's sword and the sword belt shivered with light. "And the dark house that falls from the sky, in the Wayfolk man's tale."

The Holder stared at her, her face waxen against her dark, scattered hair.

"What Wayfolk man?" Rush demanded, and the Holder turned, looking, in the cast of firelight, fierce, dishevelled, oddly like Nyx. Rush swallowed. He said again, more quietly, "What Wayfolk man?"

"A man with Nyx. Meguet saw him."

Rush's face whitened. Meguet found herself on her feet again, speaking as calmly as she could. "A young man wanting a spell from Nyx. He spoke of a little dark house falling out of the sky—"

"That's a song," Calyx said wonderingly. "The house you never leave." She paused, blinking at something in the fire. "And it's a Hold Sign. The Gold King."

"His eyes were gold," Meguet said. Her voice faltered; she finished in a whisper. "The tinker's eyes were gold. He was roasting a lizard. When the house burned, I saw the lizard's eyes. They looked at me and they were gold."

"Sorcery," Rush said flatly. The Holder said nothing. Her eyes searched Meguet a moment, then hid their thoughts. She pulled at another pin; it glittered to the floor.

"Nyx could fight it," Calyx suggested. "She would come home for this."

"No," the Holder said sharply.

"But, Mother, she has studied sorcery for nine years! If she can protect this house, she will, I know it—"

"I don't want her fighting anyone! I will not bring Nyx into danger."

"But if this house is in danger, we need someone to protect it, and Nyx—"

"No."

"Are you afraid," Rush asked abruptly, "that it's not this house she would fight for?"

The Holder's face flamed. He had struck her wordless; wordless, she struck back. The force of her blow rocked him a step and shook a few pins out of her hair. Rush dropped his face in his hands; she rubbed her wrist. She spoke first, grimly. "This is not the time, Rush Yarr, to show me my worst nightmare."

Rush reappeared; Meguet, shocked motionless, saw the blood between his fingers. Calyx, looking cross, pulled a square of lace from her sleeve and he applied it to his nose. "You hit like a blacksmith," he commented. Meguet, gripping the sheathed sword with both hands, eased her grip and set it down.

"We cannot start fighting each other," she breathed.

"No," Rush said. "I'm sorry." He sat down; so did the Holder.

"So am I," she said after a moment. "It would be easy to blame Nyx for every evil in the Delta now, but for eight years before this, her reputation has been blameless. Don't overlook that, Rush."

Calyx picked pins off the floor, began to tidy her mother's hair. "There's old Diu up in Berg Hold. Chrysom's descendant. We can send for him."

"No."

"Well, Mother, we have a sorcerer living in the thousand-year-old wood who frightened Meguet, who is not afraid of anything. What do you want to do about him?"

"I don't know yet." She looked at Meguet. "Is that why you went into the wood? Did you suspect he was there?"

"No. I didn't know where he was."

The Holder straightened, tugging her hair out of Calyx's hands. "You knew he was in this house? You didn't tell me?"

"I didn't—The Gatekeeper mentioned a tinker in a little black wagon who came into the house and vanished. I wasn't looking for him, no. But I recognized him when I saw him."

"Then why did you go into the wood?"

"The trees were beautiful," she said helplessly, puzzled. "Quiet, mysterious in the snow. They drew me in."

"They weren't quiet for long," Rush said dourly. "They rambled all over, especially after I tried to set them on fire. The tinker must have misjudged my power, or he would not have bothered to hide in his house."

"Or perhaps your ineptness terrified him," the Holder murmured.

"But why," Calyx said, setting a final pin in place, "would a sorcerer disguise himself as a tinker, drive around in a wagon reminiscent of a constellation and hide himself in the thousand-year-old wood?"

"Why," Rush asked, "would a Wayfolk man speak to Nyx of that same house?" The Holder's eye fell on him; he added carefully, "It begs an answer."

"Well," the Holder sighed, "Nyx is the one to ask. But," she added emphatically, "I do not want her back here. I would irritate her and she would upset me."

"Mother, you are being completely unreasonable," Calyx said softly.

"So is Nyx. Meguet will speak to her when the weather clears."

"She asked me to go with her," Rush said. The Holder raised a question with an eyebrow. Meguet shook her head.

"He would not leave the gate."

"Good," the Holder sighed. "It would terrify me if he did. Then go with her, Rush. But," she said severely, "do exactly as Meguet tells you, and do not antagonize Nyx."

"But what about the tinker?" Calyx persisted.

"We'll wait."

"For what?"

"For the pot to break," the Holder said darkly, "and give us something to mend."

"I found your tinker," Meguet said to the Gatekeeper, climbing up the steps to join him later. It was dusk; stone and sea and sky were all of the same raw grey. Children flung snow at each other in the yard; men stood around the forge fires, drinking ale and watching the world go dark. The Gatekeeper, lighting his pipe and trying to rise at the same time, took in smoke; she waited, standing on the top step, until he settled it.

"Sorry—"

She had disturbed him, she realized suddenly; shifting for her to enter, he did not look at her. She saw his jaw tighten in his lowered face. He drew a clean breath finally.

"You startled me. I heard you and Rush Yarr were found among the shifting trees. No one knew there was a tinker involved." He looked at her finally, eyes narrowed against his smoke. "Is that what burned?"

"His house."

"But not the tinker."

"No." He sat very still, pipe still in his hand, waiting. "You must keep watch for the tinker coming or going through the gate. But be careful of him. He is quite dangerous."

He gazed at her, his face dark against the darkening sky. "Lady Meguet," he said finally, "it's not me went in the back wood to roust out that tinker. Is he still there? Or does anyone know?"

"No." She thought of the lizard's gold eyes, and shivered lightly. "He could be anywhere."

He murmured something, shifting; forgetting her, he spat suddenly over the window ledge. "He had trouble painted all over his house, and yet I let him in. He spoke fairly enough, and gave me his reasons. . . . I should have known. A tinker wearing gold, and hardly a pot in sight. What is he, then?" She hesitated,

caught his full, angry, insistent gaze. Astonished, she heard herself answer:

"Rush Yarr thinks a sorcerer."

He still watched her. "You don't."

"No. I'm not sure what he is."

"But you guess."

Pressed, she flared at him suddenly. "I'm only seeing shadows. You are overbearing."

"Nyx," he said, and she stared at him, speechless. "You
only get like this with me when it's Nyx on your mind. That's
a broad leap to make, from this house upriver to the swamps.
From tinker to the Holder's daughter."

She stood up so abruptly she hit her head on the low, slanted
stone roof. She sat back down, tears of anger, pain, frustration
springing into her eyes. "How dare you," she demanded, rubbing
her head furiously, "tell me what I am thinking. You have no
right to judge Nyx, even if you were born among the small orange
birds."

"I'm sorry, I'm sorry—" He had one arm around her shoulder, his head close to hers; it was his hand, then, rubbing her
hair. "I'm not judging Nyx, I swear by the next thing comes off
the river bottom. I'm Gatekeeper, and it's up to me to put a name
to everything on two legs that comes in and out of this house.
There's no name for that tinker."

"You assume because the tinker is evil, that Nyx must
be—"

"No. You connected them, not me."

"Don't tell me what I'm saying."

"I'm sorry. Nobody ever taught me any manners. I only—
I would cut my heart out for this house." He was stroking her
hair now, his voice, tense with his own frustration, close to her
ear. "And it was me that let the tinker in. I have never made a
mistake before."

She lifted her head, sliding her hand under his hand; she sat
back against the stones, flushed, her hair dishevelled. He watched
her, the small lines gathered at the corners of his eyes. She stood
up again, carefully, and saw how his hands lifted as if to guide
her, then fell. She said, more calmly, "You were right about
Nyx. I am going upriver with Rush to talk to her. Don't tell me
to be careful of her."

"No," he said quickly. "I like living."

She opened her mouth, closed it. Her mouth crooked. "I'm sorry," she said. "Nyx worries me so. And this house."
"I know that." He stood up so swiftly she feared for his head, but he was used to dodging the slant. She felt his arm hover protectively around her, above her head as she ducked under the stone lintel. She went down the steps slowly, wanting to look back and not daring. She looked back finally, met his eyes.

She and Rush left two days later. The rains had slowed, but the river was still full, swirling angrily, opaque with silt. Once out of the city, she had to choose her paths carefully; the path along the river bank was under water in some places. In others, the river had spilled far over into other pools and creeks, and they had to backtrack, skirt, go south, Rush pointed out too often, to go north. It was wearisome, with the rain falling intermittently; neither of them spoke much. Rush's face was pale, set; he looked constantly ahead in his mind, seeing a woman he had not seen in nearly three years, instead of what lay under his nose. Meguet had to guide him around soggy bogs, pull him away from the crumbling hillside. It took them an entire day just to reach sight of a tavern she knew that had a couple of rush-filled mattresses, and a meal. She said with relief, "I thought it might have fallen into the water."
"What?" Rush said, roused. "That shack? That's an inn? How much farther is it? Can we get there tonight?"
"We've been slowed by the flooding. Dark falls fast here. I don't know how long it will take us to reach her house, but we can't do it tonight."
"I'd rather sleep in the rain than in that flea-bitten hut."
"Suit yourself," she said tiredly, then saw something within the trees: a black that took her breath away. Rush made a comment she did not hear; her attention was busy, trying to pick the black thing apart from the woods, make a familiar shape out of it. It moved as they moved, toward them; Rush, catching sight of it, fell silent.
It was a woman. Meguet eased in her saddle as she came closer: a woman in black, with her cloak lifted, held against her face, covering nose and mouth. She fluttered oddly, with wind that was not there. She stopped in the middle of the path, waited

for them. Meguet saw ash-white threads endlessly circling the
dark hem of her cloak; her lips parted.

"It's a witch," she breathed.

"What?"

"From Hunter Hold. Look at the pattern on her skirt and
her cloak. Look at her sandals—they make them of bitterthorn.
She must have walked all this way. . . . No." A chill ran through
her, of wonder and fear. "No. She has sent herself ahead of
time."

"She what?" Rush said incredulously.

"She is in Hunter Hold. And she is here. She sent her image
along time with a message."

"Are you sure?" Rush asked urgently. "Is it sorcery?"

"No. They only walk the path of time." She quickened her
pace then, rode alone to meet the witch.

She was an old woman, grown strong and implacable as
thorn and iron in the black desert of Hunter Hold. Her grey eyes
were milky, as if she had looked too often at the full moon. She
blinked uncertainly at the black-clad rider in front of her, as if
desert winds were blowing a fine mist of sand before her eyes.
Then she dropped her cloak from her face.

"Meguet Vervaine."

She felt her face blanch. "Yes."

"You must beware."

The witch's voice, for all her stamina, was fragile as a glass
bell. Her image flowed in the wind of another Hold. Meguet,
aware of the rain touching dead leaf and twig and water with
slow, delicate fingers, of Rush's horse stirring wet leaves on the
trail behind, answered finally, "Yes."

"You must go back. You must watch."

"What—" She drew breath. "What have you seen?"

"In the last full moon, I looked along the path of time and
I saw a lady as beautiful as night walking toward the house of
the Holders of Ro Holding. She walks along the line of time,
and the great house stands in her path, and as she walks, she
grows vast or the house grows small, small enough for her to
crush underfoot if she keeps along that path."

"A lady."

Meguet swallowed, her voice shaking. Nyx, she thought,
Nyx as dark as night. But the witch had seen a different path.

"She may know the house is there, or she may not, I could

not tell, for she is blind. You must watch for her. Will you watch,
for the Holders of Ro Holding? You can see. Will you watch?''
Meguet was wordless, shivering badly. The woman huddled into
her shapeless clothes, took a step back into her own time.
"Watch!" she pleaded, in her fine, frail voice. "Watch, for the
Cygnet!''
    "Meguet," Rush breathed, and she started.
    "Watch!" the old woman cried. "You have the eyes.''
Somehow her voice came clear, certain. "I will watch.''
    The sending faded; a darkness crumpled in the air and van-
ished. Meguet watched the place where she had been, as if she
might see the beginning and end of time appearing there. She
felt a touch on her arm and whirled, pulling her horse back.
    "Meguet." Rush stared at her, startled, disturbed. "What
did she say to you?''
    She touched her eyes, closed them and saw the dark of night,
the dark of time. "We must go back," she whispered.
    "Now?" he said sharply.
    She opened her eyes. "Rush," she said, "the witch gave
warning to the Holder's house. Warning to the Cygnet. Nyx can
wait. She is not the danger. Ro House is in danger and it can't
wait.''
    "Warning of what?''
    "I don't know. A blind woman." She turned her horse
blindly, night falling fast, and the threads of paths through the
swamp as tangled as the threads of time. "Some blind woman.
She must not enter the House. I must go back and warn.''
    "Why you?" Rush asked bewilderedly. "Why did she cross
your path, and not the Holder's?''
    "I don't know.''
    "Or the Gatekeeper's?''
    "Rush, I don't know. She told me to watch. How can I
watch anything in the middle of this swamp with night coming
on—''
    "You can't," Rush said, for once making a decision for
her. "Unless you know how to throw your image across the
Delta.''
    "No.''
    "Then," he said, resigned, for she knew he would not let
her ride back alone, with such strange things happening around

them, "we will spend the night in the shack and be home tomorrow."

They entered the gate again at nightfall, worn, mud-stained and drenched; the rains had started again. Rush rode ahead to the towers to speak to the Holder. Meguet relinquished her horse at the gate. The Gatekeeper, holding a torch above their heads, took a sharp look at her face and said cautiously,

"Is it Lady Nyx?"

"No."

"Then what?" He drew her to shelter against the wall, beneath the turret, replacing the torch in its sconce.

"You must beware," she said. His eyes widened. "Think," she pleaded. "Think. Has a blind woman entered this house since I've been gone?"

He was staring at her, so still she gripped his cloak, shook him a little, alarmed. "No," he said abruptly. "No." His hands rose, closed over her hands. "No stranger has entered or left, and no one blind."

"She's beautiful, the witch said. A blind woman, beautiful as night." She glanced at the gate; he had closed it securely behind her. "You must watch for her. She must not enter."

"No," he said again. "Who is she?"

"I don't know. The witch didn't say. She walks the path of time toward this house. Blind, she may know or may not know this house is underfoot." She felt him shudder; his hands tightened.

"But who?" he insisted. "She must have a name. Tinker has no name, the blind woman has no name—Meguet, you must find out. How can I guard against something that has no name? How can you?"

"How can I find out? I barely know they exist! I'm not like Nyx to know sorcery, or Calyx who has read everything in Chrysom's library twice—"

"You know they're dangerous. The witch came to you."

She stared at him, wordless, frustrated. "Hew, what do you expect me to do? Stand at the gate and ask her name when she enters? That's for you to do."

"It's for me," he agreed tautly. "And by then it will be too late. You must help me. You grew up in this house. You have ancient memories in your past. The witch came to you."

"She crossed my path. She said my name." She was shivering in the rain; rain rolled down his face like tears. Wind dragged torchlight over them, pulled apart the cloak of darkness they stood wrapped in. She saw them suddenly as from another angle in the yard, a cottager's window, the alehouse doorway, a tower casement: she gripping his cloak, he her hands; his face, an inch or three higher, inclined slightly, the hard spare lines of it dark and fire, reflections of the pale Delta river in his eyes.

She whispered, "Gatekeeper."

"Lady Meguet."

"I must go."

"Say my name again before you go."

"Hew."

"Meguet."

T he Holder sat late with her family that night in Chrysom's
library. Meguet, who had shed her drenched, muddy
riding clothes for black velvet and pearls, sat on a stone
seat against the stone wall. The chill kept her awake, the stones
kept her upright; demands beyond that, she felt, were unreasonable. Yet the Holder made them.

"What blind woman?"

"I don't know," Meguet said.

"Tell me again what the witch said. Tell me exactly."

She was pacing back and forth in front of the fire, the
swing of her heavy, wine-colored gown mesmerizing. Iris,
looking perplexed, was doing some needlepoint. Calyx sat in
the shadows listening intently, looking, in white velvet and dia-
monds, like something carved out of frost. Rush was frowning,
his eyes lowered in concentration; he was, Meguet thought,
about to snore.

"Beautiful," Meguet said for what seemed the third or
eighth time, "as beautiful as night, and blind."

It was then Calyx spoke. "That's simple," she said. "It's

the constellation. The Blind Lady who wears the Ring of Time. The Silver Ring of Withy Hold.''

The Holder stared at her. She was not prone to throwing things besides her voice, but she did then. The poker struck the hearth with a snarl of stone and iron that brought Rush upright, feeling for a weapon that he had taken off hours ago. He froze under the Holder's glare.

"Another Hold Sign."

"Strictly speaking," Calyx began, "the Blind Lady is not—"

"How could a constellation walk through the gate?" Iris asked.

"The tinker did."

"The tinker is not—"

"If we guard the gate," Rush said. "If the Gatekeeper watches, she can't enter."

"The tinker did," the Holder snapped.

"We weren't warned."

"The Gatekeeper let him in."

"He wasn't warned either," Rush argued reasonably. "This time, Meguet told him."

The Holder paced a step, whirled. "The Gatekeeper is responsible for whoever enters or leaves this house."

"But, Mother—" Calyx began.

"He should have known. As he recognized himself Gatekeeper, he should recognize anything this dangerous to Ro House. The Blind Lady. The Silver Ring. The Dark House. The Gold King. Something is gathering against this house—" She turned again, for Meguet had made a sound. The Holder gazed at her, waiting, her eyes hardened already against what Meguet would say.

"The Wayfolk man," she breathed. "Corleu. He spoke of these things. The Dark House. The Dancer. The Warlock."

"The Dancer is guarded by the Fire Bear," Calyx said wonderingly. "The Warlock is the Blood Fox's shadow. Berg Hold and the Delta."

The Holder's arm swept impulsively toward the mantel, where Chrysom's crystal jars and boxes and cut stones gleamed like jewels in the shadows. Meguet closed her eyes. But Rush spoke a moment later. She had checked her gesture; they were all still alive.

"We'll bring him here. The Wayfolk man."

"No," the Holder said harshly. "Not into this house."

"Under guard, bound, locked away—what more could he do?"

"I will not have him anywhere in this house."

"Then elsewhere," Rush said bewilderedly. "In the city, somewhere—"

The Holder, her mouth tight, picked up the poker, sent a small avalanche of coals rattling through the grate instead of answering.

"Somewhere safe from Nyx?" Iris asked. "Where might that be, Rush? If Nyx wants him with her, she has the power to keep him. Against you, against Meguet, against anyone."

"Thank you," the Holder said icily.

"I'm being sensible, Mother. Someone has to be." She flushed suddenly under the Holder's gaze. She continued with a stubborn, curious dignity. "All I can see is what is obvious, and that is what most of the people of Ro Holding see. You all see through the confusion in flashes of magic and learning. I can't. I just recognize the simple things. If Nyx is doing all this, none of us can stop her. If she is innocent, then she's bound to be in danger."

The Holder set the poker down with a sigh. She said nothing for a moment; her fingers worried at her elegant hair, but for once the pins were too skillfully hidden. She folded her arms instead; her eyes went to Meguet.

"You thought the Wayfolk man was not the danger."

"I think," Meguet said carefully, pulling together the dreamlike scraps of his tale, "he is trying to rescue someone. The dark house fell unexpectedly into his life. The tinker is the danger. Part of it."

"And the tinker is here."

"If we guard against the Blind Lady, keep her from entering—"

"I think we should bring them both here," Rush said implacably. "Nyx and the Wayfolk man."

"Oh, Rush, use your head," Calyx said impatiently. "You weren't listening to Iris. If she is dangerous, do we want her in the house with the tinker? And if she is not, she is much safer being away from here. And what I think—"

"If she—"

"What I think," Calyx said, raising her delicate voice as much as she ever did, "is that if Nyx and the tinker were working together, this is where she would be. Here, in this house, with him. I think we should guard the house against the blind woman. The tinker is doing nothing; maybe he can't, without her."

"What I want to know," Iris asked, "is: Are they sorcerers? Or something to do with the Holds?"

The Holder touched her eyes. "Iris, how can you say such things so calmly?"

"Well, we do have to know."

"I know." She consulted Meguet again, with her eyes. "You've seen more of this than anyone. What do you think? What are they?"

They all turned to her expectantly. She answered after a moment, softly, reluctantly. "The Wayfolk man spoke of waking the Dancer on the last day of winter. That is not sorcery. That is a tale out of Berg Hold, as old as Ro Holding."

She stood in her chambers later, staring out at the night. Rain and wind gusted across the yard. She could not see a single light on the sea. The only light in the world was in the Gate-keeper's turret, and the torches he kept lit beside the gate to guide travellers in the dark. She saw the brazier light obscured a moment, reappear. He was still there, at the cold, late hour, still watching.

She reached for her cloak.

She felt, walking through the storm, as if she walked the surface of Wolfe Sea, with all the spindrift flung about her, and the small, high fire pulling her like the moon pulling tide. He did not hear her mount the stairs; he could only have heard the booming tide, the wild wind. She stood, darkly cloaked, hooded, at the top of the stairs, at the edge of his light, and as he turned his head, she wondered if he could see her face at all, or if he would speak some name other than hers. He looked at her. Wordless, rising, he stepped into the rain. He slid her hood back with both hands, slipped her long, pale hair free until it streamed with the torch fire in the wind. She took

his face between her hands, drew it down and down until she
tasted the Delta river currents running in his mouth.

The wild rain wore them apart finally. They huddled close
to the brazier, dripping, blinking in the light. The Gatekeeper
watched Meguet; she watched the shimmering heat, too weary
to think. He said finally:

"So green, your eyes. Not a Delta green. Nothing under
these mists is that green."

She raised her eyes. There were threads of silt and gold in
his hair she hadn't noticed, a line along his mouth, a scar high
on one cheekbone, near the eye. He waited calmly, undisturbed
by her silence; his eyes, far paler green than her own, had flecks
of white in them. She said, "My great-grandfather was of Withy
Hold. His eyes got so, looking at the corn, they said. He liked
to wander, too. He was a strange man. . . . Do you mean to stay
here all night?"

"Yes."

"The blind woman must not come into this house. Calyx
says she is a Hold Sign."

He blinked, as though her words had flicked like rain across
his face. "Then I must be careful," he breathed.

"Yes." She leaned back against the wall, all her weariness
roiling through her, all her fears. She slid her hands over her
face, felt the sting of tears in the back of her eyes. She felt his
hands follow her hands, slide down her wet hair, unpin her wet,
sodden cloak.

"All in velvet, you came out," he marvelled. "In pearls.
You're soaking."

"I wanted to hear your voice." He smiled his tight, slanting
smile. She added, "I don't know why."

"The world's a wild place beyond Ro House. You've known
a good deal of it. You're not content with what's bred within
walls."

"So it seems." She drew breath as he leaned into her cloak,
caught her pearls between his teeth. "Hew."

"Meguet."

"Could you be content, in the late hours some night,
watching the gate from Chrysom's tower? You must sleep
sometime."

He lifted his head; her hands were in his hair. He drew them
down, kissed her fingers. "Will you help me watch?"

"I will." She laid her face against his hair. "From my chambers you can see the swans, you can see Wolfe Sea, you can see the barred gate and the turret where the Gatekeeper sat tonight with all the house asleep, but for one woman watching him. Watch until you can no longer watch alone. Then come to the black tower, and I will keep watch with you."

He waited until she thought he would not come. And then he came one night, unexpectedly, in some dark, lost hour adrift between midnight and dawn. She was dreaming of swans, gliding on the lake, white and black, shadows and reflections of one another, elegant, proud, secret. One black swan lifted a wing; she felt the chill of the air it had disturbed, then a play of feathers across her mouth. She lifted her hands, shaped and molded the feathery dark until a man moved under her touch and she finally woke.

He rose after a while, to stir the fire and light candles. He opened a casement to look across the yard at the gate. A mix of rain and snow tumbled past him; he stared down the hard bitter wind without flinching. He shut the casement finally, slid into bed beside Meguet, smelling of winter and cold as iron.

She rolled on top of him; slowly he stopped shivering; the warm firelight lay over both of them. He slid the furs down, fanned her hair across her back.

"Is the gate still closed?"

"Closed and barred." He went on with his task, separating the rippling strands to his liking. "Lady Meguet. Do you remember the first time you left the house on Holder's business, all in black, with the swans flying at your back and side and shoulder?"

"Yes."

"You took my breath away."

"I don't recall you looked overawed."

"I was trying to stay on my feet, not topple over in your wake. You rode through the gate like night itself. I had only just come; I was overawed by anything. You looked at me and thanked me. You wouldn't remember that."

"I do," she said, smiling. "You caught my eye. Brown and hard and half-wild, like you knew all the secret places of the backwaters. I wanted to say more, but you looked so stern and solemn.''

"So did you. You scared me silly." He began weaving strands of hair like a net. "Ten years ago, that was. Now you have been all over Ro Holding, and I have seen only as far as I can see from the gate in any direction.''

"Don't you miss the river?"

"How can I? My heart is nailed to that gate. I had to come here to find it." She bent her head to kiss him; his net unravelled.

"I could never leave this house either," she said.

"Why so? You'll marry, you'll leave—"

"Do you think so?" she asked, gazing down at him out of her cool, clear eyes. "No matter how far I go, I always come back here. Rush Yarr says that in a place as old as Ro House, and among such old families, more than faces and names are handed down. Memories, he says, echoes of the past. Sometimes I can see it. . . ."

"See what?"

"Back. Far back. As if I'm seeing through a long history." His hands were still now, his breath barely stirring her hair. "When I watched Nyx in secret, inside her house, I felt it then: that others were watching out of my eyes, evaluating what I saw, showing me what to see. . . ."

He made a soft sound, drew her hair back from her face. "Swamp's like that," he said. "Layering year after year, bone on bone; if you dig deep enough, you'd find the beginning of things. And the gate.''

"The gate?"

"Watching, I lose time, now and then. A thousand years passed through that gate. A thousand years of names spoken, shadows riding across the threshold. Sometimes I wonder if a few of those whose names I know are ghosts, riding into another century that still exists somewhere inside the house.''

She pushed her face against his chest. "Don't talk of shadows." She slid her arms around him, watching her shadow on the wall hold his shadow. "Just once, here, let's leave trouble out in the cold." He turned, easing over her, sliding his hands through her hair as he kissed her, drawing it out along the pillow, like wings.

She was half asleep when she felt him pull back the furs.
She reached out, but he was already up.

"Where are you going?"

"Just to the window."

This time she went with him, stood wrapped in furs while
the rain blew into her hair. The torches beside the gate still burned;
the bar across it had not shifted. Beyond the wind-whipped pools
of light, only a tower light or two, a cottage light, broke the wild
dark.

"Nothing could be out on a night like this."

"Someone's always up, always thinking, even in a storm
like this."

"Not tonight. There's no world left out there. Only Ro
House, in an ancient night before there were stars."

"You must be right," he said, his eyes still drawn to the
gate. "Before people. Only you and I and the swans on the
lake . . ." He turned to her, so quickly his eyes still carried
some reflection of the dark. He pulled the fur away from her
and lifted her naked in his arms like an offering to the wind
and rain and the ancient night. Cold took her breath away, and
then he did, head bowed over her body, drinking in the hard
rain.

Asleep finally, she felt him loose his hold of her, draw back
the furs. She groped for him, murmuring. The winds were singing
madly around the tower. "Don't," she pleaded, her eyes closed.
"Nothing is out there."

"I must watch." He sounded still asleep.

"Stay with me. Don't leave me yet. Not even dawn is at
the gate."

"The gate moved."

"It's only wind at the gate. Only rain."

"I must watch."

"I'll watch," she said, and felt him sink back. She pushed
against him; he wound his hand into her hair. "I'll watch," she
whispered, and drew his other arm around her.

"You watch, then," he sighed, and she felt his body ease
back into sleep. "You watch."

He was gone when she woke again. She rose, went to the
casement, and saw familiar movement within the turret. She
watched him, wondered if he were watching the black tower.
Something strange hit her hand, spilled over the stones, down

the wall; blinking, she saw her own shadow. She raised her head, and saw the sudden light fall over the sea.

She dressed quickly, ate something she did not taste. The morning lured her: a taste of spring, though the air was still brittle with cold. She went downstairs, watching for the Gatekeeper's turret in every southern window. Walking outside, between the towers, she saw him again, framed in every archway she passed along the wall. Turning into one, finally, she found her way blocked.

An old woman stood within the archway, half in shadow, half in sunlight fanning over the cobbles. She seemed to be seeking the sun with her face; her heavy eyes could not lift to see. She was dressed oddly, layered with old clothes. A cottager, Meguet thought, someone's ancient kin wandered away from the hearth.

"Are you lost?" she asked. "May I help you?" The face swung toward her, strong and hard, mottled like an apple. For a moment, Meguet felt that she was being scented.

"Ah. Meguet." The old woman lifted her hand to the ragged edge of lace trailing out of a hole in what looked like a skirt made out of sacking, over a longer gown of stained velvet. Her fingers pulled at the threads, twitching. "Lost? No. I found my way here. I came out to smell the spring."

"How did you know my name?" Meguet asked curiously. "You must remember voices. But I don't remember you."

"Your name is here." She held out the threads her restless fingers had woven together. "I have all the names." She pulled up the worn velvet; beneath it was a skirt of tapestry edged raggedly with muddy cloth of gold. Beneath her motley layered skirts, Meguet glimpsed strange boots covered in peacock feathers. "Here they all are. All of Ro House." On the hand that wove she wore a tarnished silver ring.

Meguet was silent. She closed her eyes, feeling the light on her icy face. She could still speak; the horror, a blow falling across a long distance, had not reached her yet. "They said," she whispered, swallowing the burning in her throat, "you were beautiful."

"So I was. So I was."

"How—how did we—" But she knew before she asked. She heard the Gatekeeper's dream-heavy voice: *The gate moved.*

She heard her answer. She opened her eyes, beginning to tremble. The pool of light was empty. A peacock feather watched her from the shadow, then vanished.

She pushed her face against the stones and wept.

6

I n the shadows, someone touched her. She whirled, breathing hard, back against the stones. She stared at the Gatekeeper through swollen eyes.

"You left the gate," she said, stunned. "In broad daylight."

"Moro's eyes," he said, staring back at her. "You're weeping in broad daylight." He reached out, pulled her away from the stones, held her tightly. In the yard behind him, stablehands were staring; faces clustered at the thick glass windows of the cider house. "I watched you cross the yard from Chrysom's tower in the sunlight. You disappeared under this arch and you didn't come out."

"Did you see her?"

"Who?"

She pushed against him, hands on his shoulders, to look at him. "Who." She watched the color drain out of his face. He set his hands flat against the wall on either side of her, leaned against them, not looking at her. "It was my fault," she added wearily. "I would not let you watch."

His head lifted; his back straightened, as if her words were something edged, dangerous, that had touched him unexpectedly. "Then, it was?"

"Yes." Her eyes filled again; light blurred into dark around his face. She heard him catch his breath.

"Meguet...." Then he swung his heavy cloak around her, gathered her into it. "Come with me."

She walked with him through the cottages, scarcely seeing the people that gazed, shaken, at the pair of them. He pushed a door open; she sank onto a bench, dropped her face into her hands, trying to think rather than to weep. She heard Hew stirring, hearth-sounds, the snap of fire across kindling.

She dropped her hands finally, said numbly, "I must tell the Holder."

"I'll come."

"There's no need—"

"I let trouble in," he said grimly. "Through my gate, they came. The tinker in his dark house, the Blind Lady—"

"You know her." She stared at him. "You know her."

"I know them both. I have over enough time to think up there, see pictures in my pipe-smoke and put them together. That tinker rolling across the threshold of this house in his black house with the Gold King scowling on the back door, telling his tales, then vanishing—"

"You told me. You tried to warn me."

"And the Blind Lady. 'My lady walks on the moon's road, shod, she is, in peacock feathers, all eyes, she is all eyes, but for her moonstruck eyes.'" He gave a short laugh, not smiling. "A love song, that is."

She was wordless, taking in finally the fragile, faded books that stood on oak shelves against the whitewashed walls, the dark, carved furniture with a flower winding down a chair-arm, a leg ending with a cat's face, both flower and face worn smooth by centuries. Hew poured her wine; she took a swallow; he watched her, the hard lines running along his mouth. He said again, "We'll go together to the Holder."

"Yes." She set her cup down, her eyes going to the fire. "Soon."

"Meguet."

"Soon." She raised her eyes from the fire to his face. "First I have to find them."

"Where?" he demanded. "They move in and out of shadows, they're hardly real—"

"They're in this house. They came in through the gate. They're real enough to have come from somewhere, be somewhere. They know me. I've seen them both; they've said my name. The household guard might raise the dust looking for them and never notice them."

"They're dangerous."

"I only want to find them. I only want to—" Her voice shook suddenly; she folded her hands tightly, steadying herself. "When I tell the Holder that the Blind Lady is in this house, I want to give her something more than just that. Perhaps, if I go quietly, in secret, I might learn what they want here. Why they have come into Ro House. We have to know, Hew. We must know."

He closed his eyes, breathed something. She stood up restively. "Do you have a sword?"

"For what?" he asked. "Skewering the guests?"

"A knife?"

"Bread knife." His eyes opened, withholding expression. "Where will you look? There are people moving constantly up in the towers, down in the cellars, across fields, through cottages, everywhere but Chrysom's tomb. There's no place for secrets in this house."

"Chrysom's tomb." She stopped moving to gaze at him. "The maze beneath the tower."

"That's no secret, either. Every cottage brat old enough to lose front teeth knows how to get into that maze."

"And how far do they get?"

"Never far."

"How far did you get?" she challenged him, and saw the flicker of memory in his face.

"Not past the place where all the rotting strings unwound," he said. "Seemed no one got past there. Unless you."

"No." She touched the window glass lightly with her fingers, her breath misting the blade-sharp edge of shadow the tower wall laid across the light. "Nyx and Rush and I spent days trying to get past the first few turns. We would turn a corner and wind up walking into a closet, or a pantry. Or a cupboard under a stair. Always through some door we could never find again. As if whatever Chrysom built that maze to guard is too precious, or too terrible, for humans.''

"Did he build it to guard against a tinker and a beggar woman?''

"Maybe not. Maybe. Maybe they got no farther than the first few turns. But even that's a place to hide. The black tower, where so few come.'' She turned toward the door. "I'll get— No. If I take a sword out of the armory, they'll wonder. . . . I'll get one off the council chamber wall.''

"For what?'' he asked her tersely. "Tinker doesn't burn, what makes you think he bleeds?''

"It makes me feel safer.''

"Then I'll carry the bread knife. It'll be as much protection.''

"No,'' she said, her eyes widening.

"I'm coming.''

"You can't leave the gate.''

"Am I at the gate?''

"But, Hew! Who will open and close? What will people think, seeing the turret empty in daylight? They'll think you died. What will the Holder say?''

"What will she say to you, going into that dark and lonely place alone?''

"It's my business,'' she said obstinately.

"What is? Defending the house? There's a guard for that. What makes it your business to track danger and power into such a place? Are you a sorcerer yourself?''

"No,'' she snapped. "What business is it of yours to abandon the gate for this?''

"None of mine. None of yours. So.'' He swung the door open. "My lady Meguct, let us get on with it.''

Only one door in or out of the maze never vanished: one set in the stone wall behind the dais in the ancient council chamber where Moro Ro had claimed, in the Sign of the Cygnet, all Ro Holding. As usual, the chamber, which took up the entire ground floor of the black tower, was empty. The banners of Hunter Hold and Withy Hold had been hung; the silver and gold thread winked in the morning light. The vast banner of Ro Holding hung behind the dais, hiding the door, so fragile and old that black swan melted into blue-black night, and only the tarnished threads de-

picting the stars of the Cygnet in flight seemed to hold the darkness
together.

Hew took a torch from the stairway; Meguet chose a sword
from the wall of ceremonial swords forged for each Holder, and
then held the Cygnet away from the wall until, bending, Hew
had carried the fire safely through the small door. She let it fall
behind her and entered. Fire ran down the steps ahead of them,
nibbled at an ancient dark. She smelled earth, stones, but no
wood fires, no lingering odors of cooking. She heard nothing.

Hew, moving down the steps ahead of her, stopped at the
foot of the stairs. She whispered,

"What is it?"

"I was only remembering what all the younglings hope to
find but are terrified of finding: the fearsome beings, the guardians
of Chrysom's tomb. Do you think there's truth to that?"

"Why not? The stars are falling out of the sky and turning
into tinkers. If we ever find the center of the maze, I suppose
we'll know."

"Maybe it's a Ring of Time, the center. Chrysom walked
out of Ro Holding into past or future."

She was silent, hovering at his shoulder, watching gryphons,
dragons, hawks, lions, shrug themselves out of the marble walls
of the maze. Under torch fire, they raged silently, bidding the
trespasser beware. "Why?" she wondered, forgetting to whisper.
"All this for his own tomb? What is he still guarding after a
thousand years? Are a mage's bones so precious? Do they turn
to gold?"

"I've never heard such." He took a step, then stopped,
handed the torch to Meguet. "You lead."

"Why? Neither of us is likely to wind up anywhere but in
a pantry somewhere, interrupting a cook's apprentice and a scul-
lery boy kissing."

"You're the one bearing arms," he said wryly, and, edgy
as she was, she almost laughed. She moved; he followed her.
Walls broke between passageways; she slipped at random between them. Passageways split, forked away into the silence,
forced her to choose between one shadow and another. She chose
thoughtlessly, according to the glint of light in a gryphon's eye,
the gesture of a lion's paw. At any moment, she expected, the
walls would subtly shift, dissolve and simply vanish into the
dark. A door in front of them would open to some tower or

another; they would emerge under a stairway, trailing cobwebs and blinking at the light. The small door, closing, would melt into wood or stone around it. But the walls held longer than she would have believed. Hew walked quietly beside her, watching the dark beyond the edge of light around them, sometimes watching her. He said once, softly:

"They'd never have gone this deep, surely?"

"I don't know." She added after a moment, "I've never come this far myself."

"I doubt anyone has."

"Why?"

"No threads left, no candle nubs, no smoke marks on the walls or on the floor . . ."

"It must run underground even past the tower ring. We've been walking forever, it seems."

"Into or out of forever."

She looked at him, surprised. "Do you mean like the thousand-year-old wood? Part real, part dream?"

"No. Well, maybe, or partly a different time. Or a slower time. In our own time, the House time, the maze never goes beyond the tower ring. But in a different time, it is vast and the center can be reached."

"And the House?" she asked, startled and intrigued by the intricate turn of his thoughts.

"Ro House does not exist now."

"Or the gate?"

He smiled a little. "Perhaps the gate. But open or closed? And who watches?"

A tongue of gold fire dropped out of a lion's mouth and fell, burning, at Meguet's feet.

She whirled, the torch outstretched, spinning a circle around her. She saw no one. A coiled snake of fire dropped out of a hawk's talon; a gold eye rolled from a gryphon's face, spilled fire on the floor. She drew her sword, circled again, her eyes wide, both torch and blade probing the empty dark. More fire fell, ringing them both with gold, she saw in horror. "Hew!" she cried, losing him as he circled at her back. He swung his heavy cloak around her suddenly, and gripped her, swept her off her feet. She struggled instinctively, desperately, hating to be bound, needing freedom to move, to fight. The torch slipped dangerously close to his face. He flinched back, gasping. But he

kept his grim hold; he lifted her, tossed her away from him over
the burning ring of gold. She lost her balance, tangled and
weighted in sheepskin; she stumbled to her hands and knees.
Turning, she saw only a tower of gold.

She whispered, "Hew." Within the fire something shaped:
a woman clothed in stars and night, stars clinging to her black
hair, her beautiful face moon-pale, her blind eyes closed. She
lifted her hands, pulled a glowing thread taut between them until,
under the lick of fire, it began to fray.

Meguet screamed his name. A small dark wagon with a roof
of light and a lintel of light rolled through the flames. Its door
opened. She saw the Gatekeeper of Ro House rise amid the
flames. He walked away from her for a long time, it seemed, or
into a different time, while the door in the black house opened
slowly, revealing a starlit dark.

Meguet rolled to her feet, flung herself, eyes closed, through
the fire. She careened into Hew, knocking him off his relentless
path. Groping for balance, he caught at her, dragged her down
under him as he fell. She pushed at him desperately, winded;
sagging against her, his hand on her shoulder, his arm across her
hair, he gave her no help. She edged out from under him finally.
When she dragged his arm off her hair, it fell back laxly against
the floor. He did not move.

Pulling herself to her knees beside him, reaching out to him
in bewilderment, she saw the blood on the knife in his hand.

A sound came out of her, echoed off the corners of the maze
in a harsh, terrible tangle. Laughter wove into her cry. Lifting
her head, she finally saw the Gold King.

He stood within the fire. He wore armor hammered of gold;
his hair and eyes and the seven-starred crown on his head were
gold. Only his laughing mouth was dark, a hollow that might
open into another world, another time, and she knew he laughed
at her because she did not know, seeing him, if she knelt beside
death or dream. In sudden fury, she pulled the knife from Hew's
hand, flung it with deadly accuracy into the Gold King's open
mouth.

A darkness burst out of the tinker-king, flooded the walls,
buried flame and torch fire until she could see only the barest,
silvery outline of stone animals in the wall. She got to her feet
and ran.

The stones began to come alive under the strange glow. A

hawk cried; a gryphon shifted a wing; a dragon pointed her path with an upraised claw. She ran without hesitating, not even considering choice, and as she wound deeper into the maze she realized, chilled, that she recognized the path she took. *I have walked this before*, she thought, prickling with terror, knowing it was not true. But, as memory guided her, she made choices: right at the gryphon's snarl, left at the lion's roar, between walls at the graceful shift of a unicorn's horn. *Who sees out of my eyes? Who walked this before me? Whose memories have I inherited?* And then, rounding a corner beneath a dragon's outspread wing, she knew that she had shifted into a different time.

That was why the stones moved, she realized; in her own life they might have spent a century lowering an eyelid. She swallowed drily, trembling, sensing movement around her from those that dwelled in the dark of this time. Walking into a small, circular chamber, she caught glimpses of colored horn, of fur, of rich cloth, of sword blades so massive she could not have lifted them. Here were the huge and terrible creatures of legend white-toothed, masked, prowling at the edge of an eerie, silver-green glow that came from a globe hanging over a black effigy and tomb. Chrysom's tomb, she thought in horror, but its guardians recognized something in her and let her pass among them. As she stepped beyond time, she stepped beyond wonder, beyond terror, beyond any thought of her own. She gazed at the effigy; then the globe above it dragged at her eyes. Staring into it, she saw back along her own history: a past full of names of those born to see, to watch, hers among them, though at that moment she could not remember which was hers.

The tomb faded into its own moment; the globe changed shape.

A huge, faceted crystal, suspended from nothing upon nothing, glowed like a moon at the center of the maze. Its facets blazed with a white light that slowly faded, until, blinking away splinters of light, she could see the black swan flying in every plane. The swans faded; faces began to appear within the globe, of men and women she should not have recognized but did: Rydel the gardener; the mage Ais; Tries, physician to Jain Ro; the Lady Scirie, historian and poet; Paro Ro's horse trainer Jhen; Eleria Ro's cousin Shadox; all of them descendants of Astor Ro, all secret guardians of the Cygnet. She saw her own face last, broad-boned, green-eyed, and then realized, from the pearls braided into the long hair, and the darker, straighter brows, that she looked at Astor Ro.

Motionless, submerged in her heritage, she felt no surprise. The face within the crystal spoke:

"Who are you?"

She answered, her voice expressionless, a dreamer's voice. "I am Meguet Vervaine."

"Why were you born?"

The answer, like her movement to the heart of the maze, came without hesitation. "I was born to serve the Cygnet."

"To what are you sworn?"

"To guard the Cygnet. With my life. For all of my days. Beyond my days and my life."

"You will walk in the Cygnet's eye. You will guard. You will defend."

"Yes."

"Our memories are yours, our eyes are yours. Your heart is ours and your body and the strength of your hand."

"Yes."

"Our gifts are yours. Our experience is yours. We will guide you, watch with you."

"Yes."

"You will obey us."

"Yes."

"Why have you come here?"

"The Cygnet is in danger."

"What must you do?"

She felt an ancient rage within her, honed thin and sharp as the mage-forged blades she sometimes practiced with. She said, "I will seek the danger to the Cygnet. I will hunt it down. I will destroy it. For this we were born."

"Meguet Vervaine, Guardian. Put your hands to the Cygnet's eye."

She reached out, placed her hands on the cold planes of the prism. Astor Ro's face faded. Through the white fire that flooded the crystal, the black Cygnet flew, imprinting itself in her eye, in her mind. A whispering began, within the prism or her mind. The fierce light died. She held the night sky and the constellations between her hands. As the stars slowly revolved, she drank in knowledge with the night.

The crystal vanished when she finally dropped her hands. The moment of time that had opened for her closed again, hid its treasure. In another moment, she saw Chrysom's effigy on a tomb of black marble, the globe above it, the huge, strange guardians moving restlessly around it. And then that layer of time also hid itself. She stood in the dark at the center of the maze, and watched torchlight mold the stone animals out of the darkness at the top of the wall, before the torchbearer turned the final corner and illumined the moment around her.

She stood in a small circular chamber. The guardians of Chrysom's tomb no longer moved; they surrounded her, half-sculpted out of the marble wall and painted. There was no sign of globe or tomb or effigy. There was only a shadow slanting across the ceiling, which the busy torchlight searched and shaped into the Cygnet in flight.

The Holder carried the torch.

She said softly, "I thought so."

Meguet felt the last, familiar layer of time slide into place; she stood again in her own present. "You know what I am."

"I know," the Holder said. "The powers that protect the Cygnet do not keep the Holders ignorant of its guardian. For some time now I have wondered about you." She paused. There was not a pin left in her hair; it flowed wildly down her back. Her eyes looked weary, bruised by conjecture. She added, "You would not have come down here, the Gatekeeper would not have left the gate, unless there was dire need."

Meguet put the back of her hand to her mouth. "The Blind Lady has entered." Her voice trembled. "We looked for her. They were both here, in the maze. Blind Lady and tinker."

The Holder stepped closer; firelight ran over Meguet's dishevelled hair, her singed skirt. "You found them," she said harshly.

"The Gate—Hew—I left him. He was hurt. Dead, maybe." She swallowed, calmed her voice from habit, though she had

begun to shake. "I must find him. I had to run—"
"Yes."
"I ran—beyond time, I think. Into the heart of the maze."
"Here."
"Yes, only—within. Within this place. I must go back and find Hew. He fell on his knife."
The Holder closed her eyes. "Moro's name. You cannot go back there."
"I must find him."
"No. I'll send the guard."
"They won't get far enough. They won't get past the periphery. No one does. Except you."
"I came another way," the Holder said obscurely. "Gatekeepers don't kill themselves without regard for the gate."
"He didn't—I knocked him down."
"Oh."
"He was walking into the tinker's house. I—he might have been dead then, I don't know. I tried to kill the tinker."
"It does seem futile." She touched her eyes delicately with her fingers. "The powers you have inherited are formidable, but I don't think you are able to use them to rescue a Gatekeeper. They rouse to protect the Cygnet."
"I know, but—"
"Those two may be waiting for you."
Meguet felt a familiar stillness settle through her, as when she had chosen a path or an action and choice lay in the past, in another time. "Then," she said, "I will meet them."
"Meguet Vervaine, I forbid you to do this!"
"Will you let me take the torch, anyway?" She added, under the Holder's outraged stare, "I am overly fond of your Gate keeper."
"So you would leave me in the dark."
"I'll light your way back first. It's not far, is it? The way you came in?" She looked around, at the strange menacing figures surrounding them, wearing their bright masks of paint. She had seen them many times, she knew, through many centuries. "It's quite close. . . ." she said surprisedly. The Holder watched her, face impassive. Her fingers lifted, worried her hair for a phantom pin. She gave up, tossing her hand in the air.
"I dislike changing Gatekeepers." She gave Meguet the torch. "Lead."

Meguet bowed her head; the torch shook in her hand, then finally steadied. She turned, and, stepping forward, flung a circle of light around the Gatekeeper.

She stopped, catching breath. He kept moving, slowly, with a weary, dragging persistence, until he was close enough to reach out, gather her against him with one arm. She whispered, "Hew." She put her free arm around him tightly and felt him wince.

She drew back, still holding him lightly. He carried his singed cloak under one arm; there was blood in his hair, a streak of blood along one torn side of his tunic. He smiled a little, then started as the Holder stepped into the light.

They looked at each other for a long time. Then the Gatekeeper let go of Meguet, bent his head respectfully, and the Holder said, "Hew, what are you doing here? This place is for mages and Holders, not Gatekeepers."

"I heard Meguet's voice, my lady. I followed it. Hours, it seems I followed."

"Are you badly hurt?"

"I've been worse, my lady."

"I thought you were dead," Meguet said numbly. "I saw you walking into the tinker's house."

He looked at her wearily. "It's not a tinker you were fighting, my lady Meguet. It's not a tinker lives in that dark house. Down here, there's no one to keep secrets from, unless this cheerful crowd around us."

"That may well be," the Holder said grimly, "but until I know better what danger we're in, I prefer to have only a tinker under my house."

"And a blind weaver, my lady. She got past my sleeping eye."

"I'm not surprised."

"How did you escape from them?" Meguet asked. He shook his head.

"I didn't. I woke up and it was dark and they were gone. So were you. I thought they had you. Then I began to hear your voice. Here, around this corner, there around that, words I couldn't quite hear . . . I was circling you, I think, forever it felt. You never sounded frightened. Never troubled. You were safe, I thought, but I could never find you. It helped me, hearing you, kept me from sitting down and falling asleep." He was holding his arm tightly against his side. Meguet saw him blink away sweat. The Holder said abruptly:

"The house must be in a turmoil by now. Meguet, lead us back up."

Meguet raised the torch above her head, illumined the tall, still, half-human figures ringing them. A horned face, its human part blue, its horns gold, gazed back at her out of blue and gold eyes. She reached out impulsively, touched its clawed, jewelled hand.

It swung gently aside, revealing steps. The Gatekeeper made a sudden noise, of recognition and wonder. "We came down those," he breathed. "My lady Meguet, is there a maze or is there not? Or is this all in the mage's mind?"

"You should know; you walked as much of it as any of us."

"While you spoke, who were you speaking to all that time?"

The lie came easily to her, she found, as they must come, she realized, for the rest of her life. "Only myself," she said, "guiding myself, feeling my way..." She opened the small door at the top of the stairs, pushed the heavy, dark banner aside. Through the open doors of the tower, the Gatekeeper's empty turret hung like a delicate carving against a blue-grey dusk.

With the Holder's permission, Meguet helped him back to his cottage. He sat stiffly on the hearth bench, the jagged tear in his side cleaned and dressed, watching her gaze dubiously at his pots.

"I can cook what I have hunted," she confessed finally. "But I'm no good in a kitchen."

"Never mind," he said. He stretched out his good arm. "Sit with me a little, Meguet." She dropped beside him on the bench. Her skirt was torn at the knee where she had fallen; her braid was coming apart; there were, she was certain, smudges of sweat and dust on her face. He kissed her for a long time. Night laid dark wings against the windows; the world was oddly silent.

"No wind," she said at last, surprised. "No rain."

"Stars, maybe. Entire constellations..." But neither of them moved to look. "Spring, soon."

She leaned against him, watching the fire, thinking of the tinker's fire. "What happened to you," she asked, "in that gold ring of fire? I saw you walking toward the Gold King's house.

Do you remember the open door of his house? It was full of night
and stars.''

"All I remember is falling.''

"That was after, when I pushed you away from the house.''

"No, before. When I threw you away from the fire. You
hit me with something.''

"I didn't.''

"You did. That sword you carried. I saw its pommel coming
at me. That was that for me until I woke alone in the dark.''

"Then you walked in your sleep. Or maybe it was an illusion
of you, walking. Or a sending through time, like the Hunter Hold
witches. The Blind Lady pulled a thread between her hands while
you walked. . . .''

"They didn't harm me.'' He looked down at her wryly.
"You did most of it.''

"I did,'' she said, startled.

"They didn't hurt you?''

"No. I threw your knife at the Gold King. He was armed
in gold, then, and crowned, and laughing at me. I hit him.''

"Did he drop dead?''

"Not noticeably.''

"Then what?''

"Then I ran.''

"Did they follow you?''

"I don't—I don't think so.''

He grunted. "They were in hiding. Waiting, it seems like.
We disturbed them, they showed us a trick or two and then hid
themselves again.''

"Waiting.''

"So it seems.''

She was silent. A finger of fire caught color from sap and
turned gold. She started. She turned abruptly, caught his arms
so tightly he winced. "Hew. When is spring? When is the last
day of winter?''

"I don't know. Soon.''

"How soon?'' She shook him a little, when he didn't answer. "That's what they're waiting for! The Dancer, the Blood
Fox's human shadow, the Warlock—''

"The Warlock?''

"The other Hold Signs!'' She loosed him, sprang up to pace,

thinking furiously. "How many weeks of winter left?"

"Days, more like." He watched her, nursing his side, his face hard, expressionless as always when he was disturbed. "I must watch for a Warlock now, at the gate. And all the Hold Councils themselves beginning to come soon. What do you see in all this, Meguet?"

She whirled, her face white. "I have to stop him."

"Who?"

"The Wayfolk man with Nyx. He's going to Berg Hold, to wake the Dancer. On the last day of winter."

"He'd be gone by now," Hew said, and brought her to a halt in front of him. "Unless he can fly across Ro Holding. Wayfolk don't fly. But they're not afraid to travel."

She swung to the hearth, brought her fist down on the stones. Then she dropped her face against her arm. "I'll leave now. Tonight."

"You'll never make it. Never to Berg Hold by winter's end. You might make it past the Delta."

"Then what?" she said bitterly. "Will we stop the Dancer coming in the way we stopped the Blind Lady? I can't do anything right. I try and try and only make things worse."

"Why is it you who should be trying? You, more than the Holder or Nyx or Rush Yarr? Why, Meguet? Why is it you must stop the Wayfolk man in Berg Hold?"

Because I can! she said fiercely, but only to herself, her eyes still hidden in the crook of her arm. She felt him pull at her gently.

"Don't. Not twice in one day. I'll watch, this time. I swear. Day and night."

She turned her head, gazed down at him, dry-eyed. "I must get to Berg Hold."

"But how?"

"Rush. Maybe he learned something useful from Nyx. Or the witches of Hunter Hold. Maybe they know a way I could walk through time. I could get to Hunter Hold before winter's end."

"Rush Yarr's sorcery might land you in the middle of Wolfe Sea."

"I have to risk something! It's because of the Wayfolk man these things are happening. I don't know how or why, but he is dangerous, and I must stop him."

"With what?" he demanded. "With what power? Moro
Ro's sword that you have to hold steady with both hands? Why
you? Why you that must fling yourself across Ro Holding into
the endless snows of Berg Hold to keep the Dancer from dancing?"

"For the same reason that you watch the gate, night and
day, summer and winter. Because you must. I have old eyes in
me, Hew. Old voices. They make me see, they make me do what
I can. I was born rooted to the past in this house." She added,
"The Wayfolk man needs no power to be stopped. I could
threaten him with Moro Ro's sword and he would take it seri-
ously. All I need to do is get there. . . ."

"Take the house," he suggested. "It used to fly for Moro
Ro." She stared at him. "That way I wouldn't have to fret about
you."

"Chrysom moved it."

"Did he?"

"During the Hold Wars."

"Well," he said, "from the sound of it, that's what we may
be heading toward. Did he take that power with him when he
died? Or did he leave something to the next Holder, in case of
trouble in the Delta?"

"I don't—I don't know."

"Who would know?"

"I don't know." She pushed her hands against her eyes.
"Rush Yarr?"

Her hands dropped. She gazed down at him, then she bent
swiftly and kissed him. "Calyx."

"You want to move my house where?" the Holder said
incredulously.

"The highest peak in Berg Hold," Calyx said. She was at
a table in Chrysom's library, walling herself up with books.

"It would fall off," Iris said practically.

"Well, then as close as possible to the top. Meguet could
climb the rest of the way. If people are meant to consult the
Dancer, there must be a way for them to get up."

"I'm coming with Meguet," Rush said. "To protect her
from the Fire Bear."

"This house hasn't moved in centuries!"

"Does everything go?" Iris wondered. "Barns, hen coops, the thousand-year-old wood?"

"Tinker and Blind Lady?" Rush asked. The Holder, gazing at Meguet, toying with the amber around her neck, shook her head.

"It's no longer possible. Is it?"

"The house was made to move."

"Across Ro Holding?"

"Legend," Calyx murmured with satisfaction, "says so. Legend says that during a siege by the Delta armies, the house moved to the northern fields of Withy Hold."

"Legend," Iris said sharply and poked her needle through cloth. "It's a thousand-year-old tale."

"So," Rush said grimly, "is what we've got living beneath this tower."

"Either this house goes to Berg Hold," Meguet said, "or Rush must find a way to send me there."

"If you want to get there, you'd better take the house," Calyx said.

"I think it's safer to guard the gate against the Dancer," Iris said. "What will people think if Ro House vanishes?"

"We'll bring it back," Calyx said, flipping pages. "The question is: Who actually moved it, during Moro Ro's time?"

"Chrysom must have," the Holder said.

"Maybe he left a spell," Rush suggested.

"I'm looking," Calyx said. She added, "You could help, instead of pacing around and shaking Chrysom's things up." Rush, tossing something iridescent in his hand, moved to her side. Meguet watched them turning pages in rhythm, their heads bowed over books, absorbed. She saw Iris watching also, a curious smile in her eyes. She threaded her needle through cloth and put it down.

"If the witches warned of the Blind Lady, why didn't they warn of the Dancer?"

"The Blind Lady weaves time," Meguet said. "The witches explore it. They consider the Blind Lady nothing more than a childish tale of life and death. Until she walked down one of their paths, and they saw the Lady's face."

"I don't understand any of this," Iris sighed. "I don't see how you could make any sense at all of a tinker in Chrysom's maze."

"The house," Calyx said suddenly, "was moved two hundred years after the Hold Wars." Her face was suffused with a delicate rose; finding a footprint on the trail of some historical mystery gave her pleasure.

"By Chrysom?" the Holder asked.

"No. He had been dead for fifty years. By Brigen Ro's oldest son. He moved it from the Delta to the black desert of Hunter Hold."

"Why?"

"It's not clear. . . . Brigen Ro was upset and made him bring it back immediately. There is a reference by Brigen's son to one of Chrysom's books."

"Nyx probably has it," Iris said, picking up her needlework again.

"No, it's here. Brigen's son, apparently, just moved the house to see if he could. He sounds like you, Rush."

"Thank you."

"But what," Meguet asked, "made him think he could?"

"Let's find out," Calyx said, picking up a small, frail book with letters on the cover in faded silver, "what Crysom has to say."

They watched her, while she turned pages silently. Meguet, too restless to sit, moved next to the Holder beside the fire, and wished that, when she had changed out of her torn skirt, she had put on a string of beads to worry. But she stood with her usual calm, back against the hearth, hiding a terrible impatience.

Calyx made a satisfied noise. "Here we are. According to Chrysom, the power to move Ro House is passed from generation to generation of Holders' children, who are born with an innate ability, for the Holders instinctively seek out as mates those who may inspire the power within the child conceived."

The Holder looked startled. Iris murmured, "Really, Calyx."

"So Chrysom says."

The Holder cleared her throat. "All children? Or one, specifically?"

"Nyx," Rush said shortly.

"No." Calyx looked solemnly at her mother. "Always and inevitably the first."

They all gazed at Iris. She put down her needlework uncertainly, flushing. The Holder's brows had risen. She pulled a pin out of her hair absently, her mind running down the past; a smile, reminiscent, wondering, touched her eyes.

"Mother," Iris said accusingly.

"Well, I didn't know," the Holder said. "He seemed a very practical man."

"I can't move this house."

"Chrysom says you can."

"He's been dead for nine hundred years!"

"Eight hundred and fifty," Rush corrected.

"I don't have any gifts for magic! I never had any."

"You have one," Calyx said. She sat back in her chair, smoothing a strand of hair back into place. She narrowed her eyes at her sister. "Iris Ro, you are not going to sit there and tell us you won't even try! You must. For the sake of this House. It is your duty."

Iris stared back at her, mouth pinched. Then she looked at Meguet, standing motionless at the fire, her eyes enormous, dark with urgency in her pale face. She flung her needlework down and got to her feet.

"It won't work."

Calyx smiled.

Iris was still protesting on the night before the last day of winter, but with less conviction. Midnight was the preferred time, Chrysom suggested, if possible, since people and animals would be less disturbed than by leaping in broad daylight from one Hold to another. Meguet and Rush spent the day finding merchants, guests and other assorted visitors, and persuading them to shelter somewhere in the city. At dusk, when the household was sorted out, and the last visitor had departed, she had climbed wearily to the Gatekeeper's turret, sat with him silently, watching the sun go down over the grey, crumpled sea. She could smell spring now, from the swamps: a hint of perfume over the layered scents of still water and mold, all overlaid with the wash of brine from the outgoing tide. A single swan rose high above the lake; the Gatekeeper said drily, watching it, "This'll save them a flight north."

Near midnight she stood on top of Chrysom's tower, with Rush and the Holder and her children. The wind-whipped Cygnet flew above them on its black pennant. Above it the constellation itself flew in and out of thin, bright clouds. The full moon that had blinded the Lady of Withy Hold hung white as bone in the sky.

Iris stood silently, apart from them. She must, Calyx instructed her endlessly, root herself as fast as Chrysom's rose vines to every stone, mouse, dirty pot, child and chick, sleeping peacock, weed, swan and thousand-year-old tree within the rambling walls of Ro House. Iris had explained as endlessly that she couldn't, no one could, it was not possible. . . . But she said nothing now; her profile, under flickering light, looked unfamiliar in its calm. She was gazing down at the yard, one hand on the stones, as if she were watching a horse race, or children playing. She had stood like that for an hour.

Clouds swarmed over the moon, swallowed it. Meguet, watching a fleet of night fishers on the sea, saw them vanish suddenly, as if they had all slid down into the black water. Her lips parted; she held the parapet stones, waiting for the wind to hit. She heard Rush's sudden breath. But no wind came: There was only a dark like the darkness in dreams through which they floated, a quick scratch of light across the ground below now and then, and all the constellations shifting in a stately dance above. She smelled a hint of green from Withy Hold, no more than a thought of leaves in the quickening trees. In the charmed silence no one spoke. Meguet sensed stirrings behind her, a gathering that she dared not turn to see, as if the ghosts that frequented Chrysom's tower—mages, guardians, the odd son or daughter drawn to sorcery—had come up to watch the stars. If she turned, she knew, she would see nothing: They might have been there, in the endlessly folded tissue of time, or they had never been there.

She smelled snow. In a moment or two the wind struck: a blast as bare and merciless as frozen stone. A white peak loomed over Ro House like a jagged tooth. The stars had disappeared. Snow, torn like spindrift off the crest of the mountain, scattered over them. Calyx reached out to Iris, gripped her hand, and she lifted her head, startled. They all ran for the stairs.

They huddled next to the fire, shivering, drinking wine. The shadowed, vulnerable expression in Iris's eyes caused the Holder to say fretfully, "You will only have to do this once more. Then never again, I hope."

Iris, crouched close to the flames, looked at her. She said softly, "I carried everyone's dreams . . . it was like moving the world in a bubble. I even saw my child's dream. I know where that ring you lost is, Calyx. I know where all the mice live, in every crevice. I know what the peacocks see in the dark. I sensed those in the house that do not belong here. Only they were hidden. Only they . . . And the Gatekeeper. I had trouble keeping track of the Gatekeeper. I kept mistaking him for other things.''

"The gate, most likely," Meguet suggested. "Sometimes I think he himself gets lost in it."

"And you, Meguet. I kept mistaking you for ghosts."

"Ghosts," Rush repeated. The wild winds fluting through the tower seemed to echo the word. Iris smiled at him tranquilly.

"Oh, yes. They all came, too."

Meguet woke before dawn. She could scarcely see the Gatekeeper at the wall, though by the faint red glow of his brazier she knew that Iris had not forgotten him. She dressed swiftly, went down to the armory where she found Rush choosing a sword. Horses were already saddled, waiting for them. The household, considerably startled at finding itself snowbound, had not ceased its smooth operation. The early winds eased as the sun rose. A wave of fire washed down the mountain, splashed around them: the warning of the Fire Bear.

The Gatekeeper opened the gate, his face impassive as Meguet rode through. She looked at him briefly, her own face settled into a stiff, deceptive calm. Neither spoke.

The path up the mountain was narrow, rubble-filled, steep. The edge of the world fell away from them, it seemed, on one side; on the other, bare slabs of rock, the bones of the mountain, pushed upward toward the top of the sky. They rode until the path grew too rough for the horses. A gold, raging face sprang at them as they rounded a turn on foot, breathed fire over the white world below. Meguet, shielding her face from the sun, said breathlessly, "I can smell it. I can almost taste it."

"What?"

"The end of winter." A sudden panic seized her; she pulled herself over crumbled boulder, past the solitary, twisted, stunted trees. "Hurry, Rush."

"We'll break our necks."

"Hurry."

Shadows were peeling off the mountain as the sun climbed higher. Meguet, sun in her face constantly, wondered if the Fire

Bear had roared this golden light at the Cygnet. She increased her pace, breath tearing at her, and saw, from the very top of the mountain, a blinding flash of silver.

She cried, "Rush!" He was beside her, then not, as she pulled herself up, clinging to anything solid: rock, icicle, even, she thought, the blinding surface of the snow, light, and shadow.

Something bulky blocked the sun, hissed at her. She nearly slid down the mountain. The Fire Bear was white as snow, with red eyes and red claws; it paced just above her on a flat, bald slab of granite, shaking its shaggy head, trying to hiss fire. Then, fretfully, it turned away, its attention caught, and she pulled herself onto the stones, the breath running in and out of her like fire. She heard Rush call her name, but she could neither move nor speak.

The Fire Bear was busy eating fire. It was a blue-black flame the Wayfolk man had laid on the snow, and it seemed to take its fuel from the snow. Corleu's back was to her; the Fire Bear was between them. He stood looking down at a smooth ice sculpture that lay like a statue on the top of the peak. He spoke.

Meguet moved forward. The Fire Bear saw her move, but busily ate its fire. Corleu's eyes were on the beautiful face trapped within the ice at his feet; he said, as Meguet stepped beside him, "Is that all you can tell me?"

He was shivering, lightly clad; his face looked raw in the cold. Meguet wondered suddenly how he had climbed the mountain in those clothes, and what he had done with his footprints.

"Ask the Blood Fox," the Dancer murmured, her eyes open, but unseeing. "Take him a gift."

"What gift?" There was no answer; he raised his voice desperately. "What gift?" Then he saw Meguet, a tall, black-clad figure holding with both her hands a sword that hovered near his heart.

He stepped back, his breath scraping in horror. He recognized her; she saw that in his eyes, as well as a reckless despair that made him tense to run, to attack. But there was nowhere to run, and Moro Ro's sword was dogging his every move.

"In the name of the Holder and the Cygnet, you must come with me."

The Fire Bear roared.

Black flame washed over them. Blind, Meguet leaped, felt cloth, bone in her grasp. Then she stumbled; they both fell against the ice-statue, who turned under them, murmuring, then turned again. Corleu pulled free; Meguet, finding him again in the dispersing mist, saw him stop mid-pace, stare at the Dancer.

She rose in a fluid, graceful movement. Smiling, she stepped out of the pool of melting ice. Her hair fell to her feet, one side white, the other black. She shook it back, laughing, and raised her hands to the sun.

Corleu shouted, "No!" He backed a step, another. And then a silver circle floated around him, and he vanished into it. The Dancer turned a circle, faster and faster, until her hair whipped around her, black and white. The black and white blurred into snow and shadow.

The Fire Bear blew a final breath of night and shambled over the edge of the world.

Meguet stood alone, on the top of a mountain on the top of the world, listening to the spring wind.

PART THREE

HEART OF THE CYGNET

"Who is she?" Corleu demanded. "She stood in front of me with her eyes the only color in the world. She came out of nowhere to the top of that mountain like she knew I would be there, on that one day of all days in the year, she knew I would step across time from Delta to Berg Hold, and she came to meet me. I turned and there she was, holding that blade at my heart and all I could see was green, like the green of the cornfields of Withy Hold in late summer." He was pacing; Nyx, curled in a chair, listened without moving, except her eyes, following him as he wove a convoluted path between chairs and book piles and the tiny round jar holding time. "Her eyes and her hair like when you tear the green leaves off corn and the pale silk holds to your fingers."

"Why," Nyx asked curiously, "are you comparing my cousin Meguet to a corncob?"

"Because that's what I think of when I see her. My great-gran's tale of Rider in the Corn. Green, she said, his eyes corn leaves and his hair corn silk. That's all she ever said of him. He lay with her among the corn and then rode on."

Nyx gazed at him expressionlessly out of her colorless eyes.
Her fingers found a loose button on her sleeve, toyed with it.
"That's a preposterous idea."

"I know."

"You and Meguet related."

"Moonbrained."

"She is a descendant of Moro Ro's wife."

"And I'm nothing but Wayfolk. Almost nothing."

A thin line ran across her brow. "What I want to know is
what she was doing on that mountain. Did she hear you speak
to the Dancer?"

He closed his eyes, sank into one of the chairs that for some
reason were cluttering the workroom that morning. "I don't
know." He dropped his hand over his eyes. "Dancer is freed."

"What did you expect when you gave that fire to the Fire
Bear?" she asked. He stared at her, felt the blood leap furiously
into his face.

"You did—You knew—" He was on his feet suddenly,
his fists clenched. Her cold eyes did not flicker. He whirled,
found a door and let his fists slam into it. From within he heard
the fluttering of startled birds. He dropped his face against the
door, felt the sting of tears in the back of his eyes.

"Corleu," she said softly, "to get what you want, you must
give what they want. What did the Dancer say?"

"She said," he whispered into the wood, " 'ask the Blood
Fox.' " She was silent. He turned finally, found her gazing in
conjecture at a twisted candle.

"Blood Fox . . . Last of the Hold Signs." She drew breath.
"So. That is why Meguet went to meet you in Berg Hold. Those
powers you are waking must be finding their way into Ro House."
She rose abruptly, turned to him; he saw a shadow of color the
candlelight dragged into her eyes. "You ask the Blood Fox."

"That'll be Warlock." He swallowed drily. "I saw his
shadow once."

"Did the Dancer say anything else?"

"She said, 'The thing sought lies always in the same place,
but always in a different place, and that place is never far from
the Cygnet.' It's no help."

"Of course it is. Something near the Cygnet . . . a web. The
Cygnet flies above it day and night. . . . What gift did she say to
give the Blood Fox?"

"She didn't. But I figured out that one. Any smallfolk knows. 'Shadow fox, fox shadow, hide your face, hide your shadow—' It's a hiding a game."

"Go on."

" 'Red star, blood star, find your eyes and see, find your—' "

"The Blood Star."

"Cygnet broke the Warlock into pieces and trapped him in the Blood Star. What—what will happen—"

"I don't know." Her face seemed colorless in the shadows. "But it's too late to undo."

"How do I get the Blood Star to give it?" he asked her.

"Hang on the horns of the moon and pick it out of the sky?"

"You make it." She began pacing then, her feet following an independent path of thought. "And you make it fast. I don't know how Meguet got to Berg Hold, but I doubt that she took the long way. Rush helped her, maybe. When she returns to the Delta, she'll come to this house. She knows where to find you. And she wants you."

"Why her? Why did she come for me?"

"I don't know. She's a mystery to me. She never was before this. She was only Meguet."

"There's nothing 'only' about her," he said. "She nearly sent me diving off the mountain, with her eyes and her sword. How do I make a Blood Star? With a wish and an adage?"

"Almost. It's a very old, very primitive sorcery. The Blood Star does not threaten, foretell, defend. It is all but useless except as a kind of lantern or guide between separated lovers. The effort far exceeds the results, which is why the making is rarely heard of, now. There are much simpler ways of keeping track of people than fusing your heart's blood into a glass ball."

"Mine."

"A drop or three."

"I can spare that, likely. Where do I take it, though? Where would Blood Fox be, in the Delta?"

"There's a place upriver, a strange place that resonates with ancient power. Long ago someone sensed the power, and carved statues among the trees there. One statue was of the Blood Fox as human. Or as warlock."

He nodded. "Trappers passed that place when they brought me here. I remember the Blood Fox."

"You'll make the Blood Star there. The Blood Fox will find you."

He was silent, remembering the shift of tree into blood fox into man, all one, all rooted in the still water. "She'll know this is the last of them."

"Meguet?"

"Will she know this place?"

"She has roamed in and out of the swamps since we were children. She'd know it, I think, but perhaps only as a garden of statues, not as a place of power."

"Because she has no power," he said evenly.

She eyed him. "Maybe it's not such a moonbrained idea after all. She does have some kin in Withy Hold. Do you want to see her again?"

"No."

"Then I suggest we assume she will be at your heels like your shadow. Get something to eat. Then I will teach you how to make the Blood Star."

Later, he borrowed the boat from the silent ghost, who bestirred herself in her pearls and laces to fade into the afternoon. He placed a lit, shuttered lantern at the bow and rowed through slow, tangled paths where the hanging vines were just beginning to flush with green. On a sandy bank beside the statue grove, he pulled the boat ashore. In the dying light he gathered wood. The night fell quickly, a dense darkness unrelieved by stars or moon. The bitter cold that he felt did not disperse when he lit the fire with the boat lantern. The fire itself—made from odd things— was yellow as a hunter's moon.

He carried pale, damp, rough sand from the bank and added river water to it. He worked it into a ball the size of his fist. As he molded and smoothed it, he murmured under his breath, over and over, the old rhyme he had known since he could find his feet and walk. Sweating, fire-scorched, mesmerized by his own monotonous voice, he laid the ball of sand in the fire. He watched it thoughtlessly, still murmuring, as the gold fire licked it. When it had turned black, he lifted it out again and broke it in half.

He slid a tough razor-edged piece of marsh grass over the forefinger of his left hand. Then he teased a bit of flame out of the fire onto the grass, laid the flame carefully in the center of one of the broken halves. He fed the flame three drops of his blood. The flame ran from gold to blood red. He closed the halves, laid the ball into the fire again. After a time, during which swamp animals came rustling to the edge of his light to watch, he pulled the ball out again. This time, with the heated blade of the silver knife he had taken from the house, he began to sculpt the sides of the ball. Molten silver from the blade, blood from his hand, streaked the dark sand as he worked. Sweat rolled into it from his face; words seeped into it, mingling with the river water. He layered the sphere with flat planes angling against one another. When he finished that, he was ringed with watching eyes.

He put the faceted ball into the fire. His voice stilled finally. Around him the night was soundless, in the slow, lightless empty hours between midnight and dawn. The fire flared, flared again, washing silver, crimson, black. The small dark ball in the heart of it began to glow.

The eyes around him blinked suddenly out, like vanishing stars. He heard the sighing passage through the underbrush of many small, invisible animals. Then he heard something else: a blood fox's sharp bark in the distance. Another answered, just behind his back.

He heard that as from a distance, too. Everything seemed detached from him: the heat of the fire, the burns on his hands, his dry aching throat, the appalling, lonely silence of the night. More eyes ringed the fire, some high as his knee and higher, others close to the ground. All were a smoky, red-tinged amber.

The ball in the fire had turned clear as glass, red as blood. He did not touch it. The fire sank around it, yellow again. He stood up. A great blood fox walked into the light. The fur on its massive shoulders was bristling. Its eyes were cloudy, yellow with the fire. It was dancing a little, singing its high, eerie whine before it barked and attacked. The shadow stretching from its hind paws beyond the fire's circle was not an animal's.

"Shadow Fox, fox shadow," Corleu said to it. His voice was so hoarse it might have been the blood fox's growl.

"Hide your face, hide your shadow.
Red star, blood star,
Find your face, find your shadow,
Find your heart and follow."

He reached into the fire, drew out the star that hid a pearl of blood in its heart and caught fire in all its glittering facets.

The blood fox stood silent as the trees around it. Its eyes burned into Corleu's; they seemed suddenly faceted, like the Blood Star. For a moment, his detachment vanished under that inhuman gaze; he wanted to wrap the dark around him like a cloak and slip away before he became a human swarm of blood foxes, furious with him for disturbing the Delta night.

The Blood Fox faded away. A darkness formed where it had been, shaped a man in the firelight, a patch of night with a face that shifted, blurred, re-formed. Corleu stared at it, his thoughts reeling between terror and wonder; he felt as if he were falling again through that long, black, starry night in the Gold King's house.

"You have something I want," the shadow said. Its face stilled enough to form: long, sharp-jawed, red-browed; then the lines of it fractured again. Its voice was deep, husky, a blood fox voice. Corleu swallowed.

"I made it for you."

A shadowy hand reached toward it, passed through it, darkening it briefly. At the cold touch Corleu, trapped between shadow and fire, would have backed into the fire if he could have made himself move. He glimpsed eyes, amber flames swarming across them.

"What do you want for that?" the shadow asked with a snap of teeth.

"Just—just a small thing."

"That's a small thing. That's my heart you hold in your hand. Be careful what you ask for, or I'll set a blood fox shadowing you to nuzzle out your heart."

"I'm not—It's not for me I'm asking."

"Who then? Who sent you?"

"The King in the dark."

The shadow made a complex sound, part human, part blood fox's curious whine. "So the King goes hunting. . . . You put your heart's blood into that. Into my heart. You want something worth that much to you. Corleu. That's your name. You've said my name now and then in your life."

"I'm sorry I ever learned to talk," he said starkly, and the shadowy face gave a lean, sharp-toothed grin.

"There is no idle chatter in the world. So here you stand with my heart in your hand, asking nothing for yourself?"

"I'm to be paid later."

"To be paid. Or to pay?"

His voice shook. "Both."

"I know that King, with his heart of fire. He stalks everyone's days. What does he want? What small thing?"

"Something hidden away in secret for safekeeping. The Gold King told me to go to Withy Hold, offer the Lady there a peacock feather and ask. She told me to take fire and ask the Dreamer on the top of the world. Dreamer told me to ask you. All of them gave me pieces of a puzzle, none of them a whole answer. So I made this for you." It burned in his hand with cold fire. He wiped at sweat and smoke on his face. "I need you to finish the puzzle."

"How small is this thing that sent you wandering the world?"

"Small as the heart of something wild that flies by night over Ro Holding."

The shadow was still; even the lines hinting of bone-structure stilled briefly, and gave Corleu a clear glimpse of its honed, red-furred, feral face. It made a soft whistling noise, like a branch keening on the fire, and blurred again. "He's been thinking, that King. . . . And you are feet and hands and eyes to find it. What of yours does he hold hostage?"

"My heart," he whispered.

"Give me mine. I will tell you what I know."

"How?" he asked, his heart pounding in sudden hope. "How do I give it?"

"Lay the Blood Star in the fire."

Corleu knelt close to the flames, let the prism slide among them. Just before the flames closed over it, he saw the jumbled patchwork of a man in all its facets.

The shadow stepped into the fire. Flames flared high above his head, closed like the petals of a burning flower. Corleu flung himself back, watched, breathless, as the flames swirled and parted, died down again and the Warlock stepped out of them.

He stood over Corleu, grinning his fox's grin, lean-flanked, his shoulders bunched with muscle, the hair on his head and body the red of the blood fox's pelt. He tossed black, broken pieces of the prism in his hands, juggled them a moment into a whirling black circle.

"The thing you seek is well hidden, even from that King's gold fingers, which go everywhere. But I have heard, in all my

eons of wandering, dragged after a Blood Fox with its nose to
the wind and its ear pricked to every whisper: The thing you seek
will be reflected in the eye of the Cygnet.''
   ''Reflected in—But what does that mean?'' he cried. ''It's
only another riddle!''
   ''That's all I know.''
   He let the pieces of the prism fall into one broad palm. Then
he covered them with the other. When he opened his hands again,
the black glass had fused into a swan in flight.
   He dropped it into the fire. It exploded, flinging glass, burning wood, shards of flame, into the night. Corleu, still crouched,
ducked behind his arms. All around him he heard the whisper
and crackle of leaves as the animals scuttled away.
   ''Thanks,'' the Warlock said. ''I'll remember you.''

   ''The web. The eye. The Cygnet.''
   Nyx was pacing. Corleu, slumped in a chair, watched her.
It had taken him the rest of the night to return, and for what, he
wondered bitterly, as he climbed the shivering stairway near
dawn. What he sought was only tale. Just a story, a lie, to set
him moving, rousing all the sleeping powers in the Holds. The
thing was a dream, a lure to catch a Wayfolk fool, to trap his
thoughts, keep his eyes from seeing what his hands were waking.
   He said as much to Nyx. She stopped mid-step, looked at
him with her cold, searching, inscrutable eyes.
   ''If you think that, you are a fool. The thing itself is of more
power than what you are waking. Why else would it be so carefully hidden?''
   ''What's to be done, then?''
   ''Be quiet and let me think. . . .'' She paced barefoot, a
heavy gown of grey velvet swinging as she turned. She had been
awake all night, he judged; her eyes looked luminous, and her
temper was short. ''If these powers disturbed Ro House enough
to catch Meguet's eye, then that's where they all will gather. The
place where the Cygnet flies, day and night. That's the place of
power that draws them: Ro House. Tell me again.''
   He told her wearily, for the hundredth time. ''A secret at
the center of the web, over which Cygnet flies, day and night.
That was Blind Lady.''
   ''The Dancer.''
   ''The thing sought lies always in the same place, but always

in a different place, and that place is never far from the Cygnet.''

"The Warlock."

"The thing you seek will be reflected in the eye of the Cygnet.''

"Cygnet. Cygnet. Cygnet." She whirled, to contemplate him again, her arms folded, her mouth taut. "The thing you seek, Corleu, belongs to the Cygnet, I would guess. An ancient power that's waking other ancient powers. Not even Chrysom hinted of anything like this. I want it, as badly as I do not want the Gold King to keep it.''

"You're still not forcing me to tell you."

"That wouldn't be finding it, would it. You'd never see Tiel again, and you would hate me, and refuse to find this thing at all. Then we'd have chaos on our hands at Ro House. If not already. Ro House . . . A web. The Cygnet flying . . ." She stood still then, still as one of the carved, dead trees in the statue grove, her hands open at her sides, her head bowed, contemplating her reflection in the water. He couldn't hear her breathe. Finally he heard the statue speak. "The maze."

"What?"

She lifted her head, her face white, still. He had never seen such color in her eyes. "Chrysom's maze. The black tower. The Cygnet pennant that flies on the tower roof, summer, winter, day and night. The secret of where to find this thing is at the center of Chrysom's maze.''

"Where is that?" he asked wearily. "Where do I go this time?''

"To the house of the Holders of Ro Holding.''

2

M eguet stood at the edge of the lake beyond the thousand-year-old wood, watching the swans. Iris had brought the house back to the Delta; the swans, casting black and white shadows on the surface of the water, wove a tranquil dance among themselves. Used to flight, they seemed unsettled by the flight of Ro House. Meguet, drawn out of sleep by a dream of them, had slipped out at dawn. Every image in the dream, every word, had transformed itself into swan, until their elegant, masked, enigmatic faces had crowded into her mind. She had carried all their faces across the misty pastures, past the dark, dreaming wood. Finally, at the lake, the swans had shifted from her mind into her eyes: The great company clustered in the lake as usual, busily feeding. She felt her mind empty of them, grow still, peaceful.

A swan detached itself from the group in the middle of the lake. It glided toward the shore where Meguet stood. She watched it thoughtlessly. It was huge, as black as if it had flown straight out of midnight. Its smooth, steady drift toward her was soothing, almost a dream itself. It drew quite close, so close she could see the dark, steady gaze of its reflection. She blinked, surprised, for the swans kept to the far shore. It breasted the shallows, came on, its graceful head lifted as if to meet her eyes. Fully awake now, she watched it, not moving, not breathing. It stirred the muddy bottom, so close she might have touched it, or it her, extending its strong, quick, dangerous neck.

It roused so suddenly that she started. For a moment the air was black with feathers. Its wings beat; rising, it drew a wet wing tip across her lips. Darkness thundered around her, tangled in her hair. She caught her breath; lifting her face, she saw the sky again. Sunlight shot across the lake. She tasted lake water on her lips, felt it on her face. The great swan had vanished, like the night, into light.

She turned finally, startled, wondering. Sunlight raced across meadow, pasture, illumined the back towers, but could not reach across them to Chrysom's tower, still shrouded in its darkness. As she looked at it, wings filled her mind again: dark crow wings rustling with uneasiness.

In the west tower, all the kitchen chimneys were smoking. The first of the Hold Councils was due soon. A messenger, arriving to request a guide through the swamps for a Council, assorted family, curious kin, retinue, bag and baggage, had spent a night wondering where Ro House had gone. The house was back the next morning. Meguet, greeting the messenger, had seen him torn between asking and appearing lunatic. "Hunter Hold Council," he said, and the household bustled with preparations.

Meguet, walking into that tower in search of breakfast, found the Holder, surrounded by half the tower staff. She caught Meguet's eye, sent them all flying, and gestured Meguet into an antechamber.

It was a tiny room off the main tower door, close as a bear cave and chilly even in midsummer, with a double thickness of stone. Even the chairs were stone: ledges beside the fire, in the windowless walls. There Moro Ro had taken council with Chrysom, where not even a mouse could overhear without being seen.

The Holder swung the door to with a thud that cut short all sound. It was, Meguet thought, like being entombed.

"Tell me what you dreamed," the Holder said abruptly. She looked pale, edgy; Meguet tensed at the question.

"I dreamed of swans."

"Living or dead?"

She felt the blood leave her face. "Living."

"I dreamed all my children were dead." She turned, grabbed the poker, toppled the neatly burning pile of logs on the grate so that they nearly slid onto the floor. "Rush dreamed that Nyx had become something so terrible that he did not recognize her. He shouted at me this morning because I refused to let him ride upriver with you. If this is something—" She stopped, began again. "If this is something of Nyx's doing, I can't let him go there."

"No," Meguet said flatly, and the Holder looked at her, hope waging against suspicion in her eyes. "I would sooner suspect the Gatekeeper of intending harm to this house."

"Then what is troubling this house?" the Holder demanded, her voice rising in relief. "Even Iris was in tears this morning. Iris hasn't cried since she was two. I haven't even seen Calyx. She shut herself up in Chrysom's library."

"The Dancer is troubling this house. The Dreamer of Berg Hold. We brought her with us."

"But how? How did she get in? The Gatekeeper never left the gate, he never opened the gate—that was my command."

"I don't know." She rubbed her eyes wearily. "I don't know how she got in. Maybe she followed me off the mountain top. I couldn't even stop an unarmed Wayfolk man from getting away from me. How could I stop the Dancer?"

"You're supposed to know such things! It's your heritage, your duty to protect the Cygnet."

"I know," she whispered.

"Then, where were those in you who should advise you? Weren't you listening to them?"

"I thought—I thought so. Maybe I haven't learned how yet."

"You'd better learn fast. We have the Hunter Hold Council on our doorstep and a mad dreamer under our beds. What's next?"

"Worse," Meguet said tightly. The Holder's eyes widened. "What worse?"

"The Warlock."

The Holder pulled a pearl out of her hair and flung it across the room. "Send the Gatekeeper to me."

Meguet gave him the message, then sat in the turret, watching the gate and waiting for him. A company of hunters rode out; no one requested entry. The Gatekeeper returned soon, his face impassive. Meguet asked him, as he joined her:

"What did you dream?"

"Of you." He reached across, took her hands, warmed his own. "No good watching for the Warlock."

"Why not?"

"He'll get in. Like the Dancer, he'll come when he comes."

Meguet slumped back against the stones. "Did you tell the Holder that?"

"Yes."

"Did she believe you?"

"No. I told her Dancer must have danced herself over the wall, because I kept a lizard's eye on that gate night and day in Berg Hold. What did you dream?"

"Just swans."

He smiled his quick, tight smile. He leaned forward, kissed her gently. "Don't blame yourself so."

"If we hadn't gone to Berg Hold—"

"The Dancer would have come to us here." He watched her. "And if, and when the Warlock comes?"

She shuddered. "Don't say it. Words come to life, these days."

"What then? What are they gathering for, like crows on a carcass? What's in that maze but a wizard's time-picked bones?"

"It's a place to hide."

"For what? Until when?"

"I don't know!" she flared. "Don't push at me with questions, I am so tired of hearing that answer from myself. I don't know, I don't know, I don't know." He was silent; she raised her eyes finally, found a curious, dispassionate expression in his light eyes.

"You beg such questions," he said abruptly. "If only because you're the one in this house thinking for the house. And you get angry with me because I see that."

"I told you," she said helplessly, "I am part of this house. A lintel, a casement, a stone seat in a stone wall, some old walled-up grate that hasn't been on fire since Chrysom's time."

"A lintel." He pulled her hands to his mouth. "An old grate. A tower, more like. Chrysom's tower, strong, mysterious and covered with roses." He opened her hand against his mouth, said, breathlessly, head bowed, "Will I come to you, or will you come to me?"

"Come to me." She opened her other hand, laid it against her eyes. "At least in the tower you can see the gate."

"For whatever use."

"The Holder should send for Nyx."

He removed her ring finger from his mouth. "Nyx."

"She could fight a Warlock. She's a sorceress."

"And bog witch, which is of more use. They don't fight clean." He kissed the center of her palm, then relinquished her hand. "She's coming home for the Council. So I heard. Gossip about Nyx doesn't stand around idle."

"I think," Meguet said, "that won't be soon enough." She rose, edged past him. "We've given the yard enough to talk about this morning. I'm leaving tomorrow to ride upriver."

"With Rush Yarrow?"

"No. With an armed guard. I want that Wayfolk man. He's the one who can answer questions."

"When will you leave?"

"At dawn."

"So," he said, meeting her eyes. "Meguet."

A swan wing, glistening, crossed her mind. She said, "Midnight."

She rode across the yard the next morning with twenty of the household guard behind her, all in black, with a black, silken pennant flying overhead. The Gatekeeper, crossing in front of her to open the gate, looked up at her briefly. She saw night in his eyes, swamp leaves, secret, wind-stirred pools. His thoughts dragged at her; she closed her eyes, set her face resolutely toward the gate. Behind her eyes were moving, fire-edged shadows. A silver goblet spilled wine over white fur. She heard the gate open. She rode forward mechanically, her eyes on the road between the gateposts, where the Gatekeeper, moving, laid his shadow across her path.

Slowed as they were by spring-swollen ground, by water flooded with storm-pushed tides and snow melting in the upper lands, they reached Nyx's house at mid-morning two days later. It looked more shrunken than mysterious in the spring light. Vines tugged at it here and there, threatening to encroach beneath a window sash, to pull off a corner beam. A motley gathering of old boats set the company on the dock. Meguet took two guards with her; they climbed the stairs cautiously.

Nyx came out to meet them on the porch. She looked dishevelled, dressed in threadbare velvet; her long dark hair fell untidily past her waist. Her face was pale, lean, smudged with tiredness and what looked like old ashes. She said, frowning:

"Meguet." She cast a glance at the group on the dock, and her frown grew pinched. "If you've come for me, that's far too many for courtesy, and far too few to do any good. I told you I would return home in spring."

"If I had come for you," Meguet said evenly, "I would have come alone. And unarmed. I have come for the Wayfolk man."

"Why?"

"The Holder wishes to see him."

"The Wayfolk man is gone."

"Gone where?"

"He stepped through his circle of time. He might have gone anywhere."

"He might have." Nyx's colorless eyes met hers, expressionless. "He might have gone upriver. He might have gone into a room in this rambling, changing, shifting house. He might have—"

Nyx's eyes narrowed. "How do you know this house shifts itself?"

"I came back to spy on you."

"Really." She drew breath. "Really, Meguet. You do take chances. Did it ever occur to you that wandering around in a bog witch's house might be dangerous?"

"Has it occurred to you yet that the Wayfolk man is dangerous? I came back that night when I saw you last, for only one reason: I looked at him and was warned."

Nyx was silent. She pushed her hair back from her face absently, studying Meguet. "You never even spoke to him."

"I know."

"You saw him last in Berg Hold. He told me."

"Yes. I came for him then. He disappeared into silver."

"That was the Ring of Time. He stepped through it again two days ago. I cannot tell you where he went."

"And why did he leave you so precipitously?"

"He is only Wayfolk," Nyx said. "My work must have troubled him."

"He stayed with you a long time before it troubled him."

"Did my mother instruct you to question me?"

"She instructed me to find Corleu. I will find him."

Nyx's eyes flickered, a touch of color in them. "You even know his name."

"Yes."

"He is Wayfolk. Powerless."

"He made a Ring of Time. He wakes power wherever he goes. And those powers are disturbing Ro House. I want him. Let me search the house."

Nyx did not move. She said softly, "Meguet. You must not stand between the Wayfolk man and those powers."

"Someone must," Meguet said tautly. "Will you? Where do you stand? With the Wayfolk man, with those powers, or with Ro House?"

"I stand for myself," Nyx said sharply and stood aside.

Meguet beckoned the guard up from the dock. She went first into the house. When she passed through the hallway, she heard Nyx's cold voice behind her: "Stop."

She held one arm across the door. Meguet waited, poised for anything from Nyx: charm, nightmare, a moment's private conversation. Nyx spoke privately to the air. "These belong to the woman who entered. You will not harm them."

She dropped her arm, turned away, letting the guards enter. Meguet's skin prickled. "Who were you talking to?"

"My doorkeepers. They guard me, day and night. They never sleep. No one passes them without my permission." She put her hands on Meguet's shoulders, held her lightly. Her eyes seemed enormous, mist-cold. "Except you, my cousin Meguet. Except you. I have often wondered why." She loosed her, as the guard, taking the stairs cautiously, began to file in. "Search."

"The rooms in the house shift constantly," Meguet said to the guard. "Don't let it alarm you. If you get lost, you will be found."

"By what?" someone wondered dourly.

"I will find you." Nyx glanced at her sharply. She said no more, led the way through the single door opening out of the workroom. The hearth had been cold, she noticed, empty even of ashes. The air smelled only of a slight cellar damp. *Nyx*, she thought, *is leaving.* The guard separated, opened other doors, scattered themselves through rambling corridors, where the threads of time frayed and broke and knit again. Meguet wandered with them until she was alone, in a room empty but for a great loom, the thread in the shuttle a color not used before.

She opened the only door in that room, wanting one room, expecting one room, and found it: the room full of mirrors. She felt a sudden chill down the corridor, like a wind from a broken window, or the swift turn of a sorceress's attention. She closed the door abruptly. All the mirrors were black.

"Meguet!" The door latch rattled, the door shook. "Meguet!"

She did not answer. Standing in the middle of the room, she watched the mirrors. All her thoughts were focused on one thing. The house heard her, showed it to her: the Cygnet in flight in all of its eyes.

They darkened again. *Corleu,* she thought, holding his face in her mind. *You saw where he went from this house. You heard. Show me.*

Others watched in her; she sensed their sudden waking interest, alert to her focused attention. They had watched him from the first, she realized then, before she even knew them. They had pulled her back into Nyx's house, to hear his voice, listen for his name. The Wayfolk man was the danger to the Cygnet.

Fire flared in the heart of each dark mirror. A hand held the fire. The flame moved slowly, revealed a slab of marble, a lion's paw, a gryphon's eye. The flame shifted across the mirrors, across the dark between walls. Travelling, it illumined, briefly, a Wayfolk face.

"Meguet!" There was a shock of noise that should have broken the door. But Meguet, intent on the mirrors, held the door firm with nothing more, it seemed, than blind desire, and the old house strained to do her bidding. The blood had washed from her face; she could not move, she could scarcely breathe. The Wayfolk man had stepped through time into Chrysom's maze.

The mirrors shook around her. The walls of the room shuddered, undulated. She whispered drily, "Not yet. Not yet," and they held, as if the hands of all the ghosts of her ancestors stood with the ghosts of the house to buttress them.

Faces formed under the flickering light: brightly masked, half-human, half-animal. The flame moved from one carved, motionless face to the next. Meguet put her hands to her mouth, made a sound, another. He had found his way to the center of the maze.

"How?" she shouted furiously, and found no answer within herself, only a strange, watchful silence. "How?"

"Meguet!"

She turned, flung herself against the trembling door, felt the power threatening it, pushing inward against it, beating through her, like a heart, like wings. "Who is he? Nyx, who is he?"

He stood in the dark, surrounded by statues, in the small, empty chamber that all passages but one led away from. He had found the one passage. But he could not breach time itself. He turned in the dark, she saw from the changing light, like one uncertain. "He cannot," she whispered through dry lips. "He cannot go within time." The door bucked, throwing her. "Nyx!" she cried, still watching, as she picked herself up. "Nyx!"

"Meguet!"

She clung to the door again, felt a thousand years of power within her shielding the door to watch Corleu. "Who is he? Nyx, who is the Wayfolk man?"

"He said he is kin!"

"Kin to what?"

"To you! Meguet, what are you?"

Meguet closed her eyes. The door exploded inward with a sound like all the sorrows of the house. It flung her against a mirror, and then into the mirror. For an instant she saw room after room in the overburdened house torn by the conflict of powers in it. Walls and corners drew together, flattening; walls shrank. Ghosts thinned like spun thread. Guards tumbled, crying out soundlessly, terrified. Then they merged into wood, into warped glass. Meguet screamed, "No!" She felt glass against her mouth, glass tears falling from her eyes. Then the glass itself spun and spun toward nothing. Dimly, she heard it shatter.

She sat up slowly, amid an odd debris: a few rotten boards, a pink shoe, a pair of spectacles, a broken cauldron. She was sitting on bare, muddy ground where the house had stood. As if they felt the weight of her gaze, the ancient stairs gave up their hold on the leafless shrubs, slid with a dry clatter, like a pile of old bones, onto the dock. The drowned ghost stood up in her boat, staring upward under her hand. She vanished quite suddenly. So, inexplicably, did her boat. Guards in torn, mud-streaked uniforms pulled themselves upright, looking sour. Nyx, surrounded by a pile of old books and some broken jars, stirred near Meguet. She turned on her side, wincing. A book slid down the hillside, hit the river and floated.

She followed it a moment with her eyes. "Chrysom's," she said wearily. "They are indestructible." She sat up, brushed old leaves out of her hair, then surveyed the destruction she and Meguet had wrought between them. She turned her head finally to stare at her cousin. "What exactly are you?"

Meguet slid her hands over her face, as much to evade that sudden, intense scrutiny, as to try to contain the headache that was rioting behind her eyes. "Desperate." Her voice shook badly. "Nyx, what is the Wayfolk man doing in Chrysom's maze?"

"Looking for something."

Meguet dropped her hands, feeling the thousand-year-old fear like some icy wind, blowing off a place the sun never touched. Nyx's eyes, catching at hers, seemed the color of that wind. "Looking for what?" she asked sharply.

The force of Nyx's attention lessened finally. "He never told me. He is under duress not to tell. Something of Chrysom's, I would guess, of great, secret power he may have hidden in the maze. Except that . . ."

"Except?"

"Not even Chrysom had power like yours," Nyx said simply. Meguet, staring back at her, felt the chill again: this time, oddly, not an ancient fear for the Cygnet, but one a small night-hunter might feel for its bones, at owl wings darkening the moon. She got up too abruptly, had to quell the brawling in her head.

"It was only your power," she said recklessly, "seeped into that crazed old house. I could not cast a spell of my own to save my life." She counted heads swiftly, saw with relief that no one had been rendered into glass and framed. She held out a hand to Nyx. "We're getting no farther than nowhere, sitting in the mud."

For a moment it seemed the hand grasping hers was of stone, and the weight she pulled at was the stone-tortoise's ponderous, time-burdened shell. "There are two things of great power in Ro House that I never knew existed," Nyx said softly. "One is hidden in that maze. The other is you. If you will not tell me,

Meguet, I will find out what you know, how you know it. One way or another, I will find out.''

White, mute, she set her teeth, pulled against Nyx's grasp. Nyx, rising suddenly, nearly sent them both tumbling down the hillside. "Please.'' She freed herself from Nyx's hold. Her fists were clenched; the river blurred. "Please,'' she whispered. "Just come home. Help us.''

The Gatekeeper found them a day or two later, trailing the twilight into the gate, a bedraggled company that caused him to lose his habitual impassivity.

"Lady Nyx,'' he said, helping her dismount from behind Meguet. "Welcome.'' Nyx, barefoot as the house had left her, grunted sourly as her foot hit a stone.

"Hew,'' she said. She gestured a stableboy toward the great sack of books another rider carried. Then she folded her arms over her worn, archaic, velvet gown and surveyed the towers. "At least the house is still standing.''

The Gatekeeper held Meguet's stirrup. She dismounted wearily, her face stiff. She could not smile at him; she could not even speak, until he touched her gently, as to help balance her, and then she could look at him, let him calculate the impossible distance the hand's-breadth between them was. His hand rose toward her cheek, cupped air, dropped.

"You had a rough journey,'' he breathed. She nodded, looking away from him until she could answer steadily.

"It isn't over yet. Did the Hunter Hold Council arrive?''

"Not a sign of them. They'll be a few days crossing the swamp. Lady Nyx, do you want a mount to ride to the towers?''

She shook her head. "I'd rather crawl, after that ride. I'm used to walking barefoot.'' She took a step and stumbled, grasping at Meguet to keep her balance. Brows pinched in pain, she turned up a dirty foot. Blood welled across it.

She eased down, still clinging to Meguet, and picked up the glass she had stepped on. "What is this?'' she asked, and Meguet tensed at the sharpness in her voice.

She took it from Nyx; red, it was, with curved, jagged edges. "It looks like part of a glass cup,'' she said, puzzled. "A hollow ball of some kind. Why—''

"One of the juggler's,'' the Gatekeeper said shortly. "I missed it, lying there. I beg your pardon, my—''

"What juggler?" Nyx interrupted. Meguet stared at him. "You let a stranger in the gate?"

"Not that I know," he said, and she saw how his eyes had darkened with weariness, and the skin hugged the sharp bones of his face. "Unless he slid like a shadow under the gate. I took him for a cottager, juggling for the children. Smith, by the look of his shoulders."

"You don't know him," she whispered, cold. "You don't know his name."

He hesitated. He put his hand to his eyes and said tiredly, "I never saw his face. Only his back and his juggling. Always those red glass balls. If he is a stranger, I don't know how he got in."

"You said it: a shadow under the gate." Nyx took the glass from Meguet, dropped it. It shattered into fine sand, lay sparkling in the torchlight. "He is no stranger," she said grimly. "He's the Warlock with a heart of glass, and he has just laid blood across this threshold."

Corleu sat in the center of the maze. The mage-fire he had made and carried through time into the maze burnt on bare stone in front of him. Other fires he had not made lit the strange statues circling him. Their eyes, slitted like goat or cat, painted unexpected colors, seemed to watch him.

The Dancer leaned among them, sometimes putting on one of their nightmare faces. The tinker sat next to Corleu, sharing bread and cheese, or providing it from somewhere, since he ate little but a bread crumb now and then. The Blind Lady sat mumbling names to herself, weaving from an underskirt of muddy linen. The juggler paced. Sometimes his shadow, pacing over Corleu, was the Blood Fox's.

"It's here," the tinker said patiently. He broke more bread off a loaf, passed it to Corleu. "I can feel it."

"Thread ends here," the Blind Lady said. She cocked her head at some mysterious trembling in time, and found a dangling thread in her sleeve. She snapped it abruptly; Corleu jerked. "Time, for that one."

"I can smell it," the Warlock said, standing over Corleu.

He dropped his hands on Corleu's shoulders, and sniffed at the air above the fire. "Mage-fire," he said.

"I made it."

"I know. But who taught you?"

"My great-gran," he said recklessly, and the Warlock grinned his fox's grin.

"Great-gran taught you to make the Ring of Time," the Dancer said. She turned a scarlet face to him among the shadows, with gold-rimmed eyes and delicate gold cat's ears. She settled her long, lissome body along a statue. "I heard Great-gran's dreams. I danced in them. White-haired man among the corn she dreamed, now and then, all her life. Her last dream was of green corn. I was kind to Great-gran. She never dreamed the Ring of Time."

"She was Wayfolk," the Blind Lady said, chuckling. "They see into time in little toad hops. A morsel of future here, there. Never great daylong strides of it."

"Did Great-gran teach you to make my heart?" the Warlock marvelled. His fingers dug painfully into Corleu's shoulders, then let go suddenly. He paced again. Corleu chewed stolidly, his mouth dry.

"Great-gran," he said, swallowing with an effort, "had odd talents."

"You take after her, then," the tinker said, passing him a water skin. "Thirsty? What other talents did Great-gran have?"

"She could read. She gave my granda books. Odd books, with odd things in them."

"Many odd things," the Warlock agreed, turning noiselessly on bare feet. "A wizard's blood in amber, for instance," Corleu, tilting the water skin, lowered it without drinking. He met the Warlock's eyes a moment; they were smoky amber red. He lifted the skin again, drank.

"You owe me," he said shortly. "You all do. I promised to find what I would find, not loose you into the world."

"You haven't found it," the tinker commented, carving a sliver of cheese with his knife.

"I'm near enough. I found the place."

"We found it before you."

He was silent, swallowing bitterness with his bread. "So," he said to the tinker, "you knew this place all along. You only needed me to wake your friends. If you know so much, you don't need me now. You can find the Cygnet's heart by yourself.''

Hissing, the Warlock was behind him again, one hand over his mouth, the other tightening over his throat. The tinker put a finger to his lips.

"Things listen, in here.''

Corleu heard only the blood drumming in his ears. The Warlock loosed him finally; he sagged forward, blinking, until the darkening fire burned bright again.

"I made your heart,'' he said hoarsely. "You said you would be grateful.''

"I smell a trap,'' the Warlock growled. "I smell sorcery.''

"What sorcery could stand up to you when I find this thing for you?''

"What sorcery?'' the tinker said genially. "You can answer that one.'' Corleu picked up bread silently. "You won't answer.'' He cocked a brow at the Dancer. "What sorcerers have been dreaming of this thing we want?''

She discarded her mask, let her face flow into various faces. Nyx's face came and went quickly; Corleu froze mid-bite, then chewed again, expressionless. "None dreaming,'' the Dancer said, "not of this.''

"Of him?''

"Only one,'' she said smiling, "still dreaming. Like me, before you woke me.'' She wore Tiel's face. Corleu caught his breath on a bread crumb.

"Easy,'' the tinker said, pounding on his back, handing him the water.

"I told—I told no one.''

"Not even Great-gran? Not even whispered to her grave? Not even to a green stalk of corn?''

"No one.''

"Then who taught you?'' the Warlock demanded. "Whose sorcery brought us awake?''

"You wanted that,'' Corleu said tersely. "You wanted freedom. I couldn't do it without learning somewhere, from someone. You said find it. I chose how.''

"Silver Ring of Time is a powerful magic.''

"So are you. I couldn't free things of power without power.''

"What did you pay this teacher?''

"Nothing.''

"What did you promise?"

"What does it matter?" he said. "It's my promise, my payment. Nothing to do with you."

They were silent, looking at one another, even the Blind Lady, casting about with her fallen eyes.

"He paid for sorcery," the tinker said, "with nothing we need worry about." He cocked a brow around the chamber, then regarded Corleu, hand rasping at the dark stubble on his cheeks.

"What would Wayfolk pay with?" the Dancer asked. "All they own is time."

"A man searching for treasure could promise that in payment," the Warlock said, prowling the edge of the light. His eyes flared at Corleu. "Did you?" Corleu stared back at him. He turned to the tinker.

"You didn't pay me for this," he said. The Warlock snarled beyond the fire, then barked the Blood Fox's attack, and he felt the cold sweat break on his face. But he kept his eyes steady on the tinker, who smiled a faint, thin smile.

"Wayfolk. Always one for a bargain." He waved a remonstrating hand at the Warlock. "You should be a little grateful."

"I'll be grateful," the Warlock said with a snap of teeth, "when he finds this."

"You owe me," Corleu said baldly, "not just tinker, you all do." He reached for the knife, his hand trembling in the shadows. "You told me ask for myself."

The Warlock, snarling, leaped over the fire. Corleu jumped to his feet, the knife in his hand. A blood fox's weight crashed against him, bore him back against one of the statues. Its orange lizard's face smiled over his shoulder, its cloven hand pushed into his backbone. The knife burned like a coal in his hand; he dropped it, crying out, and heard it shatter like glass on the stones. A blood fox's eyes looked into his, feral, furious.

"You alone in this. Not with some faceless mage behind you. Who is it?"

The tinker chuckled. "Don't eat him. We need him yet. Who, Corleu?"

"You may not need to know." He stopped, catching his breath; the Blood Fox eyes still glared into his, all he could see. "Ever. How could—how could anyone threaten you, once you have it?"

The Dancer pirouetted along the statues, turning herself
gracefully from embrace to embrace until she brought herself
against Corleu. She put her hand on his hair, murmured against
his mouth, "But how will we know who to protect, if we are
threatened?" Her face became green suddenly, with fierce blue
oval eyes and a sharp raven's beak. He jerked his head back,
banged it against the stones. She laughed.

"Pass the knife," the tinker asked politely, "if you're done
with it."

The Warlock loosed Corleu slowly. He bent, growling,
picked up shards of glass and flung them to the tinker. They
reshaped in the air; the tinker picked the knife out of it, cut more
cheese.

The Dancer turned across Corleu, continued her dance. Corleu slid down to the feet of the statue, closed his eyes.

"Now," he heard the tinker say, "let's begin again. You
want something more for your pains. For the worry and trouble.
That seems fair. We told you you might want more. But here is
the point we stick at, Corleu. There's the small matter of the
thing itself." He cocked an eye up at the painted Cygnet flying
across the small round ceiling, then down at the floor. "Even
Wayfolk know not to barter with air. You find this small thing.
Then ask."

Corleu looked at him, wondering if any Wayfolk in all history had ever strayed down such a mysterious path to end sitting
in the dark beneath the Holder's house, surrounded by tales come
alive and speaking. He said slowly, "You knew this place before
I did. Why do you need me now? You gave me pieces of the
puzzle. Is that all the pieces you have? If it's not here, I don't
know where to look. I don't have your magic. You could find it
easily as me, now."

"It's here," the Blind Lady murmured, and snapped another
thread absently. The tinker's yellow eyes smiled their faint, glint-
ing smile.

"Another fine point. But so easily answered, you answer."

"You can't find it without me." He shook his head, bewildered, as the tinker's smile broadened. "I'm Wayfolk," he
protested. "That means back roads, herb magic, no corners.
Ignorance, field dirt, living and dying in a wagon. I'm nothing.
If you want me for more than my feet and hands, there's little
to find. Why me? Why me to find it?" They were silent. The

tinker gazed into the fire; the Dancer beside a statue imitated its distant stare. The Blind Lady picked at thread; the Warlock picked a red glass ball out of a gryphon's mouth, set it flaming in a niche in the wall. Corleu's hands closed tightly. "You do need me," he breathed. "So I have more than air to barter with." The Warlock's face flashed toward him, snarling, but noiselessly, and he did not move. The tinker picked his teeth thoughtfully with the knife.

"It's an unusual position to bargain from. You alone can find this thing. But you don't know how to get at it."

"Hear him," the Dancer murmured. "It costs nothing. And it may amuse." She strayed to Corleu, traced his ear with her thumb. "What more does the Wayfolk man want? A house? A palace?"

"I don't like walls."

"Wealth?"

"Wayfolk can't count. They use coins for buttons."

"A sorcercr's power?"

"I've had a bellyful of sorcery."

"Knowledge?"

"I'm getting that, just breathing."

"Then what, Corleu?" the tinker asked. His smile was gone; his voice had thinned. He tossed the knife in the air, caught it. For a moment, wheeling in the firelight, it turned gold. Corleu's hands clenched; he looked at them blindly, testing the demand silently, against the straight doorposts and towers, the safety of the ancient house above his head.

"I want," he said, "a promise. That no harm will come to the one who helped me, or to her house, or to any who know her name."

There was dead silence from the gathering he had wakened; they gazed at him, remote and eerie as the statues around him.

Behind him, the statue he leaned against seemed to shift.

Meguet and Nyx entered Chrysom's tower. Nyx had paused to heal her foot, standing in the middle of the yard, with one hand on Mcguet's arm. No one greeted her; no one stared; no one, Meguet found bemusedly, noticed either of them. Then she saw the yard as from another angle, a world without them, and she said, feeling an odd mingling of uneasiness and freedom: "Have you made us invisible?"

"For a moment," Nyx answered absently. "Just until we reach Chrysom's tower. I have things to do; I don't want to be distracted."

"You will see the Holder first."

"No."

Meguet caught her breath. "Nyx, she has waited years!" Nyx's grip on her tightened slightly; she stared down at the dark head, hair swept impatiently behind one ear, what she could see of the pale, lean face quiet, absorbed in work. Nyx answered finally:

"She will be here when I have finished. If I don't begin, neither she nor I may be here in the end."

"And if you don't return from the maze? You will not go to her first, even to let her see your face? Nyx Ro, that is cruel."

Nyx straightened, tested her foot on the bare ground. "I haven't your warmth," she said, "which you extend so unexpectedly. Even to Gatekeepers, apparently. Even to me." She added, at Meguet's silence, the ghost of a smile touching her mouth, "Hew, I can understand. But you use so carelessly, at times, something that to me is simply another source of power."

"Love?" She felt the blood in her face, a confusion of anger and helplessness, as if she were without arms or armor in some vital battle. But the word touched Nyx; her eyes flickered, following a thought.

"Not even Chrysom suggested that as a source of power," she commented. "It's an interesting thought. I only meant that you allow yourself to be distracted by so many small things. To focus power you must first focus your attention."

"I am," Meguet said shortly. "It's all in that maze. If you are finished."

"First I must go to Chrysom's library."

"Moro's eyes! We have no time! If you haven't learned it by now, you don't need it."

"But I do." She looked at Meguet, her eyes distant, unreadable. "There is something vital in that library. I will need it in the maze. It may save our lives."

Meguet hesitated. Her attention drained inward, to the still, secret place where a great prism hung in darkness. She sensed disturbance in a layer of time around it, but, so far, it was itself undisturbed.

"All right," she said tensely. "But hurry."

In the library, she paced, picking bog leaf out of her hair and rebraiding it. Nyx searched through books, letting pages dance through her fingers, a mysterious task which spun Meguet's calm to a fine, frayed thread.

"Nyx," she breathed. "We must go." Nyx did not answer. She closed a book, opened another. Meguet closed her eyes, turned on her heel. Her hands fell to her sides, clenched. She forced them open. Nothing had happened, yet. Nothing, yet... "Nyx."

"Be patient," Nyx murmured. "In matters of sorcery there's nothing more dangerous than haste."

"What are you looking for?"

"A puzzle piece."

Meguet drew breath, held it. She listened to the silence a few more minutes. Then she wheeled, went to the door, opened it. She got Nyx's attention then.

"Where are you going?"

"Down. Catch up with me."

"Wait, Meguet. Please wait. We may lose each other in the maze."

"Will you at least let me send word to the Holder?"

"The guards must have told her by now." She waited, her eyes on Meguet, looking faintly troubled, until Meguet's hold on the latch loosened. She resumed reading. Meguet stood gazing at the half-open door. She closed it finally, leaned against it, head and shoulder against the wood as if she might hear voices from far below carried upward through the ancient stones.

"Rydel." Nyx's flat voice nearly made her start. She closed a book sharply. "Secret powers. Powers not to be known. To be used only for Ro Holding." Meguet turned incredulously to face her. "Rydel," Nyx reminded her, "was your ancestor. Chrysom himself, Timor Ro said, stood in her shadow." She took a step toward Meguet, her eyes wide, speculative. "The enormous powers of the mage Chrysom were overshadowed by the powers of Timor Ro's eccentric gardener. That's how you could walk past my doorkeepers."

"Your doorkeepers," Meguet whispered. Then she heard herself shout, an unfamiliar sound. "Nyx, what are you doing wasting time reading about gardening? This house is in danger!"

"Gardening is not at issue, and the acquisition of knowledge is never a waste of time. You stood against me in my house.

You. My cousin Meguet, who could never find your way through a book, let alone a spell. I want to know how. I want to know before we go into the maze. I want to take this thing Corleu is searching for, and I need power. Power like Rydel's. Like yours."

Meguet stared at her, stunned. She whirled abruptly. "You stay and look for it, then. I'm going down." She wrenched the door so hard it should have swung back to boom against the stones. Instead it pulled her off balance, brought her up hard against it.

She leaned into the wood after a moment, her heart pounding. "Nyx."

"Open it."

"I can't!"

"You could fight me in my house."

"I wasn't fighting you! I was watching! I can't—"

"Open the door."

"I can't use those powers at will!" She stopped, appalled at what she had relinquished: an ancient privacy, a secret between Holder and Guardian. But it had already been relinquished, by consent, in Nyx's house. She stood quietly then, her face against the wood, calming herself out of long habit, as for a bout. She turned finally, trembling slightly, her face white, feeling unskilled and clumsy at battles of will instead of movement. She said softly, waiting for an inner uproar of voices that did not come, "The powers are ancient. I may use them for one purpose. Only one purpose. I can't use them at my own need. They are kept always secret, and through some generations they are never used."

"Power is power," Nyx said. She stood as calm as the stone Cygnet carved above her head, unfamiliar, suddenly, as if her own past in that room, in that house, could no longer lay claim to her. "It can be worked with, changed, manipulated, shaped in whatever ways you choose. I only need to know its source."

The black prism, the Cygnet's eye, formed in Meguet's mind. She said, trying to find Nyx in the dangerous stranger in front of her, "The source itself is ancient. I obtained power by being born, only that. It is my heritage. And but what for you and the Wayfolk man have wakened, I might have lived and died without using it."

"Use it now. You can. Open the door."

"I can't. The power is not mine to summon."

"It could be. Only learn how. If the need is there, the power will come. You know that yourself. Desperation spawns power. Open the door."

The Cygnet's eye was still dark, untroubled, in its secret rings of time. . . . She shook her head, not trusting herself to speak further, for desperation would spawn nothing more magical than anger and anger was a beggar's blade. Without moving, it seemed, Nyx stood in front of her. She laid her hands against the door, on either side of Meguet's face. Her eyes, misty, unblinking, drew at Meguet.

"There must have been a place where you first knew your powers. A moment in time when you first recognized them for what they are. When was the time? Where is the place?" Meguet turned her face away; Nyx lifted one hand from the door, turned it back gently to meet her gaze. "Tell me."

"I cannot," she whispered.

"Why? Who stops you? What?"

Meguet closed her eyes, shaking with anger. In one of her lithe, skilled movements, she had ducked away from Nyx, put distance, mentally and physically between them in this peculiar battle, before Nyx realized she had moved.

But she had not: She had only thought the movement. She was still backed against the door, pinned under Nyx's gaze, with the anger in her turning into a nightmarish panic. She tried again to move. Her voice broke away from her in terror.

"Nyx, I can't—"

"You can move. If you choose. Find the way."

"How can you do this to me, how can you—"

"Don't panic. Find the power. Use the source."

"It is not—I cannot—it is not mine to use!"

"It is yours. Take it. Have the courage to take. To use."

"You don't understand—You think you know so much, you understand nothing."

"What? What don't I understand?"

"How to know without using."

"Power is to be known, is to be used, is even to be shared. You must share this knowledge with me, Meguet. It might save my life. If that, at this particular moment, does not move you, then think of the safety of this house. I can help, but you must help me.''

"Nyx—'' She could not even blink; she felt as immobile as one of the strange statues in the maze. She could only speak, and her voice shook badly. ''You have brought your swamp ways into this house. The power does not belong to me. If even the thought of using it so crossed my heart, I would lose it. Do you think I would risk my own heritage only because I can't move a finger or open a door? Ask me what my heart is worth to me, or my life. Then make me an offer. Ask me." Nyx, a hair-fine line between her brows, said nothing, waited. Meguet's breath caught suddenly, painfully; she was going to cry, in sheer frustration, she realized furiously, and she could not even wipe away her own tears, or turn her face to hide them. "I never judged you before," she whispered. "I never knew the things you know. It seemed that what you sought might be worth a long journey, a stay in the desert, a lonely life, even the life of an animal or two. But now I judge you. I know you as the small birds know you. You cut out their tongues so they cannot speak, you cut off their wings so they cannot fly. They look at you and know you. You make what you are. When you burn their hearts, it is your own heart burning in the fire."

Color flared into Nyx's face. Her eyes seemed enormous, luminous. The door latch rattled suddenly and she started. She pushed herself away from the door.

"Nyx!" It was the Holder. "Open the door!"

She pounded on it impatiently. Meguet, freed suddenly, turned her whole body, hid her face against the wood. She reached out, at the insistent pounding, pulled the door open with shaking hands. The Holder stood on the threshold, looking at the lank-haired, barefoot woman whose back was turned to her. "Nyx?" she said tentatively. "The Gatekeeper told me you had come."

Nyx turned slowly, met her mother's eyes. They were both silent then, their faces reflecting the same faint surprise at the still unbroken bond between them. The Holder spoke first, her voice soft, shaken:

"Nyx." She looked at Meguet then, her eyes suddenly vulnerable, haunted. "You went upriver for the Wayfolk man. Not Nyx. Not now."

"The Wayfolk man is here," Nyx said.

"Here! Where?"

"In Chrysom's maze. He came to look for something."

The Holder's face whitened. "What is he looking for in my house?"

"I don't know. He never told me. He is coerced. I promised him help. That's why I came back with Meguet. We are going together into the maze—"

"No," the Holder said sharply. "Meguet will go. I don't want you in danger."

Nyx paused, looked at her oddly, a touch of color in her eyes. Then she linked her hands tightly together; her brows pinched. She answered carefully, "Meguet will need help."

"Meguet may need help, but—"

"Mother, I did not spend nine years wandering Ro Holding for no reason. Almost nothing can stand against me. Almost nothing. And I promised—"

"I don't care what you promised the Wayfolk man and I don't care if you can harry Chrysom himself out of his tomb, I want you here with me. Or better yet, out of this house. Go back to the swamp."

Nyx's eyes narrowed. "I thought you wanted me out of the swamp. Your fey third daughter eating toads under a full moon, causing gossip across four Holds—"

"Then, take that as a reason to be sent back to the swamp," the Holder said sharply. "Better there than here. This house is not safe."

"That is why I came back. To deal with the danger. When I have done that, I will be gone. If that is what you want."

The Holder closed her eyes. "Moro's name. I have wanted you home for nine years. Now I want you home tomorrow. Not now."

"Why?" Nyx asked, and answered herself, coldly, evenly. "You don't trust me. You don't know me anymore. You don't know anymore which daughter is yours: the one who lived so innocently among the witches, or the one who dwelled among bones in the swamp. Which one will go into the maze? Which will fight in this house?"

The Holder was silent; Meguet saw the confusion of anguish and guilt in her eyes. So did Nyx; her head bowed slightly, away from her mother's expression. She added softly,

"There is only one way for you to find out. You must let me go into that maze."

The Holder's face looked pale, brittle as the pearls she twisted between her fingers. "No," she said. "For many reasons." Nyx did not move, or change expression, but Meguet, watching her, felt something twist in her own heart.

She said abruptly, "Nyx is right. I will need her with me."

The Holder turned to her, startled. "Meguet, no. You cannot take her. She has only a mage's powers."

"And at this moment, I have none at all." She paused. She had fought back tears, but her face was colorless, and her voice unsteady with anger and shock. The Holder said sharply:

"What's wrong?"

Meguet's shoulders straightened, lined to the stones at her back. Nyx gazed at her expressionlessly, asking nothing, forcing nothing. Meguet said evenly, "Everything is wrong. I keep blundering a step behind the Wayfolk man. I could not stop him in Berg Hold, I missed him in the swamp, and I may well miss him again unless I get into that maze. If it is only sorcery to be dealt with in the maze, I will have only a sword to fight it. I will be helpless without Nyx."

The Holder drew breath, her eyes flicking between them. The strand in her fingers broke suddenly; pearls ran like mice at her feet. She threw the last of them down.

"Then go," she said huskily to Nyx. She did not look at her daughter. "If you do not return, you will break my heart."

They were nearly at the foot of the tower stairs before Nyx spoke. "You could have told her. I thought you would. It would have been just. And," she added dispassionately, "she has already judged me."

"I fight my own battles," Meguet said shortly. "And I may well need you. I have no idea what is down there in the dark by now."

"I do not mean to harass you." She touched Meguet's arm lightly and for a breath, once again, Meguet froze, so precariously balanced between steps that if Nyx had shifted a finger she would have tumbled headlong to the floor. She felt the dark anger beat like insect wings in the back of her throat, in her wrists. "I only want to understand you, and the great secret power that uses you. I want to see its face."

*   *   *

In the heart of the tower, Corleu saw the small chamber he sat in waver around him. The fires went out, hiding the still faces of both stone and the living. Time closed over him like water. A globe lit the room now, silver-green, hanging from the center of the ceiling above a marble effigy and tomb.

The stone statues began to move.

4

The tomb guardians, colorful and fierce, prowling silently around the tomb on their half-human legs, the black stone effigy itself, of a tall old man frowning faintly, it looked, at the doings in the tower, impressed Corleu fully but briefly. His eyes kept returning to the globe.

Just a light, his brain told him. But his hands wanted to hold it; he wanted to see into it. Nothing in it but a green-white mage-flame, his eyes told him, but his attention fluttered around it like some frantic moth. *There,* he wanted to say, *there.* But it wasn't there.

"Nothing there but fire," the tinker said. Corleu dragged his eyes from it finally, turning. He opened his mouth to answer, then could not, stunned finally in that chamber full of wonders.

The Gold King stood in his gold spiked armor, masked in gold, crowned with the seven gold stars of his house. The edges of his scabbard rippled like flame. The chain he dragged went just so far across the marble floor, then simply stopped in the middle of a link, as if it continued elsewhere, in another chamber, perhaps, or somewhere among the stars.

Behind him the Warlock, dressed in the black of his night-shadow, juggled the stars that limned the shadow, and the one red star that was his heart.

"We're close," he said. His red-furred, feral face looked intent, watchful, the blood fox scenting the hunters, perhaps, or the prey. It was an ancient expression, Corleu thought suddenly, seeing the first blood fox in the Delta waiting, wide-eyed, still, for what it smelled flying low over the swamps on the wind.

His heart pounded. There was too much power. Tinker, he had told Nyx; old blind beggar woman. The Blind Lady wore peacock feathers from throat to foot. Her long black hair tumbled away from a delicate oval face. Her eyes were closed, a faint frown between her brows. Her ringed hand wove threads of palest silver; like the Gold King's chain, they stopped short in the air, continued elsewhere. Her face was so calm she seemed elsewhere as well, but she spoke. "A little farther, Wayfolk man. Take us farther."

He stared at her, not knowing how he had gotten even that far. "You must promise," he said desperately. "You haven't promised what I asked."

The Dancer chuckled. One side of her hair was black as night, the other white as snow. She wore a Fire Bear pelt; her fingers were its curved ice-white claws. She looked old as night one moment, then, at a shift of light or expression, as young as morning. "We gained ground without a promise."

"Then I won't move. I'll go no farther." He sat down at the foot of the effigy, his arms folded. "I'll stay here with the dead until you promise." His face was blanched; his old man's hair, he thought, would have turned white anyway at this point. The Gold King turned his imperious mask of gold at Corleu, and he had to drag at air, just at the movement.

"Tell us who might be waiting for us," the Gold King said. "Tell us who might have taken an interest in whatever you searched for, who might have turned a thought toward taking this thing I want. How can we promise without a name?"

"I won't name until you promise." He had reached out, clung to something solid on the tomb, in the face of the Gold King's wrath. The guardians swung their horned, beaked, goat-eyed heads at him as they roamed around the tomb. But no fire came out of their mouths, no roars of warning. "And she doesn't know what or where. She can't be there waiting."

The Warlock paced, juggling, with one hand, small worlds of fire.

"Then why are you afraid for her? This ignorant, innocent sorceress who has no interest in why we wake? If she's nowhere, how could we harm her? I know mages, witches, sorcerers. Their minds are always turning, always busy, nosing out this, that. She pointed your way here. You'd have spent years searching on your own for this maze. But she would not come with you if only to see for herself what you might find? She was not curious? She had better things to do? And why," he added, tossing a star and catching it, "would we harm her for helping us?" Corleu, gripping stone, stared at him, dry-mouthed. "No answer from the Wayfolk? Then I'll answer. Because she intends us harm."

He threw a glass ball in his hand hard across the chamber, straight at the globe. Corleu, on his feet before he realized it, saw the ball pass through the globe as if it were air, and rebound against the wall. The Warlock caught it. Corleu molded stone in his hand, still searching the globe, for a crack, injury, a wavering of its light. He moved finally, took a step toward it, touched it with one hand.

He flinched away from hot glass; it was only mage-light, burning for centuries, likely old as the maze. He turned, found an audience out of nightmare watching him.

"What do you see," the Dancer asked softly, "in there, Wayfolk? It's only a round globe of light."

"Nothing." He sat down again, cooling his hand against the cold marble: It was the effigy's left foot, he realized, he had hold of like a spar off a swamped ship. He moved his hand quickly before the effigy stirred in annoyance.

"I looked into a round globe of light once," the Blind Lady said in her low, grave voice. "I saw what I saw and never saw again. Be careful, Wayfolk, what you look too closely into."

"It's too late for care." His eyes wandered back to the globe, then dragged away from it, to meet the Gold King's expressionless, armored face.

"There," the Gold King said softly. "In there, Corleu?"

"No."

"Maybe in its shadow?"

He did not answer; his face turned resolutely from it. But

it burned in his thoughts. "You must promise," he said doggedly, "or none of us will ever know. She could never harm the likes of you. She could never take from you."

"Could she not?" They consulted one another silently; so did the fey-eyed tomb guardians.

"Never harm," the Warlock said thinly, tossing balls again. "Never take."

"But would she try?" the Dancer asked, revealing her ancient furrowed face. "There's the question. If we promise, and she tries to harm, then what, Wayfolk man? Will you come to our rescue?"

"She can't harm you," he said again, wearily. "No one could. You're old as story. You never die. Nothing's got more power than a dream. Or time. Or sun. You'll take what you want and walk through her like glass through that globe. She'd maybe throw a spell or two, but what's that to do with you? You'll go on forever. Promise."

"Name her."

"Promise. Her, and her house, and all who know her name."

"Name her."

"Nyx."

Rush's voice, pleading, breathless, caught them across the black tower. Meguet, pushing the Cygnet banner away from the door, saw Nyx's eyes widen, expression cross her face, before she finally turned.

"Rush." It sounded like a sigh. He was armed, but for his heart, which had no defense against Nyx anywhere, it seemed.

"I heard you had come home to fight for this house."

"Rush, we cannot wait—"

"I'll come with you."

Meguet closed her eyes. An impatience like some deadly acrid desert wind shook her. The Wayfolk man had breached time. She saw his face, turned upward, gazing, pale, entranced, puzzled, at the silver-green globe over Chrysom's effigy. "Nyx," she whispered. "We have no time left—"

Rush swept a torch out of its sconce, crossed the floor toward them. "You'll need help. I have some power, Nyx—"

"No."

"I won't let you go there alone."

"Rush," Nyx said, her voice cold as the gate hinges in midwinter, "you have been saying that for nine years. And for nine years I have gone my way and I have gone alone. You don't have the power to follow us. I will not be distracted trying to guard you."

"You won't." He had reached her. His eyes narrowed slightly, as if he were trying to fit a face of memory over the sharp-boned, expressionless, intent face in front of him. "I'll take care of myself. I'll guard Meguet—she has only her sword against those sorcerers."

"I need only Meguet," Nyx said flatly. His temper flared a little, sending blood to his face.

"I'll come with what I have: The house is in danger. You can't return after three years, give me a glimpse of your back and your shadow and then disappear into that convoluted puzzle out of a dead mage's brain, and expect me to wait—"

"I never expected you to wait!" Nyx's cold, calm voice, raised in sudden, genuine despair, startled Meguet. "I never wanted you to wait! You kept thinking I would return to love you—if it was love I wanted, I would never have left! You can't understand, you never could, that I could want knowledge more than you, experience and power more than you. You love a shadow that left this house nine years ago. I have nothing in me of that woman. I have travelled a strange country, and I have changed myself to live in that magic country. Love is not what I have learned in nine years, Rush. It's what I left behind."

"I don't believe that," Rush said. He was shaken, white, but grim, clinging with a blood fox's death grip to something that, to Meguet's eye, had given up life years ago without a protest. Nyx's mouth thinned; her eyes looked silvery in the torchlight. "For nine years, yours was the first face I saw waking, the last I saw sleeping, no matter who lay beside me. How could I be that mistaken? You must have given me something, each time you returned—the way you spoke my name, the way you turned your head to catch my voice—You can't have turned so far from love—"

"You did," she said flatly. "It was you who turned away from love, these nine years, turned away from those who might have truly loved you, to wring love out of a memory, a ghost, air. You loved nothing, Rush. You loved no one. Not even me. At least in nine years I learned something.''

She turned abruptly, pulled aside the banner. Rush stood blinking, his face patchy, as if she had thrown more than words at him. For a moment he almost heard her: Meguet saw the hesitation in his movement. Then, obdurately, he stepped forward. Nyx spun so fast she blurred; there was a sound like air ripping. A line smoldered across the stone in front of Rush.

"You will wait," she said, her voice shaking with anger, "and you will wait, and you will wait in this dark tower—"

"Nyx," Meguet breathed.

"Until the woman you will love freely frees you from your waiting."

"Nyx, what have you done?" He stood very still, looking half perplexed, half frightened, as if he had come to that moment, to that place, by choice, and then could not remember why. Nyx turned again.

"Nothing more," she said with grim weariness, "than what he has laid on himself for nine years. You said to hurry." Meguet, with a final, stunned glance back at Rush, followed her down the steps. "We'll have to elude Chrysom's tricks," Nyx added, "to reach the center. We might have used Corleu's Ring of Time, but it frayed when the house and all its odd time-paths broke apart." She paused at the bottom of the steps; a mage-fire in her palm illumined a lion's face at the first wall, turned to gaze back at her. "However, there are other ways of passing through time—"

Meguet, impelled by a thousand years of voices incoherent in their urgency, did not bother to speak. She gripped Nyx's arm, pulled her forward through the wall into the center of the maze. For a moment, the strange statues appeared around them, then Meguet, all her attention focused on the prism, changed that moment. The statues disappeared; black walls rose around them, enclosing the black eye of the Cygnet. It slowly paled, turned its fire-white gaze on them.

Meguet let go of Nyx then, her eyes flickering at the shadows. She drew Moro Ro's sword, out of habit. Nyx, standing stone-still, her back to the prism, blinked at the sound.

"He's close, the Wayfolk man," Meguet said, prowling, tense. "He changed time at the center. I don't know how." Nyx moved, turned her head slightly to follow Meguet's movements. "Only a Guardian can do that."

"Meguet." The word was almost inaudible, but in that chamber any word ran clear as crystal to the ear. "What is this place?"

"The heart of the maze."

"How did you find it?" Still she had not moved; expression had not yet come back into her face. "Who showed you the way?"

"You did," Meguet said a little bitterly. "Those that you and Corleu woke hid themselves here. I came here to search for them. They attacked, I had to run. Time opened. I ran here." She stopped pacing finally, leaned against the wall, watching Nyx. "You should not know about this place. I could have left you behind easily. But you said you wanted to see the face of power. I don't know its face. But there is its eye."

Nyx turned. She moved then, swiftly, to stand beside Meguet, staring at the great prism that, moonlike, was affixed to nothing but time. "What is it?"

"The eye of the Cygnet."

Nyx was silent, testing it, Meguet knew, recognizing the intent, detached expression, as if she were trying to breathe it like air, swallow it with her mind. "It yields nothing," she whispered. "Who made it?"

"Astor Ro. Chrysom made the maze to protect it. She was the first of us."

"The first—"

"Of the Guardians."

"What is it—exactly that you guard?"

"The Cygnet."

Nyx stared at her. "You never even wanted power. You never cared. You couldn't get through the maze when we were young. Is this what gave you power?"

"Yes. It needs hands, eyes, a mind living in the world. Other minds, older Guardians, woke in me to give me advice."

"What advice are they giving now?"

"They are silent. Listening."

"Listening?"

"To you. For any sign of danger from you."

"Toward you?" Nyx asked with a certain wariness. "Or toward the Cygnet?"

"Toward both."

"They did not help you before."

"The danger was only to me, not the Cygnet. Now, it would be to both, but"—she shrugged slightly, a small gesture she regretted—"now you could not touch me."

Nyx's gaze flicked away, back to the eye. "Why you?" she asked. "Why were you chosen?"

"We are all related, in some way, to Astor Ro. Beyond that, I don't know why."

"And you never knew. As we grew up together, you never sensed this power."

"I never needed it. The Cygnet was never in danger."

Nyx was silent, searching her face. The fire-white prism drew any hint of color from her eyes. "The thing he seeks belongs to the Cygnet," she said slowly. "Or is it a danger to the Cygnet? Does the Cygnet give holding power to the Holders of Ro Holding? The power of the Holders turns on a tale? A constellation? But where is the Cygnet? Four Hold Signs and their faces of power are gathered in this maze. But where is the Cygnet's face? You, Meguet?"

She shook her head, wondering, herself, what mask the Cygnet might choose. "No. I'm simply a Guardian."

"My mother?"

"Perhaps. But these powers only wear their faces to give them a human aspect. Tear the mask away, and you would have other words for them. Take those words away and—what?"

"The power itself," Nyx said softly. She looked at the prism, her arms folded, her face intent in a way that made Meguet alert, uneasy. She was no longer overawed; her busy mind had begun to weave again. "The eye of the Cygnet . . . What is in there?" Meguet did not answer. Nyx threw her a curious glance. "May I look into it?"

"Be careful."

"Is it dangerous?"

"No. But that's what the Wayfolk man is reaching toward, through time."

"Where is he?"

"Here."

"Here?" Nyx said, startled.

"In this chamber. In the same moment, but in a different circle of it. The wall is a Ring of Time. Not like you make them, from one place to another. But in one place, one moment, and deeper into the same moment. It is part of the knowledge within that eye.'' She paused, wishing she had bitten the word in two and swallowed it before she flung it to Nyx like bait. She added carefully, ''As I said, all the power it gives is transitory; it can be used only for one purpose.''

''Perhaps. I think power is malleable; it can be used to suit purpose. How much knowledge must have collected there, in a thousand years . . . And you might never have such power again in your life. This place could close like an eye closing, never to be seen again while we live. How much of it do you know, Meguet?''

''I have no idea,'' Meguet said shortly. ''But it will be enough to stop the Wayfolk man.''

Nyx was silent. All her attention had withdrawn from the prism to focus, suddenly, on Meguet. She put her hand on Meguet's arm, gently, as if to coax her to turn, to look at something. ''Meguet''—she picked words slowly—''whatever Corleu is searching for, he has been compelled to find. He is not acting by choice.''

''Compelled,'' Meguet said flatly, ''he may have been, but he has found his way step by step to this time, to this place, and he has always known exactly what he wanted. And I am born to defend it.''

''He is Wayfolk, powerless. I had to teach him spells a cottage brat could work, to get him this far.''

''He should never have taken the first step.'' Nyx's fingers tightened on her arm; she moved slightly, left them closing on air. She eased into shadows again, her face shadowed. ''He threatens the Cygnet. That is what the powers within me will see.''

''Meguet.'' Nyx's face, with the color washing into her eyes, seemed candle-pale. ''He is an innocent—''

''How would you recognize innocence anymore? You have no mercy for any who love you, why would you defend someone you yourself coerced, except to get what you want?''

''I did not coerce him. He needed me so he could rescue some Wayfolk girl—''

''And that moved you, I suppose.''

''It did, oddly,'' Nyx admitted. Her brows were pinched; expression had broken through the cool detachment in her eyes.

"I know he looks for something of great, dangerous power. But he wants nothing from it. All he wants is to rescue his Wayfolk love. It is a kind of innocence. A kind I never knew. I thought I could take what he found, and then use the power in it to protect him, send him unharmed back to his life. Back into that innocence. It seemed—even to me, living that way in the swamp— something worth protecting."

Meguet closed her eyes. "Then why," she breathed, "did you send him here? He could never have known about the maze without you. What kind of innocent dream does this look like to you? You knew I wanted him. What did you think I would do when I found him in this house? Why should I believe what you tell me, rather than what I see with all the power within me? He is here. He is searching not for the face of power, but for its heart. You have sent him here to die."

Nyx caught her breath, a small, unguarded sound, a half-formed word. She vanished abruptly. Meguet, startled, had time only to tense, and then she found herself adjusting her vision like a telescope, pulling Nyx out of the air, focusing clearer and clearer, until she could see even the changing expression in Nyx's eyes.

The great swan-etched broadsword wrenched itself out of her hands. It stroked the air with silver, a line drawn straight toward the shining prism. Fast as it moved, Meguet was faster, folding the moment in her mind, stepping across time to seize the sword with both hands, stop it an instant before its tip broke the facets of the prism. It resisted her, in midair, dragging against her on its determined path. Then the desire that had held a door against Nyx's power filled her; the need to see, to protect, became stronger than the threat, and she pulled the blade down and whirled.

"Nyx!" She caught her breath, furious and terrified. Nyx had disappeared again; Meguet's eyes picked her out from behind an illusion of black stone wall. She looked unfamiliar in concentration, detached, unreachable.

"You can move like thought," Nyx said softly. "You can see through illusion, your strength is formidable. You can walk through stone, you can walk through time. What else can you do? What else did that eye teach you that not even I know how to test? You guard a living power. I want it."

"Nyx, be careful," Meguet begged, white, trembling. "Please stop—"

"What mind is in that eye?"

"You will go too far—too far even for me to protect you. Nyx, please—"

The dark walls blinked, hid Nyx. Meguet turned, drawn as always toward the Cygnet's eye, and found her there, reaching out to it with both hands.

Finally the voices within her spoke. They checked her, stilled a thought that would have transfixed Nyx within that moment, left her always reaching, never grasping. *Wait,* the Guardians said. She waited; their voices stilled, left a silence in her like the silence in the face of the moon. Nyx's hands touched the prism, held it.

In the misty light between her hands, the Cygnet flew.

Corleu saw it within the globe. It left him no time to think, no time to move; he stood at the globe, reaching for it, his hands settling on it before he had even gotten off the tomb. He never felt the hot glass. Here, it was, he knew: The thing that trapped him and would set him free, the Cygnet, flying through that mist between time, to the place where it had hidden its heart.

A face formed out of the mist; mist lingered in the eyes. "Nyx," he said, a small word startled out of him that seemed to echo in whispers behind him. She also looked surprised, at something he could not see.

And then he saw.

5

H e dropped his hands, spun in horror and nearly impaled himself on the blade burrowing against his throat. Down the length of it, he saw Meguet's eyes.

They stared at one another: he seeing green, hearing the green rustling corn leaves and knowing what they whispered of in their dry, ancient voices. *Nothing,* he heard, *nothing, nothing, nothing,* because that is what he glimpsed between him and the blade poised so surely in her hands that the light on it did not even tremble. She saw him dead. He had crept into the heart of time and held the Cygnet's secret between his hands, revealing it to the wild, dangerous powers he had brought with him. She saw, held him transfixed with what was in her eyes. But her hands did not move to complete the image.

Kill, she heard within her, and felt the ancient, killing anger sweep through her. Light shook down the sword. He saw Tiel's face, smelled the lavender in her hair, and then sorrow thrust a sharp, heavy blade into his throat. He opened his mouth, breath grating through him, and realized that he was still alive.

He was powerless against her, she sensed. Powerless to lift

a finger to help himself: He did not even carry a knife. Still
stunned by what he had seen, he could not even speak, beg,
bargain for his life. Only his eyes spoke: of a terrible despair.
Powerless as a swamp bird in Nyx's house, and yet he had made
his way to a place not even Nyx herself had found. He had known
where to look. He had recognized what he had seen. . . .

She heard her own voice finally, among the clamoring winds
of centuries. The voices cried at her; she beat them back with
her own: *I am your eyes and feet, I am your killing hand. I live
in this world, I look into the eyes of those you tell me to kill. I
have the right to be heard. How could he have reached this place
without a Guardian's powers? He has looked into the Cygnet's
eye. He is born to guard.*

She could barely speak, among the wild voices. Neither had
moved, except him to take a breath. Together they had formed
a private moment within a slow, slow drawing out of time around
them. Nyx still held the prism, walls were still changing, Chrysom's effigy shadowed the air, faces were still coming visible
around her. "Wayfolk." Her voice shook. "What are you?"

"I—" He stuck, mute, forgetting how to talk as his eyes
ran again over her face, her hair. "I never knew," he said helplessly.

"What did you see in the eye?"

"The heart of the Cygnet."

"What you have searched for."

"Yes," he whispered. Light flashed from her blade again;
it bit at him and he jerked, feeling the sweat run down his face.

"I should kill you."

"Likely."

"Why do I recognize you?"

So he told story, his life hanging on his great-gran's tale.
Her green eyes narrowed at him through the tale; her face was
hard and pale as marble. But it reached her. He felt the blade
shift slightly against him. Something flicked into her eyes, memory, expression, something that was not death.

"My great-grandfather," she said tautly. "He was a restless
man, with odd, stray power. He lived in Withy Hold until heritage
drew him here. He would have taken a Wayfolk girl in a cornfield."

"How she remembered," he said, "was she saw and took
as well. It was what she came back to all her life. The place

where time stops. Where green never fades. Where story begins. When I saw you in that house, I saw what she told: corn-leaf eyes and corn-silk hair. But that wasn't all. It wasn't even close to all, what I saw in you.''

"No.'' The voices within her were all silent now, waiting, it seemed, for judgment from her of this dangerous, bastard power. She lifted the blade finally, held it an inch or two away from him, still tense, still watchful. ''You found what you need here. What will you—''

"How can you ask?'' he cried, seeing it again: the black swan flying into the mist of Nyx's eyes. "I couldn't lift a finger against her. When I told the tinker yes, it was stories I was thinking of: the heart kept inside a nut inside a tree, or locked in a box on one side of the world with the key in the other. I didn't know it would be in someone living! And she—she wanted this thing I looked for. She said she wanted its power.''

Meguet was silent. She lowered the blade, let the tip fall to the floor, her eyes wide, troubled. "Nyx,'' she said softly.

"You'd think a bird would have chosen better.''

"She wasn't always so . . .'' Her eyes searched around them: Nyx's hands had fallen, the effigy had seeped back into its own time. The forces gathered against the Cygnet had pulled themselves clear into the moment. She said quickly, "Hide. Go back through time.''

He shook his head. "I can't. You know I can't. Cygnet is in danger.''

"Do you have a Guardian's full power?''

"I'll find out, likely. If not,'' he added bleakly, "maybe I'll stand a better chance at finding Tiel as a ghost. But who is it the Cygnet is in most danger from? Gold King's heart or Nyx's?''

He was unprepared for time roiling back over them like a fierce, moon-tossed tide. Nyx's hands finished falling away from the prism. She turned, her face still wearing a private, startled expression at what she had seen within it. Then the Warlock stepped out of the shadows.

Her hands were moving before she even changed expression. A huge red ball formed around him; he snarled soundlessly, testing it with his hands. The Gold King drew a sword that was a blinding stroke of light, and dragged his chain toward the Cygnet's eye. Meguet, stunned by his flat, metallic sun-face, the lines wrought into it of fury and cruelty, recognized the tinker only by the gold he wore, and the tricks he played with light. She moved into his path, her back to the prism, holding the broadsword between them with both hands. She heard him laugh. The Warlock exploded out of his glass prison, throwing splinters of fire everywhere. The Blind Lady, gathering them out of the air, began to weave a net of flame.

The Gold King's sword wheeled, moving so fast it left its reflection across an arc of air. It caught one of the Cygnet wings along the grip of Meguet's sword and wrenched it from her hands. It flew across the room toward the Dancer. As she looked at it, the swans on the hilt and pommel, etched along the blade, startled away from it, flocked together as they flew, tiny birds turning desperately along the curved walls.

Meguet pulled the Gold King's relentless path along a fine, slow, narrow line of time; he walked his halting pace toward the prism, but the distance he crossed was minute. The Blind Lady lifted a hand toward them, reshaped the Gold King's path, and he pulled himself close to Meguet. He was molten, she saw; blisters of gold appeared and disappeared along his armor. Nyx swung toward them. Her face seemed as detached as ever, concentrating, as she juggled spells, but her eyes were wide, and there was a desperate edginess to her movements. She flung out a hand, frowning. The Gold King's chain lifted ponderously, began to wrap itself around him.

He only laughed again, the dark, jangled, echoing laughter that Meguet had heard before. He was so close to her, she could feel the heat within him. She would not back; Corleu, behind her, gripped her finally, pulled her a step or two closer to the Cygnet's eye. The Warlock sent the small birds scattering out of the air, dead at Nyx's feet.

She stared down at them, a moment that cost her. The Blind Lady flung her web. It fell over Nyx, a weave of fire and light that tangled around her. She cried out suddenly. Meguet, her heart pounding at the sound, left the Cygnet's eye to Corleu and moved to her, so quickly that the Gold King, swinging his chain at her, tripped only empty air.

"Wayfolk," the Gold King said, facing him. He put out a burning hand; Corleu flinched back from it. His shadow, flung forward by the light within the prism, fell over the Gold King. For an instant he was tinker again, with shaggy night-black hair and smiling golden eyes. "You found what I wanted. Why fight me? I'll return what's yours."

"I didn't promise you someone living!"

The tinker shrugged. "Who will miss her? She's swamp-mired. Her heart is full of little bones. Who would want her ruling Ro Holding?"

"The Cygnet—"

"A bird, like the ones she pulled apart?"

"It's more than bird," he said desperately, but the tinker smiled his mocking smile and shifted out of Corleu's shadow. Armed again, masked in light, he swung his hand at Corleu, his upturned face glowing pale in the light from the prism. The spiked armor hit Corleu like stone. Thrown out of the Gold King's path, he hit the wall and clung, blinking, trying to stay on his feet while the wall moved against him. The floor bucked suddenly; he fell to his knees.

Wayfolk, he heard suddenly, deep in him: the frail, whispering winds of voices. *Watch his shadow.*

It lay under his hands, the Gold King's shadow, stretching away from him. Its hands reached toward the prism's reflection, a complex dance of light thrown along the wall. The shadow of a swan flew into the fractured light. Shadow-hands closed around it. The bird eluded, flew again into the light. Again the hands grasped. The bird flew.

The rhythm of it transfixed Corleu; the action seemed of a world apart, a different time—small, silent movements he could draw out, he felt, if he wanted. In his mind, he changed one color trembling on the wall. The Cygnet flew, the hands grasped. He changed another color, made it a different reflection, in a different time. The hands grasped, closed, empty; the bird flew. He change a color. A different shadow, a different time, a different world. The hands closed. The bird flew.

How many worlds? he wondered, fascinated. How many times?

Then a blood fox's shadow leaped across the wall. Corleu heard its bark. His mind, a sparkling prism, moved too slowly to shift into the Warlock's time. Something struck him. He slid helplessly on a tide of splintered light. The wave broke, slammed him against the wall, then let him fall onto his back, half-stunned, blind, heaving for breath. He smelled blood fox, felt a warm, snarling weight on his chest. And then he felt its sharp claw over his heart.

Meguet saw him fall. The Warlock was invisible, but its blood-fox shadow hunched over Corleu, clear on the wall. Her mind was tangled in the Blind Lady's net, tracing its threads of fire and time one by one, breaking them. As fast as she broke, the Blind Lady wove. Nyx and the Dancer were fighting over Moro Ro's sword. Birds flew, fell dead; the blade formed, turned to peacock feather; the blade formed again, made of fire, streaked the air toward Meguet. Flame crumpled against something invisible, blew out, re-formed. It was an idle but desperate game, to keep Nyx from freeing herself from the net. The time in its threads was slowing her movements, measuring them to its flow. Soon, Meguet knew, the sword would form, slip beyond her, strike.

She glimpsed the Dancer's chaos then: panic, nightmare. *I cannot hold them,* she thought, almost in wonder, for failure was unthinkable. She saw Corleu move under the blood fox, like a drowned man touched curiously by fingers of tide. Then he lay still again. The blood fox lifted its muzzle, barked.

I need help! she cried down the centuries, then saw the Gold King's hands close within the prism.

No bird flew.

Her desperate unweaving faltered; unravelled lines of time snarled in her mind. She heard Nyx cry, "Meguet!" The great, flaming blade flew at her again. Nyx's hand, rising to stop it, was a scant moment late. It bore onward. Meguet, her attention snared between Nyx trapped in time, and the small bird trapped in the Gold King's hands, hesitated, torn. Nyx turned to follow the sword's path, tightening the net around her. She swayed, her face glistening, white with exhaustion, as if time were wearing at her. "Meguet!" Her voice was husky with weariness and horror. "Use your power! Save yourself!"

But she had been given no time for herself: Time was divided between the Cygnet and its heart. She could only pick apart one final thread in the web of time around Nyx, and then the great sword severed the future in front of her eyes. She did not see it swerve; it impaled her breath as it flew past her, or through her, left a deadly edge of silver in her vision. She closed her eyes, shaken by her own heartbeat, and felt time knit itself again as she found her breath. Opening her eyes, she saw Corleu lift his head finally, groggy, bewildered. Silver caught his eye. He turned his head, saw it come.

"No!" Nyx snapped. A thread in the fiery net snapped in response. She dredged a word from somewhere deep in her; Meguet did not recognize her voice. Another thread snapped. She threw both hands upward, shaped the word out of shadows, it seemed, and white fire torn across the air out of the shining prism. The starry fire fell over Nyx, dissolving the net of time. She reached up again, drew at air with her entire body. Air sculpted her, lifted her. Meguet saw her eyes as she flew past, pale lavender, strange in a swan's face.

Then the white wings shifted time as they fell; in a fractured movement, the swan was across the room, ahead of the flaming sword, swerving in the air to push it out of its deadly path. But the sword, searing the air in front of Corleu's eyes, was faster. He caught a confused image of silver fire, white feathers; he heard Meguet's voice, crying out with his own.

The sword formed its own wings. A swan's neck extended along the blade. It came so close that for an instant Corleu saw a night-black eye, with a pearl of light in it from the prism's light. Then it pulled itself up, climbed the air, its black wings thundering past his face. He gasped. The swans wheeled together in the small chamber, one black, one white, turning and turning endless circles that gradually lost their frantic speed, slowed to an endless, timeless spiral, as if they had all the night and all the stars to fly through.

Then there was only one swan, and its black shadow; one angled down to meet the other. The white swan touched its shadow; Nyx reappeared, standing beside Corleu.

There was not a sound in the chamber; Gold King and Blind Lady might have been among the statues Chrysom had made. Meguet stood as still, feeling something build in the silence, like another wild, powerful, mysterious word. Nyx felt it, too. She looked around her, hands poised to work, her shadow falling protectively over Corleu. But no one moved; faces only stared back at her, wordless, motionless, masked.

She began to tremble suddenly, gazing back, incredulously, at what she had been fighting. "What are you?" she breathed. "What is it you are looking for?" She looked at Corleu when they did not answer. The Blood Fox, its human shadow lying beneath Nyx's feet, moved its paw from his chest. It sat back on its haunches, grinning its fox grin as Corleu pulled himself up. Even he could not stop staring at her.

"You saved my life," he said in wonder. "You did all that, became swan, just to save a muckerheaded Wayfolk man who brought all this on you—"

"But what—" Her voice broke away from her, echoed off the high stones. "Corleu, what have you been searching for?"

"The heart of the—" He paused. His eyes widened on her face, as all the threads of the tale they had made among them wove into place. She wavered under his sudden, burning tears. He whispered, "Your heart."

It was such a rare and startling sight, Nyx weeping, that Meguet felt her own throat tighten. Wordless, spellbound, she watched the Gold King loose what he held in his hands: A shaft of sunlight struck the prism. Color danced along the walls. Her eyes widened; she put her hands suddenly to her mouth.

"Just story, you see," he said to her, and was tinker again. "Just a piece of sky." He reached up, snapped the gold chain around his neck. The sound it made as it hit the floor boomed ponderously against the walls, then faded into the rustling wings of small birds. The Blind Lady was busy reweaving her net, gathering its fiery, broken threads into a patch over a hole in one of her skirts. She whispered as she worked, whispered story, Corleu knew, all the story in the world.

"But you always fight the Cygnet," he said dazedly, as the tinker reached down, helped him to his feet. "In all the tales."

"Look again," the tinker said, "and it's Cygnet fighting us: whatever sun touches, whatever dreams, whatever works magic, whatever flies. . . . When the heart casts a shadow instead of dancing light, there story begins."

The Blind Lady finished her weaving. She took the ring off her finger, tossed it in the air. The Ring of Time opened in the heart of the maze, a blinding silver that enclosed the night. She stepped back. The Fire Bear lumbered through it, sending a soundless roar of its black fire across the stars. The Blood Fox leaped through, dragging its tantalizing shadow. The shadow flung something behind it before night swallowed it. A small red prism cracked in two on the stone floor, a drop of darker red glistening within it.

The Blind Lady's sightless face turned toward Meguet before she left. "You have some talent," she commented, "with my threads." A white peacock feather drifted to the floor as she vanished.

The tinker stepped toward the Ring. "Wait!" Corleu cried, and he turned, his eyes luminous, smiling his thin, equivocal smile.

"Don't fret, Wayfolk. I always pay my debts." He put his hand over his heart, bowed his head to them both. "Thanks," he said, and added to Meguet, "I'll do a bit of tinkering for you, when I go."

He walked through the Ring, into a darkness squared by stars, one gold star rising above it. The Ring dwindled; stone walls patched the night. The Ring fell to the floor, a tiny circle, then a stroke of silver, then wings and circling swans on a flawless, sun-forged blade.

Corleu picked it up, held it out to Meguet. She met his stunned and weary gaze; she took the sword in one hand, and slipped her other arm around his shoulders. Their pale heads touched. Together they watched Nyx wipe her face on a threadbare velvet sleeve. She turned away from them without speaking, moved into some private vision under the Cygnet's eye.

The Holder and her children stood waiting beside Rush in the black tower. It was morning, Meguet saw, startled, as she pushed aside the Cygnet banner. The rich spring light tumbled down from the high, narrow windows, lay in slabs across the stones. They all looked worn, fretted, sleepless. Even Calyx's hair had tumbled down.

Nyx went to the Holder. She said huskily, her head bowed, "In my house in the swamp, there was a room full of mirrors. I looked into them. I never saw what they reflected. Their reflections seemed to have brought me here, forced me to look again."

The Holder touched her hair, drew it back from her face. "I don't understand," she said wearily. "But you are safe and Meguet is safe, and that is all I need to know now."

"The House is safe." She added, "The Wayfolk man fought for the Cygnet."

The Holder looked at Corleu. His face burned; he felt Wayfolk to his bones under that dark, powerful gaze. Then she moved it to Meguet and he could breathe again.

"How?" she demanded.

"It seems," Meguet said, "my great-grandfather met his great-gran. In a cornfield."

The Holder made a blackbird's noise. "It's unprecedented."

"His hair is like yours, Meguet," Calyx exclaimed. "Are we all related, then?"

Corleu stared at her delicate face, which surely must bruise under a whisper. Iris said tiredly, "Work it out later, Calyx. What I want to know is how, when Meguet and Nyx went into the maze, Meguet and Nyx and a Wayfolk man came out of it."

"What I want to know," Calyx said, "is will you take the spell off Rush, now?" She patted his arm soothingly as he stood there, silent and pale, looking, to Corleu's startled eye, remarkably like the Warlock's distant descendant. "I can understand why you didn't want him wandering around in the maze, setting things on fire at random, but he's harmless now."

A touch of color rose in Nyx's face. "I forgot about Rush." Her eyes flicked, troubled, to the Holder; the Holder's eyes narrowed.

"Now what have you done?"

"I'm not sure. . . ." She looked at Calyx, standing close to Rush, then hid her eyes behind her hand. "I'm very tired," she sighed. "Calyx, just talk to him. I'm afraid he'll shout at me."

"Rush," Calyx said. She stood in front of him, her hands on his arms, her pale, weary, smiling face coaxing his bemused, distant gaze. "Rush, wake up. It's morning and the house is still standing. Nyx is here."

He was looking at her suddenly, blinking, as if she had just wakened him out of a dream of nine years. "Calyx?" he said, and touched her face. Meguet heard Nyx's faint sigh of relief, met her eyes a moment.

"Nyx is here," Calyx said again, her smile deepening; he lifted his face, jerking himself farther out of dreams.

"Nyx," he said. A long look passed between them. He drew breath. "You never wanted me to follow you," he said ruefully. "But last night you went too far. Farther then I could ever go."

"I know," she said softly. "I hope you will forgive me. What happened—whatever happened down in the maze was my doing also. My fault. You were right: I wandered too far. Corleu and Meguet brought me back. That is how I would tell the story," she said to Corleu, "if I were telling."

"If I were telling," he said, "I would say you brought yourself back."

"What I would say," Iris said, "is that someone should tell us what happened all night down there. Meguet?"

She shook her head quickly. "No, not me," she said, remembering the Gold King's molten face swinging toward her, masked and furious, and the tinker in the woods, smiling as he picked out the lizard's eye, and the sword flying at her, and then the swan. . . . "I only saw pieces of it."

"Corleu, then."

"No," he said with sudden intensity. "I'll never tell. It's not mine, not for me. I only want to find what I lost, which is," he added, "near enough like what was almost lost in the maze."

They were silent; the blood fox eyes moved to Nyx. "Then you," Rush said, "must tell."

She met his eyes. "It's a very long story, Rush. And not yet over. I still have things to learn."

"Nyx," the Holder breathed, "not again!"

Nyx put a hand on her arm. "I have things to learn in this house," she said gently. "You must teach me."

Horns sounded outside the gate, a startling fanfare that made the pigeons whirr outside the windows. The Holder closed her eyes, touched her wild hair.

"Not Hunter Hold. Not now."

"Now," Calyx sighed.

"Meguet—" The Holder paused, eyeing Meguet's stained uniform, her fraying braid, and flung up her hands. "At least you're dressed and armed. Go to the gate and wait for us. Corleu, don't leave this house. I want to talk to you. Nyx, did you come all the way from the swamp without shoes?"

A stable girl led her horse out as Meguet ran across the yard. It was saddled and caparisoned; the Gatekeeper had seen the Council coming. She pulled herself up wearily, rode to the gate. The impatient, golden flurry sounded again. The Gatekeeper did not come down yet. But he looked down, and his impassive expression strained badly at the sight of her.

The Holder joined Meguet finally, after the horns had sounded a third time. Her children and Rush Yarr sat mounted behind her, in such astonishingly tidy attire that Meguet suspected a sorceress's hand in it. She looked for Corleu, saw him standing with some cottagers near the smithy. Too far, she judged, to slip through the gate unnoticed, in the tangle of entry.

The Holder nodded. Meguet rode to one side of the gate, stood guard, according to ancient ritual, Moro Ro's sword outstretched before the gate. The Gatekeeper opened the gate.

The Gold King stood outside: the Hold Sign of Hunter Hold, the crowned King in his dark house on a field of dark blue, newly sewn, for the silver thread depicting the stars glittered like water in the sun. Cedar Kell's two young children held it, one on each side, their faces immobile with terror at the sight of the Holder before them. The Holder began the ritual that in Moro Ro's time had cost blood for every word.

"Who speaks for Hunter Hold?"

Cedar Kell stepped in front of the banner, looking tired, dusty from travelling, but cheerful.

"Kell speaks for Hunter Hold," she said in her booming voice, that must have laid threats on her children, for not a smile or a tear touched their faces.

"Under what sign?"

"The sign of the Gold King."

"Under what stars?"

"The yellow star its lintel, the yellow star its roof, the four stars of red and pale its walls, the blue star marking its door latch. Under this sign the Gold King holds Hunter Hold."

"Does the Gold King recognize the Cygnet?"

"The Gold King recognizes the Cygnet."

"Under the sign of the Cygnet, the Gold King holds Hunter Hold. For the end of time, the Cygnet holds the Gold King under its eye, beneath its wing, within its heart. None shall break this bond."

"The Gold King holds Hunter Hold, the Cygnet holds the Gold King. Under its eye, beneath its wing, within its heart. So bound are they, so bound are we. Truth in my words, peace in my heart, Lauro Ro."

"And peace in mine," the Holder said, and smiled. "Welcome to my house, Cedar Kell."

Meguet lifted the broadsword, turned her horse away to let what amounted to a small travelling village through the gate. She remained mounted, sword sheathed, until the Council members, families, kin, retinue had entered. When the baggage and supply carts started rumbling in, she dismounted, gave her horse to the stablers. She found Corleu again, looking tense and frayed in the crush.

He seemed relieved when he saw her. "I must go," he said. "Can you tell the Holder that? I'll come back, but there's only one thing in the world I want to do now—"

She put her hand on his shoulder. "I know. But you can't leave. Not yet. You are half-Guardian—"

"And all Wayfolk at this moment," he said, his face turned to the open gate. "I've been in walls too long."

"Don't be afraid. You have kin within these walls."

He looked at her, silent. Then he sighed, his body loosening finally under her touch. "Seems strange. Last night you nearly killed me. Now, you're the only reason I might stay."

"You must do better than might. Be patient. You have a formidable inheritance. You'll never be able to stray far from this house. The heart that brought you here will bind you here. Wait for the Holder." His eyes moved to the black tower. She saw him draw breath and hold it. "Wait," she said again. "The Holder will send for you soon."

"How much," he asked abruptly, "do I tell her?"

"You tell her everything. But only her. No one else in this world."

He nodded, his eyes still on the tower, with the Cygnet flying over it, by day and night. He sighed again, sagged against the smithy wall.

She left him there, to watch him from the Gatekeeper's turret. She felt, climbing the stairs, that there was no end to them. Then she was at the top, sitting thoughtlessly, watching the sea, and the Gatekeeper help ease a wagon through the gate. The sunlight touched her eyes gently, closed them.

She was asleep when the Gatekeeper came up finally. He smoothed her hair from her face, in small, gentle touches; she woke dreaming of wings. Then she saw the burning sword fly at her again and she started. Sword turned to swan, swan to Gatekeeper's taut, tired face.

She caught her breath at the vision. Then she leaned forward, quickly, into the warm, familiar dark of his embrace. She slid one hand around his neck, where she could feel the blood beat. "It's over," she said finally. "The House is safe. They've all gone."

"Have they? Through which gate?"

"The gate they came through."

"There is only one gate to this house."

She nodded against him, her eyes closed. "And you are the only Gatekeeper."

He was silent; she felt him begin to speak, hesitate. She lifted her head; he held her face between his hands, looked into her eyes. He said at last, very softly, "Why is there a swan in your eyes?"

"There always is," she answered. "Have you never noticed? A great wild black swan, who sometimes watches me sleep . . . The only swan that never leaves this house, summer or winter." She smiled a little, at his stillness. "It's only story."

His head dropped; his lips touched hers, feather-light. She closed her eyes and heard, from some distant corner of the yard, children's voices, chanting to some game:

In a wooden ring,
Find a stone circle,
In the stone ring
Find a silver circle . . .

She felt Hew move; sun spilled over her face. She saw the back of his head as he leaned out of the turret, looking over the wall.

"What is it?"

"We have a guest, it seems."

"Who now? The whole world just came in."

"Wayfolk by the look of her."

She caught breath, leaned across him to look down as he spoke to the visitor, as courteously as he would have spoken to a lord's daughter. The girl was slight, with long, straight, heavy black hair, and wide-set dark eyes. Wayfolk to the bone, yet standing alone, and prepared to cross a threshold.

"How can I help you?"

"I'm looking for someone," she said, her voice, gentle and timid, barely carrying above the tide's voice. "We came down from Withy Hold. A Wayfolk man named Corleu. We passed a tinker said he might be here."

The Gatekeeper got up to open the gate. Meguet, trembling, closed her eyes again, felt the sun lay its hand across her face, catch her sudden tears.

Corleu, slumped against the wall, his eyes on the dark tower, turned his head at the sound of the opening gate. His heart saw before the light relinquished the dark, slender figure to his eyes: He felt the green timeless secret place bloom in him again, with all its scents and still pools and sweet, rustling shadows.

Tiel crossed the threshold as he began to run. They met within walls, in a place with no walls.